Eligibl

"The police will be here in a minute," the man said, approaching them, his eyes first resting on Hannah, then on Kiki. "Is she okay?"

Kiki's hand left one eye and she surveyed the handsome stranger. With a theatrical sweep of her arm she lifted herself onto one elbow, raising a limp wrist toward him.

"If you could assist me," she said.

Hannah narrowed her eyes. Was it possible that her sister could be flirting with one potential boyfriend while another lay dead at her feet? But surely not even Kiki was capable of that.

The stranger took Kiki's hand and pulled her forward. Apparently underestimating her weight, he faltered slightly and Hannah put her hands on the back of Kiki's hips, pushing her to a standing position.

With Kiki finally upright, he said, "We should step outside the gate. We don't want to disturb anything."

Kiki touched her hand to her forehead. "Oh, yes, please, let's get out of here. It's all too horrible. Poor Arnold must have had a heart attack."

"Heart attack?" Hannah said with disbelief. "He was lying facedown with blood all over the back of his head. Arnold Lempke was murdered."

A Very Eligible Corpse

A Very Eligible Corpse

ANNIE GRIFFIN

BERKLEY PRIME CRIME, NEW YORK

A VERY ELIGIBLE CORPSE

A Berkley Prime Crime Book / published by arrangement with
the author

PRINTING HISTORY
Berkley Prime Crime edition / September 1998

The Penguin Putnam Inc. World Wide Web site address is
http://www.penguinputnam.com

ISBN: 0-425-16535-3

Berkley Prime Crime Books are published
by The Berkley Publishing Group,
a member of Penguin Putnam Inc.,
375 Hudson Street, New York, NY 10014.
The name BERKLEY PRIME CRIME and the BERKLEY PRIME CRIME
design are trademarks belonging to Berkley Publishing Corporation.

PRINTED IN THE UNITED STATES OF AMERICA

10 9 8 7 6 5 4 3 2 1

Special thanks to Carol Lundmark, Kenton Dunkel of the Mill Valley Police Department, and to Jim Osbon.

To my husband, Jim

$\mathcal{O}$NE

$\mathcal{I}$T IS A RUEFUL FACT of life that our bodies age, that however youthful our hearts, our flesh succumbs to the progression of time and gravity. But happily the brain doesn't always accept this. So while the full-length mirror before Kiki Goldstein revealed a woman of sixty, with lines around her forehead and mouth, a slight sag to her jaw, a puffiness to the eyes, and a general shifting of everything outward and south, Kiki herself saw something quite different.

Light entered her cornea, bounced against her retinal cones; messages of reality shot at light speed to her cranial cortex, but there the wiring somehow got twisted and the message woefully distorted. What Kiki saw in the mirror at that precise moment was a dewy-skinned vixen, a delicate yet sensual peach of a woman, inexplicably youthful, blissfully voluptuous, the type of woman that drives men into carnal fevers, into sex-crazed lust machines craving a single touch of her molten flesh.

Eyes squinted, lips pursed, and with a slow, languorous sweep of her plump fingers, she luxuriated in the reflected outline of her plenteous bosom. Her breasts were, next to her starburst-diamond-and-synthetic-emerald cocktail ring, her most prized possession, a gift from her long-departed second husband, Cecil. The yellow jumpsuit she wore, ironically the color of a "yield" sign, was at least two sizes too small, thus perfectly displaying these silicone wonders, the thick fabric straining almost audibly, shoving them together so they bulged upward like yeasty loaves.

Most boutiques in upscale Hill Creek sold only shapeless fashions in trendy blacks, browns, and blues, the colors of bruises, and Kiki had dragged her sixty-one-year-old sister Hannah Malloy to five different stores before reaching this one. It was a small, chic establishment with maple floors, rose walls, and lots of track lighting, its merchandise a mixture of high-priced elegance and funkiness typical of Hill Creek, California.

Every space in the store was lined with garments, and Kiki discovered the yellow jumpsuit in a dusty box of former fifty-percent-off clothes destined for shipment to a discount retailer. But although the outfit had turned up the noses of the store's more elegant clientele, for Kiki it was manna from heaven.

She pressed her hands against the back of her hips, giving her chest a Marilyn Monroe arch upward.

"Do you think this works as cruise wear?" Kiki asked in a voice ridiculously girlish for a woman of sixty, its tone high-pitched and irrationally energetic.

Sitting comfortably in an oversized velvet chair, absorbed in a liberal newspaper editorial she heartily disagreed with, Hannah peered over the top of round tortoiseshell reading glasses, eyeing her sister with constrained amusement.

"Only if you're cruising for sailors," she replied dryly. "And then only if they've been out to sea one hell of a long time."

Her nostrils flaring, her pride only slightly wounded, Kiki straightened her shoulders in defiance and patted her blond hair, which had been bleached and poufed into a cotton-candied tribute to cosmetology.

"You're just jealous, Hannah. Pea green because I'm going to be on a fabulous cruise to Acapulco on the arm of Arnold Lempke."

Kiki had won the cruise in the Hill Creek Rose Club raffle, a club Kiki and Hannah had joined years before, though Kiki exhibited limited interest in roses. The primary interest for her was the club's social activities.

Hannah rolled her eyes then returned them to the editorial, which was less distasteful than the subject of Arnold Lempke.

"That's correct. I'm lusting to be with a man who looks like Ross Perot only without the dashing good looks." Hannah took a jelly bean from the bag in her lap, popping it her mouth and letting the flavor explode upon her tongue. Watermelon. Delicious.

Kiki stomped one wedgie-shoed foot. "Oh, go ahead and be snide, but even if you aren't jealous, the other girls at the Rose Club are. You should have seen Bertha's face when I told her Arnold was going on the cruise with me. Serves her right the way she goes on and on about how Samuel Stone drools after her."

"Samuel Stone is close to ninety. He's not drooling after her. He's just drooling," Hannah said, her eyes remaining on the newspaper.

"Go ahead, make your jokes. But I'm going to be strolling the deck wearing this juicy little outfit. Arnie will be taking my picture. All the men will be noticing me. And do you know what question they'll be asking?"

"Vixen or Volkswagen?" Hannah muttered under her breath. The remark didn't reach Kiki, who was deep in her fantasy by now, her eyes fixed once again upon her image in the mirror.

"They'll be asking, is she single, is she available?" Kiki said breathily to her reflection. "But I won't be. I'll be on the strong, manly arm of Arnold Lempke."

Hannah opened her mouth to mention that Lempke was a shrunken, brittle stick of a man and that Kiki outweighed him by at least twenty pounds, but thought better of it. From the time they were children she had found teasing Kiki excellent sport and basically harmless since you couldn't pry away Kiki's self-delusions with a crowbar.

Lauren, their twenty-eight-year-old niece, who stood to the right of the mirror, stifled a smile. "The jumpsuit looks nice, Aunt Kiki, only isn't it a little low in the chest?"

Kiki twittered. "There's no such thing, honey. At my age a woman has to show a little cleavage."

Hannah searched the newspaper for *The New York Times* crossword puzzle. "What you must understand, Lauren," she said as she riffled the pages, "and I think we're all mature enough to discuss these things openly, is that Kiki hasn't had sex in three years and is hoping to fornicate with Mr. Lempke."

Lauren looked aghast at Hannah. Kiki exhaled loudly. "You are *so* crude," she said.

Pushing her glasses a little farther down her nose, Hannah looked over them. "Excuse me, Lauren, for being vulgar. Let me put it another way. Your aunt Kiki is hoping to be blasted by Mr. Lempke's love musket."

Lauren laughed, covering her mouth when she began involuntarily to snort.

Kiki's lips twisted into a knot. "There's nothing wrong with a woman strutting her stuff a little." Just to annoy her sister she bent forward, shimmying her shoulders to maximize the fissure between her breasts.

Hannah raised an eyebrow, took a jelly bean out of the bag, and with a perfect lob, tossed it smack into the center of Kiki's bosom, the cherry-red missile disappearing as surely as if it had plunged into a canyon.

Kiki's mouth opened into a silent, horrified "oh." She dug her hand into her bra, her chin pushed into thick folds as she glared downward. Coming to Kiki's aid, Lauren examined the crevice.

"You'll need strong rope and a flashlight," Hannah said with a chuckle, her eyes still on the paper.

"Oh, very funny, ha, ha," Kiki replied as Lauren gingerly retrieved the jelly bean with two fingers. "You don't like Arnold and I can't understand why. He likes you even though he thinks you're his toughest competition in the rose contest."

Realizing that it would be impossible to finish the newspaper, Hannah folded it and placed it on the floor beside her chair.

"It's not only Arnold I have a problem with. It's how you met him."

Just then the swishing of a long skirt and the sound of clogs brushing against the carpet became audible.

"You guys doing okay?" the young salesgirl asked. Once she had sized up these three customers as nonshoplifters, she had left them alone. Even if they *were* shoplifters, the store's owner would be delighted to get the garish yellow jumpsuit out the door any way possible.

"Dandy as candy. I'll take this," Kiki told her. The girl shrugged and left to write up the bill.

"How did you meet Mr. Lempke?" Lauren asked Kiki, her tone normal but the set of her mouth suspicious. Her aunt's unbridled zeal in the pursuit of males was legendary. Big-game hunters stalked prey with less determination.

"I met him at the Baptist church," Kiki answered.

Hannah chortled and ate another jelly bean, this one green apple. "You make it sound so innocent."

Kiki turned sideways and gave her figure another appreciative look. "I can't imagine what you're getting at."

"You joined the Baptist church? I thought you were Jewish." Lauren tilted her head, puzzled.

Kiki waggled a hand at her. "Oh, well, Cecil wanted me to convert, but I never got around to it. All those classes. Anyone interested in tea? All of a sudden I'm dying for a Lemon Lift."

"The subject she's avoiding is that she joined the First

Baptist Church to keep tabs on the Sunday prayer list,''
Hannah said, and she could tell by Lauren's confused expression that she would have to explain further. ''They put
the names of very ill people on the prayer list so church
members can pray for them. One of Kiki's friends told her
it was an excellent way to meet men. You watch the prayer
list and see which men have especially sick wives, then you
start stalking them. As soon as they're widowers, you
pounce. The poor men barely have time to get their dark
suits off before a woman dives inside their boxers. Apparently the Baptist women die off sooner than the Jewish
ones, so Baptist Kiki is.''

''That is disgusting and so completely untrue!'' Kiki
said, hands petulantly on hips, although she knew it was at
least partially accurate. She had considered the idea a stroke
of genius, but once she got involved in the First Baptist
Church, she realized that she hadn't been the only woman
to think of it. With available older men at a premium, scop-
ing out the prayer list had become a local sport with some
Marin County women of a certain age, and with all that
competition, bagging a man wasn't so easy. Kiki had baked
these widowers-in-training tuna casseroles, fed their cats,
and patted their aching knees. She was only showing Christian kindness to poor men who needed it, she reasoned, and
if as a by-product she happened to snag a prize like Arnold
Lempke, who could fault her? No one except Hannah, who
insisted that every single woman over fifty should consider
herself fortunate to be free and self-sufficient. Kiki didn't
share that view.

Kiki slipped back into the dressing room behind a scanty
curtain and tried to take off the jumpsuit, but physics and
friction battled against her. Hannah could hear her groaning
and cursing as she struggled to push the fabric over her
hips.

After more grunts wafted from the dressing room, Lauren
went in to help. A few seconds later she stuck out her head.

''It won't budge,'' she announced.

"Better let me help. This requires experience," Hannah said, standing up. She pushed aside the curtain.

Kiki was in a comical state of disarray, the jumpsuit pulled down to her waist exposing her purple Wonder Bra. Kiki owned them in eight different colors.

"Help me, Hannah," she pleaded, using the same tone that had worked at the age of five.

After closing the curtain, Hannah took hold of the fabric clumped around her sister's middle. She had done this many times before, since Kiki had a habit of wedging herself into clothes—jeans, bathing suits, one time a silk jockey outfit—that were much too small.

"Okay, suck in your gut," she ordered.

In spite of her current predicament, Kiki managed to grow dignified. "I don't have a gut."

"Then please inhale deeply and contract the excess flesh protruding from your torso."

Lauren could be heard giggling on the other side of the curtain. Kiki shot Hannah a look, then closed her eyes and drew in as much breath as her lungs allowed, her cheeks pushing out, her eyes bulging. Once the garment was successfully removed, she paid for it, unthwarted by the problems it had caused her. The women then headed off for their usual haunt, the Book Stop coffeehouse.

Hannah took a deep yoga breath, inhaling the crisp air as they stepped out onto the tree-lined sidewalk. Hill Creek was a suburban village in Marin County about half an hour north of San Francisco. Hannah and Kiki had been born and raised there, each leaving the area for a few years during their marriages but returning in widowhood. After Cecil died, Kiki moved into Hannah's small house located a few blocks from town.

The relationship between the two women was not without strain. Kiki often found Hannah overly critical and high-minded. Hannah occasionally thought Kiki shallow. But underneath this surface friction the sisters loved one another and were happier with each other than without. And despite their differences, both women were good-hearted and took care of each other, although Kiki required the majority of the attention.

Since Hannah and Kiki had been girls, people always remarked on how different they were, not only in personality but physically. Tall and lean, her shoulder-length hair dyed deep auburn and pulled back from her face in a sleek chignon, Hannah was a handsome woman. She carried herself with a noble grace and she still turned a head or two as she walked along Center Avenue to do her weekly shopping. In stark contrast, Kiki was short, round, and blond, with a pretty and pug-nosed face that reminded you of a pampered lapdog.

Hannah, Kiki, and Lauren crossed the street, dodging a group of Bermuda-shorted tourists ogling the view of Mt. Tamalpais. Marin County was known for its picturesque scenery and free-spirited population, and Hill Creek was in many ways its heart and soul, for the town represented both the light and dark qualities peculiar to the area. Twenty years earlier Hill Creek had been beautiful, quaint, and slow-paced. It was still beautiful, filled with towering firs and Mt. Tam rising majestically in the background, but the small local shops had been replaced with upscale boutiques with prices to match. The streets were frequently knotted with traffic, the houses inhabited by stressed professionals who commuted in their BMWs to San Francisco and didn't mind paying fifteen dollars for a pound of coffee or the exorbitant real-estate prices. Regardless of these difficulties, the residents considered Hill Creek to be the best place to live in the world, and they had to be right, since so many people yearned to be part of its small population.

The Book Stop was one retail establishment that had stubbornly refused to give in to the lure of shiny newness. The small pink, tile-roofed building stood on a corner on Center Street and housed a small bookstore and adjacent café. Its paint was dingy, the old stone floors weary and in need of sweeping. The book section held a relatively small selection of volumes the managers considered literary or otherwise relevant, although the occasional movie star's biography sneaked its way onto the shelves, and of course, they carried *People* magazine, which stood on the rack next to the *New York Review of Books*.

The three women nabbed a table by a tall arched window overlooking the town plaza, a paved area where local residents congregated. There in the plaza well-to-do women compared plastic surgeons and fertility drugs, former hippies now eligible for senior-citizen discounts basked in the California sunshine, their brains happily rattled with occasional LSD flashbacks, and teenagers with trust funds but dressed like the homeless rode skateboards when they should have been in school.

The wall behind their table bore flyers printed on colored paper touting classes in Sufi mysticism, holistic healing, radical breatherapy, and feng shui as well as seminars in spiritual emergence trauma, body-mind alignment, and how to discover one's inner goddess. Inner goddesses had recently been a hot topic around the local espresso shops, some residents thinking the gender-based term politically incorrect. It was quickly changed to inner god/goddess, but that jargon was a mouthful, especially after a couple of dry white wines, so it was shortened to just godology. Hannah could never quite figure out what her inner god/goddess/godology was all about and quickly found she didn't care.

Lauren took on the task of getting the drinks—two waters, a Lemon Lift tea for Kiki, a double espresso for Hannah, and a "nothing" for herself, which was the term applied to plain decafs with nonfat milk. Once the drinks arrived, Kiki and Hannah took out their postmenopausal herbal capsules, downing them all in a well-practiced single swallow.

The effects of menopause once again abated, Kiki rested her chin on her palm as she drowned her tea bag in a mug of hot water.

"Lauren, did I tell you that Arnold Lempke personally

nursed his wife at home until she died? That man was by her side night and day," Kiki said, shaking her index finger for emphasis. "Wouldn't let a nurse touch her, he was so devoted." She took a sip of her tea, making a face when it burned her tongue.

"That's so wonderful. I remember Mr. Lempke from ten years ago," Lauren said.

"You used to be friends with his daughter, didn't you?" Hannah asked as she sipped an espresso as thick as bat's blood.

"Yes. Lisa. I haven't seen her in years. Her father must have loved her mother an awful lot to take care of her like that." Lauren pushed her long brown hair behind her ears, her eyes brimming with sympathy. She was a warm, loving puppy of a person, an emotional sponge soaking up whatever pain or joy was around her. It was her gift and her curse. "What did his wife die from?"

Kiki leaned close. "She had a stroke, I think," she said, her voice lowered. "Sad. But we should all be so lucky to have a husband like Arnold to take care of us when the time comes."

It crossed Hannah's mind that a woman who had had a stroke was better off with professional nursing care, but it wasn't a subject she knew much about, so she kept her opinion to herself.

"You'll get to meet Arnie if he comes to the Rose Club cocktail reception tonight," Kiki said happily. "He promised to sit at our table." Wearing a sly smile, she nudged Hannah's elbow. "And you, Hannah. I want you to be nice to him."

Hannah gave a small shudder at the thought of having to schmooze with Arnold Lempke. To her he seemed cold, aggressive, and completely self-absorbed, though apparently he had a way with women. Hannah personally couldn't see it. She wasn't especially interested in attending the cocktail reception in the first place and she had been hoping that Kiki would forget she had agreed to go. No such luck.

She attempted an evasive maneuver. "You know, I forgot that I have to order next season's bulbs tonight, and—"

Kiki set down her mug with a clatter. "You have to go! I won it fair and square. I had a full house to your three tens!"

Hannah winced. "You wouldn't have known you had one if I hadn't explained it to you."

"It doesn't matter. We agreed if I won the game you would go to the reception. You can't back out. I beat you."

Hannah nodded with resignation. There was no denying that Kiki had won the hand during last week's poker game, and a bet was a bet.

"You can wear the dark purple sheath." Lauren, another Wednesday-night poker participant, was equally encouraging about getting Hannah out and socializing more.

Kiki clutched her hands in front of her chest. "Oh yes, the purple sheath. A little boring, but very flattering, Hannah. Makes you look a little like Jane Fonda. Maybe you could wear your hair loose for a change."

Just then an elegant woman in her early thirties dressed in white leggings and matching pullover sat down at the table next to them and said hello to Lauren. Lauren introduced her to her aunts. Her name was Marlene.

"Is this your poet aunt?" Marlene asked, her voice silky. Hannah smiled. Lauren loved to tell her friends about her poetry-writing relative. Hannah was only an amateur poet, but her work was printed twice a month in a local weekly newspaper. It seemed to her that remarkably few people actually read the poems, which didn't bother her. The work won her an occasional free cup of coffee at the Book Stop.

"I've always thought I've had poetry in me. Something primal," Marlene said, putting a low throaty emphasis on the last word. "I have an hour free while my little Todd is in his African drum class, so I thought I'd have some java and soak up the atmosphere."

"And how old is Todd?" Hannah asked, trying to be friendly. She was truly appreciative when anyone showed interest in her poetry

"Two," Marlene answered. Hannah blinked. But then, a two-year-old in an African drum class was fairly average for Hill Creek.

Hannah, Kiki, and Lauren returned their attention to each other so Marlene could soak up atmosphere.

"Back to the reception," Kiki said. "There will be several eligible men there, if you know what I mean."

"Eligible for Medicare," Hannah replied.

Kiki made a face. "Age has nothing to do with anything. Men need women. Women need men."

"Women don't need anything except exercise and interesting work," Hannah told her.

Kiki made a "twiffle" sound. "They're some things women need and you know what I'm talking about."

"Let's drop the subject."

"You've been hiding yourself away lately, Hannah," Kiki said. "You need to go out with men."

"I've gone out with men."

"But you never go out with them more than once."

"Once is enough." Hannah downed the last gulp of coffee.

Leaning forward, her elbows on the table, Kiki glanced around to make certain no one was listening. "What was the point of getting that darn tattoo if no man's ever going to see it?" she said, voice lowered.

"You should at least let us see it, Aunt Hannah," Lauren said eagerly. Both she and Kiki were dying to get a glimpse of the artistic results of Hannah's two trips the month before to a tattoo shop in San Francisco. She had been very open about having the tattoo done, but now refused to show it to anyone or even say where it was located, which made her sister that much more intent on seeing it. She had followed Hannah into the bathroom and demanded a viewing, but that had been futile. She had repeatedly cracked open

Hannah's bedroom door to get a peek as Hannah dressed for bed, but Hannah always managed to catch her. It was all very exasperating.

"I'll show you my tattoo when I'm good and ready, and I'm currently not," Hannah said. "Do we have time for me to have another coffee?"

"Oh, forget coffee," Kiki said with frustration. "I just don't believe any woman gets a tattoo unless deep down she wants a man to see it."

"Well, you're wrong," Hannah told her.

Kiki eyed her sister with a stern expression. "The problem with you is that you never give men a chance."

Hannah rolled her eyes. "I've had two husbands and a dozen lovers. That's been plenty. The problem with you is that you're obsessed with men. It's not healthy, and one of these days it's going to get you in trouble."

"Obsessed? *Moi?* I just know what I want, and I want Arnold Lempke. And it's not going to hurt you to get out a little. You know what they say. Use it or lose it."

Although she would never admit it out loud, Hannah knew Kiki was right about one thing. Hannah could stand to get out more and see people. Not that she didn't like her life. The problem was that she liked it too much. She adored her gardening, her pets, her poetry, and her volunteer work, but she rarely socialized and she sometimes feared she was turning into a recluse.

"Well, you can live your life any way you want to, but I like men and I'm hanging on to the one I've got," Kiki declared proudly. "And with my new jumpsuit I'm going to knock Arnold Lempke dead."

Two

$\mathscr{B}$ENEATH AN INDOOR ARBOR OF pure white chrysanthemums, Hannah sipped a Calistoga water and surveyed the crowd at the Rose Club cocktail reception. She was wearing the purple sheath along with her dressiest shoes and her best beaded necklace, and she felt positively chic. Although her hair was in its usual chignon, she had adorned it with a single lavender iris, which completed her outfit to perfection. Kiki had tried her best to talk her into wearing a pair of black panty hose, but that's where Hannah drew the line. When she retired from her job as an executive secretary several years earlier, she had vowed solemnly never to wear panty hose again, and so far she had stuck to the promise.

It was fun to be dressed up and at a party, Hannah realized as she watched the club members milling about the ballroom, some huddled by the table of appetizers, others chatting in small groups or sitting at tables. The club attracted a homogeneous membership, mostly front-line baby boomers putting the effort into their gardens they once put into their sex lives. It was an elegantly dressed group, most of the women in simple but expensive cocktail dresses, the men in dark suits or white dinner jackets. But Hannah smiled at all this pomp and finery, since most of them probably had fertilizer under their fingernails. Certainly they all looked like they were having a good time.

The band had just started playing a polkalike version of "Satisfaction" and people began dancing. Most of the dancers out on the floor were over fifty and they gyrated somewhat stiffly to the music, their heads filled with vague remembrances of Woodstock and the Summer of Love. But now they were much more interested in free trade than free love, and at last year's "Back to the Sixties" bash almost everyone got their peace symbols confused with the Mercedes emblem.

The cocktail party was naturally held in the Rose Club clubhouse, which members liked to call the "cottage." The latter was actually a formidable six-thousand-square-foot Tudor-style home that had been built in the twenties and donated to the club thirty years before by a rose lover who preferred plants to his children. All large social functions held by the Rose Club took place in the ballroom located in the east wing. To make money for maintenance and to pay taxes the room was occasionally rented out at an extravagant price for wedding receptions and anniversary functions. People willingly paid the money, with a long waiting list for the privilege, since whatever signs of wealth Marin County residents couldn't actually afford to buy, they tried desperately to rent. The ballroom was lavish, with tall leaded windows, a grand piano at one end, a herringbone wood floor, and massive crystal chandeliers that twinkled and glistened in sun or candlelight.

While standing in the corner of this opulence, Hannah watched the dancers, easily picking out five married pairs who were recombinations from previous Rose Club couples, and two of whom were on their third go-round. Marin residents tended toward multiple marriages, trading in spouses as easily as last year's Lexus. But the Rose Club crowd had a curious tendency to pick their significant others from within the club membership.

It wasn't surprising when you considered it, Hannah thought, since gardeners tended to have similar natures. She found the best gardeners to be nurturing, agreeable people, and it seemed natural for them to marry. And the resulting offspring knew how to mulch well and spray properly for blackspot. The club had an impressive junior gardening group that had planted Russian sage and lantana along the Hill Creek medians, making the drive through town spectacular in spring and summer.

A tuxedoed waiter came by with a tray of ice-cold champagne, offering a glass to Hannah, which she refused with a smile. She then turned her attention to the ballroom itself and admired the decorations. The decorating committee had outdone themselves and the room was festooned with hundreds of fresh flowers—roses, lilies, and chrysanthemums, not only in arrangements on the tables but woven onto trellises standing on opposite sides of the dance floor, with hundreds more tied onto garlands that draped outward from the center of the ceiling. Hannah didn't cut many flowers from her own garden, preferring to see them in the ground, but she had to admit the cut flowers in such profusion were lovely.

Seeing the crowd of old friends, she felt wonderfully contented, the evening having gone better than she had expected. As soon as they arrived, Kiki had raced off in search of Arnold Lempke, so Hannah had been free to do as she liked. She hadn't attended one of the club's formal functions in several years and everyone seemed so glad to see her. She had chatted with several friends she hadn't seen in ages. One of them had invited her to work in the Learning Garden at the local elementary school and Hannah surprised herself at how quickly she accepted.

There was no denying that in spite of her earlier reticence, she was enjoying the party immensely. The lighting was dimmed to that point where everybody's looks were remarkably improved. The food was good, the music pass-able, and she had gotten into several absorbing conversa-tions, especially the one with a woman regarding the use of oil sprays on spider mites.

Hannah heard a familiar bangling of bracelets and then felt a hand on her shoulder.

"Oh, Hannah, don't stand here by yourself," Kiki said. She was wearing a beige-and-gold chiffon cocktail dress belted at the waist, reminding Hannah of an Oscar Meyer wiener cinched in the middle, although she would never tell that to Kiki. The dress was frothily unfashionable, something Doris Day would have donned in the late fifties for a frisky scene with Rock Hudson. And to complete the effect, Kiki's bottle-blond hair was teased and sprayed to the point where it no longer seemed attached to her scalp but seemed more like a parachute in full flight, dropping her skull to safety.

Hannah smiled at her sister then warily eyed her half-full champagne glass. Kiki had a low threshold for alcohol, anything more than two drinks inducing powerful urges for strip limbo.

"Go enjoy yourself. I'm perfectly content people watch-ing," Hannah said.

"But you can't be. No, I won't let you stand here by yourself."

Hannah smiled. "I've only been by myself a moment. Trust me, I've been chatting up a storm."

"We've got a big table in the corner." Kiki wrapped her arm around Hannah's waist and whispered in her ear, "Ar-nold's here. And he's sitting right next to me."

Not waiting for arguments, she grabbed Hannah's hand and dragged her through the dancers, wiggling, eyes closed, to a Lawrence Welkish rendition of "White Rabbit." When she and Hannah reached a large round table in the corner, a woman leaped up from her chair, swept over, and gave Hannah a bear hug.

"Hannah, I knew you would be here tonight. I saw it

with my inner eye,'' said Naomi, their next-door neighbor. Her largish figure was draped in a long flowing red caftan with ribbons dangling from the neck and sleeves, her hair piled on top of her head and held in place with wooden picks that had little silk flags dangling from the ends. The effect was at first startling, then quite gay as the flags bobbed with every movement of her head.

"You are a vision. Purple is your color. Perfectly complements your aura,'' Naomi exclaimed, then leaned her face close to Hannah's ear. "I have to talk to you about the festival next week. Ginger has me down for duty at the dunking booth, and you know my back. I just can't handle the standing, and I was wondering if you'd be a dear and trade with me.''

Hannah suspected that Naomi's back was perfectly fine and that what she couldn't handle was the fact that dunking booth duty was the least favored of all events at the annual Rose Club festival. It required dealing with hundreds of squealing children who had never been properly disciplined by school or parents for fear of damaging their self-esteem. The job also entailed frequent splashings. All the volunteers had drawn lots to see who would work which sections. Hannah had lucked into the beer concession, which was one of the most sought-after positions, nice and quiet since most people in Marin preferred dry white wine with buttery undertones and an amusing hint of oak.

"I thought you had allergic reactions to yeast,'' Hannah said, calling her bluff, but Naomi reacted fast under pressure.

"I was thinking of wearing cotton gloves to protect myself.''

"I'll think about it,'' Hannah said, and Naomi beamed, temporarily satisfied. She knew that although Hannah could be a tough nut on the surface, underneath she was soft as marshmallow, and all it would take was a few well-timed groans about back pain to get her to relent.

By this time Kiki had flounced down into the chair next

to Arnold Lempke, who was gnawing on a celery stick, one hand gripping a fresh Scotch on the rocks. Hannah tightened up just looking at him, and she tried to understand exactly why he repelled her so. She knew lots of people with less-than-pleasant personalities, but she had a special distaste for Lempke.

Across from him sat Wanda Backus, the Rose Club vice-chairperson and her husband, Walter. Hannah didn't know the youngish couple sitting next to them, which was quickly remedied.

"This is Sandy and David Dawson. They're new members who just moved to Hill Creek and we're so thrilled!" Kiki gushed daintily for Lempke's benefit. Sandy and David smiled politely, each of them looking as if something sharp was lodged in an inconvenient orifice. Hannah assumed Wanda had been describing her and Walter's sex therapy, which after a cocktail she was apt to do loudly and graphically, using her knife and fork for demonstration purposes.

Kiki leaned toward Lempke. "It's always nice meeting new people, isn't it, Arnold? When I think of all the new people we'll meet on our cruise."

This was mostly said for the benefit of Wanda, who liked to pummel Kiki with the fact that she had a husband in tow, *in tow* being the operative words, since Wanda dragged Walter around as if he were a lassoed calf. Wanda was a prime example of a much-married Marinite, with poor beleaguered Walter being her fifth nuptial plunge. She had yet to tolerate a husband more than three years, but it wasn't for any lack of ability to commit, for she had been devoted to the same incontinent poodle named Bon Bon for over ten.

Lempke smiled tightly without looking at Kiki. As Hannah sat down in the only available chair, unfortunately located on the other side of him, she noticed Kiki's hand squeezing his knee under the table.

Although Hannah couldn't explain it, at that moment a

small chill swept through her and she was seized by a feeling that something unpleasant was brewing. Lempke was always a fairly cheerless man, but he normally had decent social graces. Tonight he looked unusually grim, the small smile on his face seeming forced, and beneath Kiki's ebullience there was an air of desperation. She was trying too hard to flaunt their relationship and apparently Arnold wasn't in the flaunting mood.

"So, Hannah, tell us about your tattoo. Kiki says you're being very mysterious about it," Naomi said. Hannah cast her sister a reprimanding glance as Naomi continued. "I have the entire zodiac tattooed across my buttocks."

After that statement, Hannah's tattoo was forgotten as everyone animatedly discussed Naomi's posterior, which she kindly offered to expose to the table. It was only the shocked protest of Sandy Dawson that prevented her.

All ears then turned to Wanda, who told a story about grubworms at the roots of her impatiens. Everyone, including Hannah, listened intently, since garden pests was on everyone's list of favorite topics.

It was during Wanda's story that out of the corner of her eye Hannah saw Lempke, apparently thinking everyone enraptured with grubworms, take a handful of cheeseballs from the plate in front of him, wrap them in a cloth napkin, and stick them in his coat pocket. It amazed her that the man would steal cocktail appetizers when everybody knew he was rolling in money. But then she remembered that his wife had died in the past year. Maybe the poor man wasn't getting enough decent food at home. She made a mental note to tell Kiki to make him some casseroles he could freeze.

The cheeseballs successfully pilfered, Lempke turned to her. "I have suspicions about some downy mildew on my new hybrid," he said, his tone serious. "I'd like you to come over tomorrow morning and have a look."

It surprised Hannah that Lempke wanted her advice on his roses, since he fancied himself the greatest authority in

Northern California. In fact, she was so surprised that she stumbled around a few seconds before politely declining with an excuse that she was doing counseling with the breast-cancer help group the next morning. This wasn't perfectly true, but she immediately planned to make it so by calling the center in the morning and offering to work extra hours. To be honest, she was interested in inspecting Lempke's downy mildew. It was a new rose disease much feared by rose growers across the country, and she had only seen photographs of it in gardening magazines, yet she found Lempke too annoying to spend any time with. She knew it was an uncharitable attitude, but it was one she couldn't help.

Lempke smirked at her refusal. "Don't help me, if that's the way you want it," he said. "I'm going to beat you in the rose competition this year, sweetheart. You may have won three years in a row, but this year's mine."

"I wish you luck," Hannah said with sincerity. She didn't grow roses to win contests. She grew them because she loved them. The Rose Club's annual festival was the only contest she ever entered, and she did it only because the festival proceeds went to charity.

She liked winning. She couldn't deny it. When her "Mr. Lincoln" won Queen of Show last year, she found herself bursting with pride. But she felt winning shouldn't be taken too seriously. The fun was in the growing of the rose. Still, a bit of recognition from one's fellow gardeners was appreciated, especially since Hill Creek rose growers all faced similar challenges of cool nights and frequent summer fogs, creating a less-than-ideal environment for their beloved flowers.

The band began to play an old Beatles tune. More people moved toward the dance floor, but everyone at Hannah's table stayed put.

"You want to dance, Arnie?" Kiki asked loud enough so everyone could hear. "Good practice for the cruise."

"No," he answered with a snort. Kiki sat back in her

chair, her smile only slightly dimmed by this rejection, but Hannah could tell she was embarrassed by the way she hastily turned her attention to Naomi.

Then, to Hannah's colossal surprise, she felt a pressure on her thigh. She almost hoped she was having some strange seizure, the only alternative being so distasteful, but looking down, she found to her disgust that it was indeed Lempke's hand. There were only two options, the first being to cool his crotch with her Calistoga. She chose option two and pushed his hand away. Lempke responded with a wicked grin.

"You're a good-looking woman. Would you like to do a round on the dance floor? I can shake it when I need to," he whispered, his voice low so Kiki wouldn't hear.

Hannah made certain Kiki was deep in conversation with Naomi before responding. "I'd rather swallow a lug nut," she told him.

Undaunted, Lempke smiled devilishly, making her feel like upchucking the sun-dried-tomato focaccia appetizer she had eaten earlier.

Luckily the awkward moment was broken by the sound of Wanda's voice breaking through the music with buzzsaw clarity.

"Naomi, darling, you must tell Sandy and David about your channeling. I've filled them in on your psychic abilities, about how much help your Red Moon has been to Walter and me," Wanda said enthusiastically, speaking as usual for both herself and her husband. Walter never seemed to mind, since his lips were usually wrapped around a cocktail glass. In addition to their sex therapy, Wanda and Walter frequently saw Naomi for psychic readings.

"We're not really sure what channeling is," Sandy said stiffly, touching the collar of her prim navy suit.

Hannah smiled. "That's because you're new to Marin County."

"We're from Cleveland," David answered, a reply that explained their ignorance of New Age practices.

Everybody in Marin knew all about channeling. Although psychic powers and spiritual transformation had for ages been part of the Northern California culture, in the past few years there had been a renaissance of interest. As the baby boomers aged, they realized that their BMWs and water-view condos hadn't provided quite the inner satisfaction they had hoped for, so they began seeking spiritual guidance. And there was plenty of spiritual guidance available in California, in all price ranges. Although with the way the stock market was going, cults where members gave up their worldly goods to gurus was strictly passé.

Naomi sat at attention, loving to talk shop. "I'm a vessel for a spirit from another world. An ancient Hopi snake shaman named Red Moon. He speaks through me."

David and Sandy looked confused.

"He takes her body," Wanda chimed in.

Confusion turned to disgust as Sandy, eyebrows lifted and lips puckered in a particularly Cleveland-like brand of disapproval, pressed a well-manicured hand to the base of her throat. "Excuse me?"

"Nothing sexual," Naomi explained with a patronizing smile. "He uses me as his instrument. His energy pours through me. Think of me as his Internet connection to the physical realm." She said the last part with a grand sweep of her arms that sent all the little silk flags in her hair quivering, then she lifted her eyes toward the garlands hanging from the ceiling. "Through me Red Moon provides heightened spiritual consciousness and a divine path to understanding one's inner mysteries."

It seemed to Hannah that at fifty dollars an hour, what Red Moon provided was a way for Naomi to pay her substantial Visa bill each month. Just then she noticed Lempke tense up, and glanced down to see if Kiki's hand had wandered some place it shouldn't have, but her sister's fingers sat benignly on his knee.

"Red Moon has such insight," Wanda said to Sandy. "Two years ago when Walter and I weren't sure whether or not to sell the rental in San Rafael, we consulted Red Moon. He directed us to a vortex in Sedona. 'At this place of power you will find answers,' Red Moon said. And he was so right. There we were, just Walter and me, high on this bluff, dressed in native Hopi wear. It was *sooo* romantic. *Sooo* healing. We did the Dance of the Deer and afterward we felt such clarity.''

Walter took an extra big sip of his martini as the memory apparently came back to him. The Dawsons looked perplexed.

It was at this point that Lempke drew his Scotch to his lips, swallowed the remainder of it as if it were the last whisky on earth, then slammed the glass down on the table.

''It's all a lot of goddamn bunk! That whole Red Moon business is a complete and total fake,'' he said way too loudly. An uncomfortable silence enveloped the table and Hannah realized from the way he was glaring at Naomi that it was her presence that must have caused his foul temper that evening. Naomi froze, at first startled by his remark, but then turned to him.

''Now, Arnold, you're directing your energy into a very negative passage. Perhaps if you closed your eyes, took a deep breath, and focused on a chakra,'' she said to him, her tone soft but with a edge, like velvet wrapped around a sharp rock.

''What's a chakra?'' Sandy asked.

''An energy point in your body,'' Wanda answered quickly, her eyes glued to Lempke and Naomi, not wanting to miss a good fight.

''Don't chakra me,'' Lempke spat. ''You're a fraud.''

Naomi gasped, closed her eyes, and seemed to be madly trying to focus on a chakra of her own.

''Why, Arnold, how can you say such a thing?'' Wanda said, coming to Naomi and Red Moon's defense since she had paid both of them a lot of money. ''Red Moon was such a comfort to your wife during those last months.''

Lempke's fingers tightened around his empty glass. ''Oh

sure, Mary paid plenty for that stupid Indian-spirit bunk. A waste of money and I always told her so, but she was so set on it and at first I didn't think there was any harm.''

"Harm?" Naomi's eyes popped open. "Red Moon helped Mary with some important emotional integration.''

Pressing his hands against the edge of the table, Lempke leaned toward her menacingly. "Crap. That's what it was. Pure unadulterated crapola. All that stuff about hyacinths blooming in the garden even though we never planted any. Supposed to be a sign of long life or whatever. Well, they never came out of the ground, did they? It just gave my poor Mary hope where there wasn't any. There's never been hyacinths in my garden and there never will be. The damn bulbs are too much trouble.''

Hannah looked at Naomi. If her poor friend was concentrating on any chakra, it could only have been one of Lempke's, and she felt certain Naomi was imagining putting a knife through it. Hannah reached over and placed a reassuring hand on Naomi's arm, but aimed her attention at Arnold.

"You're entitled to your opinion, Arnold, but you're not entitled to being hostile and obnoxious,'' she told him in a quiet but firm voice. Kiki's eyes grew large.

His face screwed itself up. "I'd think a rosarian as astute as yourself would have a little more sense,'' he replied, then turned to the astounded Dawsons. "You'll find Hill Creek in particular and Marin County in general filled with New Age flakes and losers. They'll take your kids and brainwash them. Wreck their lives.''

Sandy and David exchanged worried glances. "What do you mean?'' Sandy asked.

"Example one, people pretending that dead Indians can talk through them,'' he said, jabbing his finger against the table. "Example two, my only daughter joined a crazy church called the Church of Revelations. Full of people talking weird things, doing weird things. It's not normal.'' Lempke paused, his eyes fixed upon the tabletop. "There's something wrong going on at that church and I'm going to prove it,'' he muttered. He raised his drink to his lips, scowling when he realized he had already finished it. He put the glass back on the table then turned to Kiki. ''I can't go on that damn cruise. I want you to stop bothering me about it. I've got work to do exposing that church.''

There was a stupefied pause in the conversation. It was Walter who broke the silence.

''I think old Arnold may have some blocked feelings from unresolved birth trauma,'' he commented with a drunken giggle, speaking for the first time that evening. ''Could need a colonic cleansing.'' His wife grabbed his martini out of his hand.

Kiki's widened, tortured eyes followed Arnold as he stood up, pushing his chair back noisily. ''I need another drink, this time one with some decent Scotch in it.'' With that, he stomped off.

Dropping a bucket of excrement on the table wouldn't have disturbed everyone any more than Lempke's nastiness. The Dawsons looked dumbfounded. Naomi turned red with fury and poor Kiki fought back tears. While Wanda's mouth hung open Walter used the opportunity to slide his martini back in front of him.

Kiki jumped up from the table, spilling her champagne, and ran toward the ladies' room, her high-heeled mules slapping the floor as the band switched to a merry rumba. After exchanging an anxious look, Hannah and Naomi both followed.

The ladies' room was thankfully unoccupied, and the women congregated by the vanity. Now in the safe confines of the female sanctuary, Kiki let her distress go at full throttle, her eyes streaming, lips trembling. Grabbing a large wad of toilet paper out of a stall, she pressed it to her nose.

''I've never been so humiliated in my life!'' she blubbered, her voice muffled by the tissue.

Naomi dabbed at Kiki's running mascara with a Kleenex. ''That man has enough bad karma to choke a horse.''

"To refuse to go on the cruise is bad enough," Kiki continued. "But to do it in front of Wanda. She's probably gloating right now."

"Who cares if she's gloating? It doesn't matter what anybody thinks," Hannah told her. "The important thing is that you don't let a fool like Arnold upset you."

"That Arnold," Naomi muttered. "You should hear him run on and on about how religious he is. Well, I don't believe it. As for his problems with his daughter, from what I could see, the problem isn't the Church of Revelations. He and Lisa never got along. Mary told me."

"Are you feeling better, Kiki?" Hannah asked.

"Just let me get my face back on," she answered, scrounging through her beaded handbag for her makeup. She examined herself critically in the gilt-framed mirror, dried her eyelashes with the toilet paper, then, mouth open and her face inches from the glass, began applying a fresh layer of mascara.

"You're better off without him anyway," Hannah told her. Watching Kiki's reflection in the mirror, she saw an expression on her sister's face like that of a cow watching the space shuttle fly overhead—the senses receiving input but with absolutely no comprehension.

"Better off without him?" Kiki asked.

"Of course. You can have a perfectly good time on the cruise alone."

Kiki spun around to face her. "But I'm not going alone. I'll get Arnold back."

Naomi and Hannah exchanged incredulous looks.

"Kiki, you listen to me," Hannah said. "Chasing Arnold Lempke can't come to any good. He's a foul man and he's treated you terribly."

Turning back to the mirror, Kiki reapplied her lipstick. "Arnold can be very sweet when we're alone. I don't know what's wrong with him tonight. I think Naomi just gets on his nerves."

Naomi's eyes narrowed and Hannah patted her arm to keep her quiet.

Kiki continued. "Arnold is going on that cruise with me. I'll get him back. Just you wait and see."

With that proclamation she began furiously dabbing blusher on her cheeks until she looked clownish. Hannah took a tissue out of her handbag and, with Kiki's chin held gently in her hand, wiped off some of the makeup.

"We just need to take off a little of this pink here and over here. There. You look gorgeous," Hannah said. "Now let's go back to the party and have a lovely time."

If she had been a colder woman, she could have mentioned that Lempke had made a pass at her, but that information, however factual, would have been too cruel a blow. She could never hurt Kiki that way, so she kept it to herself. She would have to find another way to distract her sister from him.

With Kiki put back together, the three women returned to the ballroom. Lempke was back at the table, another empty glass in front of him, his mouth moving rapidly. Just as the women reached the table he leaped out of his chair.

"It's a fraud!" he growled to anyone within earshot, the words slurred. "That Church of Revelations. It's a fraud. I'm going to report all of them to the district attorney's office! And I'm going to do it tomorrow!"

And with that ominous proclamation, he stomped off, leaving the rest of the table staring after him in bewilderment.

$\mathcal{T}$HREE

THE BLOW CAME HARD AND without warning, crashing against the back of his neck, a deafening thunder roaring through his head. Time froze, everything in his slender world ceasing to exist except the burst of pain and light that enveloped him.

Then, as quickly as the pain had erupted, it ceased, and his mind began floating in a comforting stillness, all the confusion and anger of seconds ago now vanished. Only one image remained in his moments before death, that of his beloved hybrid rosebush. One last time his eyes fell upon its flowers and he admired nature's perfection—the glossy green leaves catching the sunlight, the fragrant petals a velvety white adorned with streaks of red. The red looks like blood, he thought as his body collapsed forward into the plant.

But it didn't only look like blood. It *was* blood, and it unluckily belonged to him.

"I don't want to bring up bad memories, but last night was such a catastrophe. How can you still be interested in that

detestable man?'' Hannah said as she drove Kiki's gold
1972 Cadillac Eldorado convertible away from their house
on Walnut Avenue. In a land of BMWs and Mercedes,
Kiki's choice of transportation was a curiosity in Hill
Creek, and the Cadillac had become a local landmark. The
residents smiled as Kiki, donning dark glasses and a col-
orful scarf, drove the car, top down, along Center Avenue,
waving to any person she knew and lots of people she
didn't.

When Kiki had moved in with Hannah several years before, Hannah had owned a Subaru station wagon, but the
women could afford to keep up only one car. Kiki insisted
it be the Cadillac, especially after it was requisitioned
briefly by a local filmmaker. After that, Kiki wouldn't have
given up the car on any account, so Hannah sold the Subaru
and moved her potting shed out of the back of her one-car
garage so the Cadillac, the size of a small barge, would fit.
To Hannah's surprise she grew to like the car. Although it
was unwieldy to drive and park, she loved its smell, the
interior filled with the odor of aged fabric and vinyl, of
pressed powder and perfume.

But at that particular moment, nestled in its cushioned
seats of beige simulated velvet, Hannah was not in the best
of moods. Under duress, she had agreed to accompany Kiki
on a reconnaissance mission to Arnold Lempke's. Then,
while backing out of the driveway, she had been forced to
commandeer the car's steering wheel after Kiki, fresh from
the hairdresser and feeling especially delectable, kept ad-
miring her new false eyelashes in the rearview mirror and
had run over Hannah's lilies-of-the-Nile. Only the week
before Kiki had smashed the right rear fender in the parking
lot of Lady Nails. There was no need to drive to Lempke's
in the first place since his house was only a couple of blocks
away, but Kiki refused to walk.

"Arnold didn't mean what he said," Kiki replied dis-
tractedly, taking her sweet time in responding to Hannah's
question.

Hannah shot her a look of openmouthed astonishment. "Didn't mean it? He yelled it out for all to hear," she said, her voice rising heatedly. In a spasm of disgust, she stopped the car in the middle of the street. "I can't do this," she said, rapping the steering wheel with her palm. "It's too degrading."

With a frantic waving of her hands, Kiki shouted, "Hannah, someone's honking at us! You're acting crazy."

Hannah pressed on the accelerator and the Cadillac lurched forward. "You're the one acting crazy. Catching a man isn't the only worthwhile goal in life. There are other pursuits. There's education, art, exercise."

Kiki gave her sister a mocking glance as she gazed into her compact mirror and refreshed her Tahiti Pink lipstick for the third time in six minutes.

"I'll give those a try when I'm ninety. As for now, I think I'll try activities that are a little more frisky."

Hannah groaned. "Are you that desperate to have sex? Is that what this is all about?" As she spoke, her hands flew precariously off the steering wheel. "Because if it is, it would be more dignified to dip into Cecil's pension fund and buy yourself a pool boy."

Kiki's entire body shook with revulsion. "You have *such* a dirty mind. This isn't a sex thing. This has to do with companionship."

"Oh yes, companionship," Hannah said with a smirk. "That's what you called it in high school when you were caught in the backseat of Randy Kowolsky's De Soto."

"I was in love!"

"You're always in love." Hannah immediately regretted mentioning the De Soto incident, it having been a sore point with Kiki for the last forty-five years or so. "I'm sorry, I really am. The point I'm trying to make is that last night when Arnold said he didn't want to go on the cruise, he sounded like he meant it."

Kiki let loose a false, tinkling laugh. "I can change his mind."

Gritting her teeth, Hannah did her best to squelch the apprehensions bubbling up inside her. It had taken twenty minutes of begging to convince her to participate in this surprise visit to Arnold. But Kiki had seemed so depressed after the party last night. So she finally gave in, deciding anything was worth perking her her sister up, even if it meant subordinating her own judgment. Besides, she had to admire Kiki's fortitude and persistence. If she had directed those qualities to the business world, she could have climbed high up the rungs of some corporate ladder. Now all it had gotten her was a couple of husbands she had never liked much. Yet here she was scheming to bag another one. Some women just never learned.

Hannah made a left onto Sunnyside Lane, the Cadillac sputtering and hesitating, as if reflecting Hannah's consternation.

Kiki smacked her lips together then snapped on the top of her lipstick with a satisfying click.

"I'll be the first to admit that Arnie flew off the handle. But you know how men are. All that testosterone." Kiki said this word with a singsong lilt and a suggestive lift of her eyebrows. Hannah rolled her eyes upward. Kiki had more testosterone in her little finger than Arnold had in his whole body.

"Right here," Kiki told her, wiggling her finger. "Fourth house on the right."

Hannah pulled the Cadillac to the curb. After a little more primping on Kiki's part, they got out of the car and walked up the short walkway that led to Lempke's gate, Kiki's high heels clicking against the cracked sidewalk. Her knees weren't as good as they used to be, and the shoes—coupled with the fact that she had squeezed her hips into a stretchy leopard-print skirt—resulted in her having to walk slightly stooped, with short, pigeon-toed geisha steps. She had tapped out a Mexican hat dance by the time they reached the six-foot redwood fence meant to keep out stray dogs and solicitors.

Hannah halted in front of the gate. "We're not going one step further until you button up your blouse. You're practically hanging out."

"Oh, don't be such a prude."

"It's not prudishness. It's taste. Button up or I get back in the car."

Kiki sighed with exasperation. "All right, all right. But it's strange coming from a woman who was a hippie in Haight-Ashbury. You practically ran around naked. Now you're so conservative."

"That was thirty years ago. Things have changed."

"Not all that much," Kiki said. "You still listen to Jefferson Airplane." She buttoned up one button, looked at Hannah, still saw disapproval, then buttoned up another one.

"That's better," Hannah said. "Now listen to me. I'm giving you one more chance to avoid making an idiot out of yourself. We can turn around right now, walk away, and maintain a few shreds of dignity."

"I don't want dignity. I want Arnie on that cruise." For emphasis, Kiki grabbed the gate latch and jerked it upward, pushing the gate forward, the old wood scraping against the sidewalk.

After taking a few tentative steps and seeing the front yard, Hannah gasped. Although the house itself was like Lempke—square and dull, all sharp ugly edges—the garden in front was a paradise of texture and color. Petunias, lilies, asters, wisteria, and trumpet vine filled almost every square foot, all bursting with purples and reds and yellows. If the house represented Lempke's harsh exterior, was this garden the image of his soul? Hannah wondered.

"Arnold's a better gardener than I imagined," she said, her voice softened with admiration.

Kiki smiled. "See? You'd like him if you gave him a chance."

Perhaps she would. He was not only an excellent gardener but a landscape designer as well. Hannah noticed a gravel walkway leading to a side yard and her pulse quickened.

"The garden over there faces south. That must be the roses." Eagerly she grabbed Kiki's arm, attempting to pull her along. "I'd love to see his hybrid tea. It must have taken him years of work to produce it. Everyone says it could win the competition this year."

But Kiki stood firmly where she was. "We can do that later. I'm going to ring the doorbell."

"Please, Kiki, just one minute. I want to take a good look without him staring over my shoulder."

Kiki threw up her hands but followed. "Sweet Jesus, with you it's always plants, plants, plants. You should pay a little attention to people sometime."

They walked down the path along the side of the house through a narrow shade garden filled with foxglove, ferns, and hostas. Hannah stopped to admire one especially vibrant fuchsia.

"Isn't it lovely, Kiki?" She touched one of the purple flowers. "It must be quite old. It has a trunk with bark, like a little tree."

"Trees, schmeez," Kiki replied. "Let's hurry up and look at that silly rose."

As they rounded the back of the house they entered one of the most prodigious private rose gardens Hannah had ever seen. Brilliant red and yellow climbers ran along the fence line, and a series of tiered raised wooden beds sat filled with dozens of gorgeous flowering bushes.

Hannah stared, drinking in the scented air and rich colors, but Kiki couldn't enjoy them because at that moment her view of the world suddenly darkened. She stopped in her tracks. "Oh, piddle. Is my eyelash coming off?"

Hannah pulled her eyes away from the roses and looked at her sister. "It's either that or a spider's on your cheek."

"Help me fix it."

"All right. Hold still and close your eye." Hannah got her reading glasses from her purse, put them on, and attempted to stick the eyelash back on Kiki's eyelid, but the lash resisted and Kiki's eyelid insisted on twitching.

"You're pushing me," Kiki complained

"If you'd keep your eye closed, I could manage better."

"My eye *is* closed."

"It isn't."

"I'm telling you, it is. You're pushing me into the bushes. I feel thorns. Oops. Oh, spit. Now my heel's caught and—"

Teetering on her shoes, Kiki lost her balance and soon plopped down onto the gravel walkway, legs splayed, the event accompanied by a disconcerting ripping sound.

"Oh, see what you've done. My seam is torn!" Kiki said, her arms and legs flailing like an overturned cockroach.

With a shake of her head, Hannah leaned down to help her up. "It's hardly my fault. Well, you can't see Arnold with a ripped skirt, so we might as well go home." Looking behind Kiki, she froze. "My God, what is that?"

Following Hannah's eyes, Kiki looked down to her left and let out an alarmed "oh." A khaki-clad leg stuck out of the flower bed directly behind her, and she immediately recognized the green suede Hush Puppy at the end of it.

"Arnie?" she said with some amazement that he would be lying in his flower bed in so peculiar a fashion, but then she had often seen Hannah, deep in the bushes, crawling around for what she called "snail patrol." Kiki leaned over until she saw Lempke's face pressed into the dirt at the base of a rosebush. She jumped up faster than she ever suspected herself capable of doing.

A knot lodged in Hannah's throat. After helping Kiki to a standing position, she knelt down next to the strangely limp leg.

"Arnold? Can you hear me?" she said.

Most of his body was shoved back in the rosebushes, hidden by the plants, along with a large metal box holding gardening tools. Hannah pushed the box and the plants to one side, the thorns tearing maliciously at her skin. It was then she saw the blood, fresh and red, on the back of his neck, staining the shoulders of his blue plaid shirt.

"Oh, no," she said softly, her hand to her mouth. She reached for Lempke's wrist and pressed her fingers against the still-warm flesh.

"He's dead," she said in a tone of quiet amazement. "Kiki, don't look. We have to call—"

At that moment she heard Kiki emit a loud gasp from the back of her throat. Her body stiffened before crumpling downward. Hannah was only able to stand up halfway before she could catch her, and the women were caught awkwardly, locked in this strange embrace when they were startled by a shout behind them.

"What's going on here!"

Hannah twisted her head and saw a tall, gray-haired man standing in the corner of the garden. He looked sixtyish, lean and tan, dressed in cotton slacks and a cotton shirt. A dappled brown-and-white spaniel stood at his side, straining on his leash, his nose raised and sniffing furiously.

The man's eyes left the women and moved down to Lempke's corpse, his expression altering only slightly when he saw the blood. Reaching into his pocket, he pulled out a small expensive-looking cellular phone. He directed his eyes at Hannah.

"Don't move. Don't touch anything. I'm calling the police."

While he punched numbers into his phone Hannah stepped back a few paces away from Lempke's body, lowering Kiki onto the grass.

The man took the phone from his ear. "I told you not to move."

"I don't accept commands from strangers," Hannah said, glaring at him. "My sister has fainted. Stop gaping at me and make the call."

He apparently took commands better than Hannah because he immediately dialed. Hannah knelt down beside Kiki and patted her cheek until she moaned softly.

"Sit up, Kiki," she whispered. "This is no time for histrionics. You've never fainted in your life."

"What happened?" Kiki asked, raising herself on her elbows. She hadn't really fainted, but as soon as she got another look at Lempke, she squawked and fell back again.

"Get a grip on yourself."

Kiki put her hands over her eyes. "I don't want to get a grip on myself. This is awful. Terrible." She gave her feet a little kick at the ground. "I feel sick."

"You have to pull yourself together. Poor Arnold is the one we need to think of right now."

"I know you're right, Hannie, but I just can't get up," Kiki said, her eyes still covered. "My legs feel like rubber."

"The police will be here in a minute," the man said, approaching them, his eyes resting first on Hannah then on Kiki. "Is she okay?"

Kiki's hand left one eye and she surveyed the handsome stranger. With a theatrical sweep of her arm she lifted herself onto one elbow, raising a limp wrist toward him.

"If you could assist me," she said.

Hannah narrowed her eyes. Was it possible that her sister was flirting with one potential boyfriend while another lay dead at her feet? Surely not even Kiki was capable of that.

The stranger took Kiki's hand and pulled her up. Apparently underestimating her weight, he faltered slightly and Hannah put her hands on the back of Kiki's hips, pushing her to a standing position.

With Kiki finally upright, he said, "We should step outside the gate. We don't want to disturb anything."

Kiki touched her hand to her forehead. "Oh, yes, please, let's get out of here. It's all too horrible. Poor Arnold must have had a heart attack."

"Heart attack?" Hannah said with disbelief. "He was

lying facedown with blood all over the back of his head. Arnold Lempke was murdered.''

And with that, Kiki yelped and fell backward, Hannah and the stranger each catching one of her arms.

FOUR

IN HANNAH'S LIFETIME SHE HAD attended a few funerals and viewed the guests of honor, but finding a corpse so unexpectedly and so distressingly alfresco was a far more jolting experience.

She stood just outside Lempke's gate staring past yellow crime-scene tape into the yard where his body still lay. The sun was shining, the temperature pleasantly warm, the loveliness of the day in surreal opposition to the death scene in the garden. Working zealously, the police scoured Lempke's yard for evidence, searching through the rosebushes and the other flowers. Hannah watched with sadness, for she knew that dead or alive, Lempke would have loathed the police trampling his lovingly tended garden.

With the initial shock over, she had nothing to take charge of, nothing to do to make herself useful. And while she stood there waiting as Detective Morgan had firmly instructed, she found herself feeling ill and anxious, a dull wad of nausea wedged in her stomach. What in the world had happened to Arnold Lempke?

The police had arrived within moments, the nightmare

of finding Lempke only worsening as a young detective grilled Hannah and Kiki about what they were doing there, how they had found him, what they had seen, heard, and touched. It had happened so quickly, Hannah couldn't remember all the details the detective seemed to expect from her, and Kiki was useless, erupting into tears every time the detective put a question directly to her. Hannah ended up doing most of the talking.

It was odd, but as she described the events the clearest image that came back to her was the name of the hybrid rosebush Lempke had fallen into, the rose he had spent so many years developing and was entering into the Rose Club festival. He had named it "Summer Surprise." Hannah read it on the garden marker stuck in the ground in front of the plant, and if it weren't so tragic, she might have laughed.

Detective Larry Morgan from the Hill Creek Police Department was clean-cut, blond, about thirty-five. He tried to be polite, talking to Hannah as if she were his mother, which just made her feel worse. But underneath his diplomatic words she heard an accusatory tone that insulted her.

A man carrying a metal case said a brusque "excuse me" and pushed past them, the officer guarding the gate moving the tape to allow him into the yard. Hannah saw CORONER printed in bold white letters on the back of his jacket.

She peered around the gate to get a better view of what was happening. When the officer told her to stay back, she moved down the sidewalk a few feet, stood on her tiptoes, and looked over the fence. She was busily watching the coroner crouch down beside Lempke's body when she felt a tug on her sleeve.

"Hannah, all the neighbors are staring at us. Just look at them." Kiki sniffled. "It's so embarrassing."

Hannah turned. The neighbors were indeed huddled in small groups in their yards, gaping, fascinated with the commotion. By now they knew there had been a murder, and within hours it would be all over the county. A murder in Hill Creek was not just a rare and appalling event, it was the very juiciest of scandals. But the neighbors' macabre interest was of little concern to Hannah.

"Count your blessings, Kiki. You may be embarrassed, but poor Arnold Lempke is far worse off."

Detective Morgan wouldn't allow Kiki to go home to change, so with one hand modestly grasping the large rip in her skirt, she hobbled, one high heel broken, a few steps farther from the gate.

"It's all so horrible. I think I'm feeling faint again, Hannie."

Kiki only used the name *Hannie* when she was feeling especially vulnerable. It had been an hour since they had found Lempke, and she had already managed to faint three times, the last time occurring when she was certain one of the better-looking policemen was watching and would be sure to help her.

"No one's catching you this time. You faint, you hit concrete," Hannah said firmly.

Kiki's hand dropped from her forehead. "Don't be mean."

"I'm not being mean. It's just that I can't see what's going on if I'm having to take care of you. You're absolutely fine."

"I'm not fine," Kiki said. "Why would you want to watch what's going on in there anyway? It's all so wretched." A tear rolled down her plump cheek, leaving a glistening trail through her rouge.

Seeing this, Hannah's stern demeanor melted and she pulled Kiki to her. With their arms around each other, the two of them peeked anxiously into the garden. The coroner and two officers were now kneeling by Lempke's body, talking earnestly.

"What are they doing? Do they dust bodies for fingerprints?" Kiki asked.

"Let's hope not, dear. If the poor man didn't shower last

night, your prints will still be all over him.''

Kiki slapped Hannah's arm. ''That's so rude. I hardly touched him.''

''You could have read Braille with less hand contact. Now hush. I want to hear what they're saying.''

Just then the coroner stood up and, with a stabbing gesture, showed the two policeman how he supposed Lempke had been struck. He raised his fist high, the way he would raise a knife, then plunged it downward.

It was difficult to hear all the conversation since one of the officers was facing away from her, but Hannah managed to catch some of it.

''They're discussing the height of the killer,'' she whispered.

Kiki wrapped her arms around herself. ''Oh, don't listen, Hannah.''

''I have to do something to occupy myself. I can't just stand here like a post.''

''They told us to just stand here,'' Kiki said.

''I'm not good at taking orders.''

''This is so typical. You'll get us both into trouble and—''

Hannah shushed her. It was then she noticed a small stool overturned near Lempke's body. It was dark green plastic, blending into the grass and foliage, but she noticed it because she had one much like it herself. They had been on special at Urban Farm Nursery the month before. It was a great help when digging in the flower beds because it cushioned one's knees.

The sight of it triggered an idea, sending a small tingle down the base of Hannah's neck. If the police were considering the height of the killer and the angle at which Lempke had been struck, then they should consider that the killer could have stepped on the stool.

Walking quickly back to the gate, she leaned over the police tape. Kiki followed.

''Hannah, what are you doing? We're supposed to wait here and not bother anything.''

Hannah ignored her. "Excuse me," she said to a female officer standing a few feet inside the garden. Busily taking notes, the officer looked up at her. "Could I speak with you a moment?"

"Can't just now. Stay well behind the tape, ma'am," she said, then walked away.

"See, Hannah? They're too busy," Kiki said.

"Ridiculous. I could have important information."

As another policeman brushed past her Hannah tried to get his attention, but he was in too much of a hurry to stop.

Exhaling loudly, she crossed her arms. "This is very frustrating. I am, after all, a taxpayer."

"Can I be of help?"

Both Hannah and Kiki turned and there stood the man who had found them in the garden, the eager spaniel still at his side and still eager.

"I thought I should introduce myself. I'm John Perez." His tone was businesslike but with a trace of shyness. He stuck out his hand to Hannah, but it was Kiki who grasped it, reaching out as if she were a shortstop and it were a line drive threatening to zip past her.

"I'm Kiki. I want to thank you. You were so kind to us when we found poor Arnie." Hannah mouthed the word *kind,* her expression dumbfounded. Kiki continued, one hand till holding her torn skirt together. "The way you took charge. You were such a help."

"A help? He was rude," Hannah said, not bothering to hide her annoyance.

Perez's eyes moved to her. "I wasn't thinking about my manners. I was thinking about the blood on Arnold's neck."

His use of Lempke's first name surprised Hannah. "You know him?" she asked.

"I'm a neighbor." He made the statement quickly, glancing away uneasily. Behind him a policeman warded off a group of teenagers who apparently came to catch a glimpse of the body. Alerted to the fuss, Perez's dog snapped forward, giving a worried whimper. Perez stooped down and rubbed his head.

"It's okay, boy. You're okay," he said soothingly, and it amused Hannah that his manly voice softened sweetly when talking to his dog. "Just now you were trying to get a policeman's attention," Perez said, standing up. "Maybe I can help."

"How?" she asked.

"I know some of these people."

Since no one else had been paying attention to her, Hannah told him her idea about the stool. He listened intently but then explained that the stool had been brought by the police to hold tools and bags rather than lay them on the ground and disturb the crime scene. Hannah looked again at the stool and saw the policemen using it.

"It looked so much like a gardening stool," she said, embarrassed.

Perez smiled. "It was an honest mistake."

"That's Hannah for you. Always overanalyzing," Kiki said, edging her way into the conversation. Just then Detective Morgan came through the gate. He took Perez aside and the two men spoke. It was obvious to Hannah they knew each other.

Perez walked off and Morgan came back to the women.

"We'll need to fingerprint you. We can do it right over here," he said, motioning to a police van.

"What about John Perez? Don't you need to fingerprint him?" Hannah asked.

The question seemed to surprised Morgan. "We have his fingerprints already. They're in the computer."

"He has a criminal record?" Kiki asked with a gulp.

Morgan chuckled. "No. He used to be the Tri-City police chief. He only retired a few years ago. Everybody knows him."

It would be an understatement to say that the fingerprinting did not go well. Although Hannah submitted calmly to the process, Kiki yelped when the officer pushed her first trembling finger into the black ink pad. Then, with all fingers blackened, she inadvertently pressed them to her chest before the officer had the chance to offer her a paper towel, resulting in nasty marks on her yellow silk blouse.

Afterward they were allowed to go home, the police looking as glad to see them leave as they were to exit.

At first all was quiet in the Cadillac as they headed back to Walnut Avenue, both women too stunned to say much of anything. It was Kiki who finally broke the silence.

"Naomi says fate is a woman name Fortuna," she said. Her head was pressed against the window, her eyes closed, and she had turned on the air-conditioning full blast with all vents directed at her face. "She says when Fortuna swishes her skirts, that's what makes our lives change."

"I'd say she rustled her petticoats pretty well today," Hannah replied gravely.

There was a pause. "God, I need a cocktail," Kiki blurted.

"It's barely lunchtime."

"I don't care." She pressed her hankie to her face. Kiki expected further argument, and when Hannah failed to respond, she looked at her sister and noticed her distraught expression. "What's wrong?"

Hannah cast her a look of disbelief. "What's wrong? We just found your boyfriend dead."

"But you were cool as a cucumber back there, flirting with that handsome John Perez. Now suddenly you're all ruffled." Kiki rummaged through her purse, trying to pull out her lipstick, but she was too nervous to hold on to anything, so finally snapped her purse shut.

"I did not flirt with him. I don't flirt, period. You know that," Hannah said.

"Not flirting is just another way of flirting. Anyway, I liked him."

Hannah raised her eyebrows. "The body of your last man is not even cold and you're already after someone else?"

"I'm not after him. But you have to admit he's attractive."

"When he first saw us he practically accused us of being murderers."

Kiki looked wistful. "Sometimes relationships get off to rocky starts."

"For all we know he could be the murderer himself. Lempke had only been dead about an hour when we found him. I heard the coroner say so. And when I felt his pulse his skin was still warm. Perez could have killed him then seen our car pull up. He sneaked out then came back to make it look like he was just walking by."

Kiki squeezed her eyes shut. "A former police chief? Don't say such a thing." She looked at her sister. "Besides, it's not for us to think about who killed poor Arnie. That's for the police. They're the ones responsible."

Hannah gripped the steering wheel more tightly. "But I feel responsible, too."

Kiki frowned. "Why?"

"Because if I had just gone over to see his downy mildew this morning like he asked me, maybe the killer would have seen me there and gone away. Maybe Lempke would still be alive." Hannah mulled this over a second then hit the steering wheel with her fist. "But I'm so obstinate sometimes."

Kiki's features expanded into an expression of sympathy. She patted her sister's shoulder. "Don't blame yourself, honey. You can't help it. Mama always said it was because you were a late baby. You just refused to come out of the womb. You wedged yourself in there and—"

Always disliking that particular story, Hannah cut her off. "You realize, Kiki, that after Lempke humiliated you last night at the party—in front of half of Hill Creek—you'd be a decent murder suspect yourself. Lucky for you, you were at the hairdresser's, then you were with me, so you have an alibi."

Kiki stiffened. "Well, to tell you the truth," she said,

her voice raised to a higher pitch, "I didn't come straight home after the hairdresser."

Hannah's eyes darted to her sister. When she looked at the road again, she saw a car stopped in front of her. She hit the brake. The Cadillac stopped with a screech then lurched forward, sending Kiki's purse flying.

"Why do you do this? Are you trying to kill us?" she yelled.

Hitting the gas again, Hannah drove to the end of the block and pulled the car into their driveway.

"You lied to the police. I heard you tell Detective Morgan that after the hairdresser's you came straight home."

Kiki rubbed her hand against her cheek. "Well, almost straight home. I didn't lie. I just forgot."

Hannah didn't believe this but had a more important issue to press. "If you didn't come straight home, where were you?" She turned in her seat, looking her sister straight in the eye.

Kiki squirmed. "Don't look at me that way, Hannie. You know I hate it. Remember that time in junior high before the spring dance when you took me behind the gym and gave me that look, and—"

"You stuffed your bra with the hand-trimmed linen napkins Mother gave me for my hope chest. But we're not discussing that. Where were you between the time you left the hairdresser's and the time you came home?"

"I . . . I was window shopping."

"Did anyone see you? Did you talk to anyone who would remember you?"

"I don't know. I don't think so. Besides, where were you when he was murdered?"

"For your information I was at the breast-cancer center the whole morning and two dozen people saw me. I got home only moments before you did. But you more than anyone needs to be able to prove that you were in town."

"Why does it matter?"

"Because if you can't prove you were window shopping,

it means you don't have a decent alibi for the time Lempke was murdered. And the police could think you have a motive for wanting him dead after what happened at the reception last night.''

Kiki emitted a horrified burst of air. ''You talk like you really think I might have killed him.''

Her eyes still on his sister, Hannah leaned her elbow on the steering wheel, running her hand through her hair. ''Of course I don't think you killed Arnold. But don't you understand, Kiki? It's possible that the police will.''

$\mathscr{F}$IVE

$\gtrsim\!\!\varphi$

$\mathscr{T}$HE NEXT DAY HILL CREEK hummed with the news of Arnold Lempke's murder. The story made the front page of the morning *Marin Daily News* and was on everyone's lips with their second cappuccino. Hypotheses about social decay rang through the gourmet coffee shops. Cult-related explanations percolated during Shiatsu massages. Juicily detailed recountings based on fifth-hand information passed *après* tai chi at the community center.

Certainly the town had its share of minor crime, mostly high-school vandalism and lesser drug busts. And a rich cocaine dealer had been shot dead by his jilted girlfriend eight years earlier, but his house had been deep in the hills, a distance physically and psychologically from the town proper. But Arnold Lempke had been a longtime resident and well-known member of the community. Everyone had the unsettling yet oddly titillating feeling that if it could happen to him, it could happen to anybody.

Unbeknownst to any but a privileged few, this speculation was centered smack dab in the middle of aisle four of the Hill Creek Grocery.

To understand the Hill Creek Grocery is to understand the town itself, for the grocery was the town's quiet heartbeat, its spiritual nucleus, the pure essence of Hill Creekness distilled into its narrow aisles crowded with gourmet foods. In the Hill Creek Grocery you understood that you were someplace special, a more elite ground than the rest of the vulgar, mundane world. Here in this small store the local gastronomes combed the shelves for exotic chutneys, the freshest of pestos, the rarest of European cheeses. They peered into the small frozen-food section, not for Popsicles and TV dinners, but for phyllo dough, frozen demi-glacé, or perhaps ready-made crême fraiche for those meddlesome days when feverish exploration of one's inner goddess prevented the luxury of whipping up one's own.

Sure, the chain grocery stores with their harsh fluorescents and greasy Chinese takeout thrived in the crass shopping centers close to the freeway, and many residents shopped there. But the Hill Creek diehards still frequented the grocery, where the produce was handpicked and organic, where you couldn't find Velveeta or a loaf of sliced white to save your life, but could pick from three different varieties of marscapone and four different brands of pressed seaweed for wrapping sushi.

Although Hannah preferred the Safeway for some staples because the prices were better, she shopped the grocery for fruit, vegetables, and fish. But on this particular day, the morning after Lempke's death, she and Kiki journeyed there for necessities more urgent. Kiki needed Moon Pies.

Moon Pies were hardly haute cuisine. Still, they had a certain retro appeal, so the grocery started carrying them two years earlier, much to the detriment of Kiki's thighs. But this day all hungers for physical improvement had taken a backseat to the hungers of her soul.

Kiki and Hannah stood in aisle four in front of the pastry section. Kiki, disguised in a hat and sunglasses, scanned the shelves with a well-trained eye while Hannah leaned on the grocery cart, waiting impatiently.

"You're covered with crumbs," Hannah said. "You've eaten the last two on the shelf. You'll make yourself sick. And I don't see why you can't take the stuff home and eat it there."

Kiki looked at Hannah over the top of her sunglasses. "We're not leaving until I'm sure Wanda Backus is gone."

"Why?"

"Because I can't face her, that's why. Everyone in the Rose Club must know I was at the police station this morning." Kiki shoved a last bite of Moon Pie into her mouth. "It was such a nightmare."

The police had requested a second interview with Kiki first thing that morning, and she left the meeting a nervous wreck. Someone at the Rose Club cocktail reception had called the station and told them about the scene that had taken place between Lempke and Kiki at the party. The police interviewed her for two hours and they wouldn't allow Hannah to be with her. The message was clear that she was on their list of suspects.

"I want a Ding Dong," she said, her eyes pink and puffy from crying. They had been in aisle four for a good ten minutes and Hannah was antsy to leave, but seeing her sister's distress, she was trying to be patient.

"They probably don't carry Ding Dongs," Hannah said, then pointed to the center shelf, "but the chocolate-covered biscotti look good."

Kiki grabbed a package and tore off the cellophane, tossing the wrapper into the grocery cart with the others so she could pay for everything later. Just as the entire cookie disappeared between her shiny pink lips, her eyes grew saucerlike. Cheeks bulging, she squeaked then ducked behind the cart. "There's Wanda. She's headed this way," Kiki blubbered, mouth full. She then dashed around the corner as fast as her rounded frame allowed, leaving a telltale trail of biscotti crumbs behind her. Pushing the cart, Hannah quickly followed her into a corner of the store set aside for toilet paper and napkins.

"Our names were in the paper as the discoverers of Arnold's body," Hannah said. "There's no point in hiding. You have to face people."

"No, I don't. Not until I feel stronger."

"Did you tell the police the truth about where you were yesterday?"

Kiki looked suddenly sheepish. "Not exactly."

Hannah gripped the cart handle more tightly, her disaster radar on full alert. "You didn't tell them you went window shopping after the hairdresser's?"

"Yes, I did tell them that. Only it's not quite the truth, you see."

Hannah swallowed hard, bracing herself for the worst. "What *is* the truth?"

"After the hairdresser's I looked so good. Zelda did an especially nice job on my hair, you see, fluffing it—"

"Get to the point," Hannah commanded.

"Well, I thought it would be a good time to go see Arnold and talk him back into the cruise."

Hannah covered her face with her hands, her eyes peeking through her fingers. "You didn't go over there?"

"No, no, of course not. I just drove by his house a few times trying to work up the nerve to talk to him. But I never stopped. So I came home and got you to go with me."

Now clasping her hands in front of her face as if in prayer, Hannah tried to reassure herself that things weren't really that bad, but reason wouldn't allow it. The situation was getting ugly in a hurry.

"How many times did you drive by, Kiki?"

"Only once or twice. Maybe three or four times," Kiki replied, her voice getting increasingly anxious. "Why?"

"Your car sticks out. Everybody knows that boat of yours."

"So?"

"Someone may have noticed it, which could tie you to the murder."

Kiki's face grew pale, despite the layers of Estée Lauder rose blush. "Oh, my God."

Just then Hannah heard her name called. Turning, she saw Naomi speedily pushing her grocery cart down the aisle, her yellow Indian-style tunic with matching pants flapping, the wheels of her cart creaking madly. Arms outstretched and the immense sleeves of her tunic waving, she looked like a giant yellow moth as she enfolded Kiki in one arm and Hannah in the other.

"You poor creatures. I heard everything. Fortuna has not smiled on you. Such negative energy, finding a corpse like that, even Arnold Lempke's." Her voice was oozing pity. With difficulty Hannah managed to unwrap herself, after which Naomi voluntarily released Kiki. But release was brief, because Naomi grabbed their hands. "I have a friend who does aura cleansing. You'll need it after encountering all those negative spiritual pulses."

"My aura feels squeaky-clean," Hannah said with only the slightest tinge of sarcasm. Naomi seemed oddly agitated, but Hannah supposed everyone who knew Lempke had to be upset. "But it was an awful experience, especially for Kiki."

Naomi swirled to the left, refocusing her sympathy vibrations solidly on Kiki. "Yes! Naturally, Arnold was your *amore*." At this point she paused. "Darling, you have crumbs stuck to your lip gloss."

"She's saving that for later," Hannah said. "Kiki's stress eating."

"Of course she is," Naomi said, pulling Kiki into a bear hug. "Completely understandable. But don't fret. My intuition tells me the killer will be found quickly. I'm seldom wrong about these things. I'm such a conduit for psychic energy. It just flows through me like talk through a telephone wire. Yes, I'm quite certain the police will soon solve the case."

At the very mention of the word *police* Kiki broke away

from Naomi, letting out a muffled howl. Hannah patted her shoulder consolingly.

"The police interviewed her this morning. Apparently the process wasn't pleasant," Hannah explained.

"Wasn't pleasant?" Kiki said through her hankie. "They grilled me like I was a pork chop."

"Don't exaggerate," Hannah said.

"You weren't there."

Naomi's mouth stretched into a grimace. "But why grill you?"

Kiki stared dumbly at her a few seconds then burst into fresh tears. Hannah resumed her shoulder patting with more vigor, but with little effect.

"Someone called in a tip to the police last night about how Lempke embarrassed Kiki at the cocktail party. The police feel it gives her a motive. You know, a woman scorned," Hannah said quietly, whispering the last part as delicately as if she were discussing Kiki's bowel habits.

Her ringed fingers pressed to her lips, Naomi's eyes grew large. "Who called them?" she asked in a dark tone that made Hannah think she was planning to put some voodoo curse on the betrayer.

"It was anonymous, but it had to be a Rose Club member. Quite likely someone at our table."

Naomi looked at Hannah, at Kiki, then back to Hannah.

"You realize that the police may want to interview you as well," Hannah said to Naomi. "Arnold said some terrible things to you."

"I was with a client yesterday morning," Naomi said in her defense, but she was visibly shaken at the notion. Her lips pursed and one of her eyebrows arched. "The dark kinetic flow in this incident cannot be underestimated. I think we should consult Red Moon."

"Red Moon?" Kiki asked, sniffling giving way to interest. "What could he do?"

Hannah was silently asking the same question. There was

a definite atypical turbulence about Naomi that day that aroused her curiosity.

Eyes closed, Naomi held out her hands, fingers fanned. "I feel his essence rising from deep within me," she intoned, her voice low and throaty. "I sense he wants to speak."

"Could he give us the name of the killer?" Kiki asked.

Naomi's eyes popped open. "Red Moon's not one for naming names, but he could shed light, I'm sure. But we can't dillydally. When Red Moon desires to speak, it's best to jump on it, pronto. How about tonight? It will be free of charge since you're in crisis."

Hannah eyed her neighbor with ever-increasing curiosity. Yes, definitely something was cooking in Naomi's pseudopsychic head. Naomi knew that Hannah had little faith in the existence of Red Moon, and she had never before asked Hannah to one of her little séances, although Kiki had attended several. Hannah's knee-jerk reaction was to decline a tête-à-tête with anyone long-deceased, but her interest in Naomi's odd behavior made her accept the offer. Naomi pulled her Day-Timer from her velvet backpack and they arranged a time that evening, then she briefed Hannah on how her dining room should be arranged to be most receptive to Red Moon's visit.

With other errands to run, Hannah was eager to leave the market, and Naomi agreed to check around the store and make sure Wanda had left. She took off, and a few moments later reappeared at the end of the aisle and gave a thumbs-up sign.

Hannah and Kiki were at the checkout when Hannah noticed Naomi lagging behind them, looking at the other checkout stand even though it was unmanned, and waved her over. Naomi wheeled her cart to them somewhat reluctantly, Hannah thought. Then she saw the package in the cart, its edge peeking out from under two bunches of organic broccoli.

"Are those sausages?" she asked, using a tone suitable

for identifying Nazi holdovers in the backwoods of Brazil.
She eyed Naomi suspiciously. "I thought you were a strict
vegetarian."

"They're for Red Moon," she said, looking pinched.
"He has meat cravings stemming from his days as a Hopi
warrior."

Reaching into Naomi's basket, Hannah moved aside
some tofu to get a look at the label. "Cravings for spicy
Thai sausage?" She was dubious but let the matter drop.
It wasn't any of her business if Naomi wanted to scarf
down high-priced wieners on the sly. Besides, it was hardly
the time to start a fracas when the day was just starting to
smooth out. Kiki had stopped crying, and if Hannah could
keep her calm she might coax her into stopping off at the
Jiffy Lube for an oil change for the Cadillac.

But the calm was short-lived, for as soon as they stepped
out the door, there was Wanda stooped down on the sidewalk trying to coax her toy poodle Bon Bon into making
"a weewee for Mommy" (no one deserved one more, Hannah thought) on a small beleaguered boxwood bush grap-
pling for life at the corner of the building.

Hannah spotted her first, and grabbed Kiki's elbow to
steer her in the other direction, but Fortuna failed them.
Bon Bon had just lifted his little chicken-bone leg onto
Wanda's suede Charles Jourdan pump, and as she jumped
back, shouting "naughty, naughty," she spied the sisters.

Upon seeing Wanda, Kiki let out a petite, biscotti-laced
belch of dismay. Wanda bolted forward. "Well, Kiki," she
said, her tone syrupy with feigned concern. "I hope the
police weren't too hard on you."

"How . . . how did you know?" Kiki muttered.

Wanda smiled maliciously. "Oh, Kiki, everyone knows.
My yoga instructor's sister's boyfriend is a parking-meter
collector. That's how I found out. You can't keep that sort
of thing quiet, darling. But don't worry. Innocent until
proven guilty. No matter what you've done."

Hannah's stomach clenched into the grimace she dared

not show on her face. Wanda Backus put the major media to shame when it came to the rapid dissemination of information. If she knew the police were questioning Kiki, it was only a matter of hours before the news reached the far corners of the earth, or at least of Hill Creek.

Temporarily speechless, Kiki stood there, all color drained from her face, with Bon Bon jumping up and down and bombarding her with shrill, accusatory barks, the excitement causing him to squirt urine all over the sidewalk. Despite his cutesy poodle cut, Bon Bon was known around town as a mean-spirited, particularly annoying representative of his species.

Just then Naomi emerged from the market carrying her string bag of groceries. She didn't have to be psychic to see what was happening. After taking a look at everyone's faces, she hurried over to join the fray.

"Listen here, Wanda," Hannah said, her voice dignified yet at the same time mildly threatening. "My sister is guilty of nothing except dating a man with a limited future."

"I hardly meant—" Wanda.

"I know exactly what you meant. If you start spreading rumors about Kiki, you'll get no plant cuttings from me again, ever."

Wanda inhaled sharply. This was a threat with some teeth to it, since Wanda was over at Hannah's at least once a week wheedling cuttings and horticulture advice. She lifted her chin haughtily.

"There's no need to be hostile."

But Hannah thought there was plenty of need. She said a quick good-bye to the two other women, then steered Kiki toward the parking lot.

"Oh, sweet Jesus," Kiki sputtered as they walked. "Everyone in town is going to think I killed Arnold. You have to help me, Hannah. You just have to help me."

Hannah took her hand and squeezed it. "Don't worry. We'll sort this out together."

She tried to sound comforting, but she saw with a terrible

clarity what lay in store for Kiki if the murder wasn't solved. It was possible that the police would question her again, though there couldn't possibly be any real evidence against her. But if Lempke's murderer was never caught, people in town might still think Kiki had something to do with it. Even when the gossip died away, Kiki would still have a suspicious connection to an unsolved murder, and that connection could stay with her a very long time.

"But how do we sort it out, Hannah? What can we do?"

Hannah came to a halt and Kiki followed suit. With her bag of groceries in one arm, Hannah put her free hand on her sister's shoulder and looked her in the eye. "The way I see it, there's only one thing we can do. We have to find Arnold Lempke's killer ourselves."

In times of trouble, Hannah and Kiki had always rallied together. When their parents had died, after the departures by death or evacuation of their various husbands, when ten years earlier their sister, Lauren's mother, had been killed in a car accident, the two of them bonded as families should. Who better than a sister to help a woman shoulder the uncertainties of life? There could be a powerful, immutable bond between sisters, Hannah felt, and she had never felt that bond more strongly than at the present.

This was a uniquely troubled time, the situation so public and potentially disastrous. So that afternoon they gathered with Lauren in the small, rose-filled garden located behind Hannah's Craftsman's style cottage on Walnut Avenue and began the process of commiseration.

Lauren had taken off early from her job as an accountant for a San Francisco CPA firm when she learned from Hannah about the scene that had taken place at the grocery. By four that afternoon Kiki lay sprawled on the lawn-chair recliner, looking like Camille in the death scene while Lauren and Hannah repeated words of encouragement.

Hannah, wearing her gardening clothes—old Japanese gardening pants, sweatshirt, floppy straw hat, and rubber clogs—was down on her knees digging fresh compost into the soil around her hydrangeas as she pondered how one would go about finding a murderer. Not that she didn't trust the police. She was one of their most ardent supporters and two years ago donated several of her best rosebushes to the police-station landscape project. But she knew from the newspapers that sometimes small-town police bungled murder cases. It wasn't due to lack of ability so much as lack of experience, and they most likely needed all the help they could get. And who would be better equipped to help than a local resident like herself, who knew the town and the murder victim as well as his circle of friends? But she had to figure out where to begin.

"What's your theory, Lauren?" Hannah asked as she worked the dirt, wanting to get as many ideas as possible. "Who do you think might have killed Arnold?"

Kiki pressed her hand to her forehead. "Haven't we talked enough about this for one day?"

Hannah stopped digging. "But we have to keep talking about it. Together we might be able to come up with some ideas that could help the police."

Kiki took the cold washcloth Lauren had brought her and draped it over her eyes.

Lauren sat in a garden chair near Kiki. "It could have been an act of random violence, I suppose," she began. Kiki's eyes were obscured, but Hannah saw her lips twist into a disgusted pucker. "I'm always reading about that sort of thing in the newspaper."

Unable to ignore the conversation, Kiki lifted the washcloth. "Those things happen in Los Angeles or maybe San Francisco. But random violence in Hill Creek? I hardly think so."

"We think our town is immune to such things, but perhaps Hill Creek isn't as safe as we think it is," Hannah said, with some sadness in her voice. Her trowel hit a rock and she began digging around it so it could be removed. "I wonder if it could have been a burglary?"

Kiki raised herself onto her elbows. "Arnie did talk about some stamp collection he had that was worth some money," she said with new energy. "Maybe someone killed him so they could steal it."

"But the police would check first thing to see if something was stolen, wouldn't they?" Lauren asked.

Having successfully excavated the rock, Hannah tossed it aside. "I'm sure they did. Naomi called about an hour ago and said the police had her in for an interview right after lunch. I don't think they would be doing all this questioning if they were certain it was a simple burglary. They must have some suspicions that the killer had a more personal motive."

The subject of police questioning brought up unpleasant memories for Kiki. "I need a cup of tea," she said, her voice once again weak.

Lauren jumped out of her chair. "Let me get it."

"No, dear, I'll get it myself." Kiki hauled herself up and dragged into the house.

Lauren's face registered concern. "I've never seen Aunt Kiki so depressed."

Hannah looked up from her work, resting her arm on one knee. "She's not strong enough for this kind of trouble, having her name tainted this way. To her, appearances are so important."

Lauren shuddered. "And to have your friends and neighbors gossiping about you. The scene you described at the grocery this morning sounded awful."

"It could very well get worse." Hannah sighed and dug her trowel into the dirt with renewed vigor. Her pet pig Sylvia Plath and her dog Teresa S. Eliot, both SPCA foundlings, nuzzled the dirt until Hannah waved them away.

"You're not doing that well yourself," Lauren said. "I can tell by the way you're digging. You always dig like mad when you're upset."

"Of course I'm upset." Hannah jabbed at the dirt with

her trowel to prove the point. "I have to help her, but I'm not sure where to start."

Their conversation was interrupted by Kiki's return, a dainty hand-painted teacup in her hand. As she passed by, Hannah sniffed the air.

"That's not tea in that cup. That's sherry."

Kiki collapsed back onto the garden lounge. "You and that nose of yours. I need a toddy for the body. I'm so stressed. Don't be mean, Hannie."

Tears crept out of Kiki's eyes, melting away Hannah's disapproval. She couldn't blame her sister for wanting a drink, even though it was only five o'clock. Hannah looked down at her plants and saw Sylvia testing the newly fertilized dirt with vigorous shoves of her wrinkled snout.

"Lauren, could you take the girls into the house for me? I'm too dirty to go in myself and Sylvia's doing her best to dig up the hydrangea," she said.

After making sure Kiki was comfortable, Lauren called both pets with kissy noises and, with promises of treats, herded them inside the back door. Some people found it strange that both animals had free run of the house, but Sylvia, a large and lazy black Vietnamese pig, was more intelligent and much better behaved than the dog Teresa, who had a tendency to chew shoes and leave "Tootsie Rolls" on the carpet on rainy days.

"I checked my messages at work, and Brenda Greigel called me. Haven't heard from her in years," Lauren said when she returned to the garden. "You might remember her, Kiki. She was a school friend. She ran around with Lisa Lempke and me in junior high."

Interested, Hannah stopped fertilizing. "Why did she call you?"

"Apparently there's going to be a service for Lisa's father at that church she goes to. The Church of Revelations. It's tonight. Brenda thought I might want to go."

Hannah stood up. "A service there for Lempke? He hated that place."

"Well, from what Brenda said, I think the service is really for Lisa," Lauren told her. "I think I'll go."

Hannah brushed herself off. The service sounded odd to her. Arnold Lempke had stated publicly that he was turning the church in to the DA's office for fraud, so he couldn't have a been a member himself. It hardly seemed likely they would give him a memorial service. Hannah found herself suddenly very eager to see the Church of Revelations.

"Good. I'll hurry up and shower so we'll have time for some dinner first. There's still quite a bit of that Creole pasta you brought over in the fridge."

"*You're* going?" Lauren asked.

"Of course I'm going. I think Kiki and I should both go. It's only good manners," Hannah said, but it was much more than good manners she had on her mind. If she was going to help uncover the murderer, she needed to find out as much about Lempke as possible. The night before he died, he had ranted on about his hatred for the church. You can learn a lot about a person by uncovering the things they loved, but perhaps, she thought, you could find out more by uncovering the things they hated.

Six

THE INTERIOR OF THE CHURCH of Revelations oozed self-righteous, high-priced piety, the small size of its sanctuary compensated by sumptuous decor. The walls were paneled with oak, the pews covered with rich red velvet to cushion the expensively clad derrieres of its Marin County flock. Overhead, grand iron chandeliers shaped like wheels within wheels hung from the vaulted ceiling, each holding at least forty candle-shaped lights dimmed to a lemony glow.

Sitting in a back pew, Hannah eyed her surroundings, soaking in the details. She was intensely curious about the place. The night before he died, Lempke had said this church was full of crazies. *Full of people talking weird things, doing weird things. It's not normal,* he had said only a half day before life was wrenched from him. But as Hannah inspected the people filling the pews, they seemed fairly typical of the area, most of them looking well-heeled and well educated. So what on earth had Lempke meant?

Spotlights from outside poured light through ceiling-high stained-glass windows, casting splotches of color on the floor. Along the sides of the windows flowed heavy red velvet curtains, and it was the curtains Hannah stared at as the sounds of Bach drifted into the room from a hidden organ. "They look like blood running down the walls," she muttered to no one in particular.

"What, honey?" Kiki asked. She, Hannah, Lauren, and Naomi all sat together in the pew, Naomi having insisted on coming with them when Hannah called to change their appointment with Red Moon.

Refusing on grounds of basic contrariness to wear black to any funereal event, Hannah wore a simple brown print dress. Kiki liked to fit in, but she thought black made her skin look sallow, so she wore a navy suit purchased two years earlier at Loehmann's, accessorized by oversized fake pearls she thought gave the whole outfit a definite Chanel feel. Lauren was still wearing the serious gray suit she had worn to work, and Naomi had changed her yellow tunic for one of deep forest green, a symbol of growth, she said, which was important at times of death. To mark the solemnity of the occasion, Naomi placed a small black bow in her green turban.

"It was nothing," Hannah said, responding to Kiki's question. But it *was* something. Now that she had settled into the environment and had gotten the feel of the place, she decided that even though everything looked normal, the Church of Revelations was somehow peculiar. For a moment she thought what was nagging at her was the shrimp Creole she eaten too quickly at dinner, but after giving it more thought, she realized that the people filling the pews were unusually silent. They looked normal enough. Some wore suits, while others dressed more casually, but that was fairly typical of church these days. No, it was something in their demeanor that made them different. Although it had been at least a year since Hannah had been to church, she remembered there being a pleasant buzz in the sanctuary as congregants seated themselves—people exchanging greetings, catching up on each other's news before the service began. But not this group. They all looked so somber. They didn't speak. They didn't laugh or wave to a friend. Instead they sat in their seats, their eyes expectantly facing the front of the chapel. Odd, she thought. Definitely odd. Suddenly feeling cold, she wished she had brought a sweater.

"Are people staring at me?" Kiki asked, sitting on Hannah's left. It amazed Hannah how in any situation her sister managed to remain so completely centered on herself.

Hannah noticed Naomi sitting very straight on the other side of Kiki, her chin cocked upward, her eyes off in the distance as she held up her index finger. "No," she said thoughtfully, then closed her eyes. "You're not the focus here, Kiki. The magnetic force in this room is definitely near the front. It's strong, very strong, and I'm getting some curious energy flows."

Having said this, she opened her eyes, snapping back to the common reality and more mundane issues. With great fanfare, she pulled a small pillow out of her giant handbag, painstakingly positioning it behind the small of her back. "Have you made a decision about taking my place at the dunking booth, Hannah?"

"I'm still considering it." She had to hand it to Naomi—that pillow was a savvy gesture—but Hannah still found it strange that in all the years they had known each other, Naomi had only announced these long-standing back problems when they would conveniently get her out of dunking-booth duty.

"When I die I want to be cremated," Kiki said, spitting out the words suddenly as if she had had a spasm. "And my ashes scattered in the ocean."

"Really. I'd think you'd want them scattered over Nordstrom's," Hannah replied. "That's where you spend most of your quality time."

Irked, Kiki turned toward her sister. "You shouldn't make fun of me when you know I'm vulnerable."

"My apologies. There's just something about this place that puts me on edge."

"Seems pretty normal to me," Kiki said.

"In any case, pay attention to your surroundings," Hannah told her. "We must keep a sharp eye. Gather information."

Kiki nodded eagerly and Lauren cast her aunts an alarmed look. "Gathering information for what?" she asked, but didn't get an answer because at that moment everyone around them stood up, obliging them to stand up also.

A smallish man dressed in a well-cut double-breasted navy suit walked slowly, regally across the platform, stopping behind a podium at its center. Lifting his hands, palms turned upward, he smiled Buddha-like at the congregation.

Hannah strained so she could see him better. Naomi had been right about the energy flows, because there was something compelling about this man, a magnetism that drew your attention to him. His eyes were a shining, vivid blue, his skin pale, and the subdued smile on his face seemed at the same time joyful and sad, as if he knew wondrous secrets. His eyes swept the room, stopping at times as he made silent contact with people in the pews. At these moments he let his eyes linger as he mouthed "the Lord loves you," then his gaze moved on.

Eyes reverently closing, he nodded slightly and the organ burst into "Rock of Ages," the music swelling inside the room as the congregation began to sing.

"So that's Reverend Swanson," Naomi whispered as the music enveloped them. "I've heard people talk about him like he was a saint."

"Where are the hymnbooks?" Lauren asked, searching the pew. Everyone in the congregation seemed to know the hymn by heart. Lauren quickly thumbed through the hymnal until she found the song, and the women sang. It was only Hannah and the Reverend Swanson who felt no compulsion to join with the others. His face beaming, he stood on the platform, confident and serene, watching the congregation while Hannah watched him.

The hymn over, everyone took their seats and the minister spoke about how deeply grieved he was over the loss of Lisa Lempke's father.

"We must cling together and support our dear sister Lisa in her time of need," he said, gripping the sides of the podium, his face glowing with religious fervor.

Hannah nudged Lauren, who was sitting on her right. "Why a special service for Lisa? Churches don't normally do that."

"How would you know?" Kiki interjected, whispering, yet managing to do it loudly. "You haven't stepped foot in a church in how many years?"

"I always preferred to pick up men in bars," Hannah replied dryly. A woman in the pew in front of them turned and shushed her. Hannah apologized.

"I don't know why they'd do this special service. I mean, it's her father who died. Not her," Lauren whispered to Hannah.

Hannah sat back in her seat, crossing her arms. It definitely seemed strange, unless Lisa had some unique relationship to the church or was giving the church a lot of money, which was possible. The rumor had always been that Lempke was rich as King Midas but just as stingy, and Hannah wondered if he bestowed any of his precious money on his daughter.

"On the surface this church seems perfectly normal," she whispered to Lauren, but it was at that juncture that all normalcy ceased.

Reverend Swanson paused and lifted a box from inside the podium, placing it carefully on top. It was about the size of a jewelry box and covered with purple fabric. He prayed a few moments, asking no one to join in his special communications line to God, then raised the box's lid. To Hannah's wonder, he lifted out a stone. It was wider than his hand, its surface smooth and shiny, shaped like an egg but flattened on the bottom.

With great solemnity, Reverend Swanson stepped out from behind the podium and moved toward the edge of the platform, cupping the stone with both hands, his eyes on his audience as he walked. The congregation sat motionless and attentive. He stopped at the front of center stage. His eyes closed once more and suddenly his previous stick-straight posture loosened.

Clutching the stone, his knuckles whitened, his head rolled around his shoulders, his eyelids fluttering so the whites of his eyes showed. He looked as if he were having some sort of seizure, and for a moment Hannah was afraid he was going to fall down, but no one made a move to help him. Whatever was happening, the congregation seemed to expect it.

Hannah shifted uncomfortably in her seat. She cast a glance at Naomi, Lauren, and Kiki. They were all riveted on Swanson, as was everyone else in the room.

He began to speak again but now his voice was higher-pitched. The words streamed out rapidly with a different tone and cadence, sounding like they were coming from another person altogether, yet they were obviously coming from Swanson. And as if to further confuse Hannah, she could no longer understand what he was saying.

She nudged Kiki, perplexed. "I don't get it. He's speaking English but the words don't string together into sentences."

Kiki nodded, her eyes stuck straight ahead. "It sounds like gibberish."

Hannah returned her eyes to the front of the room. "Religo-babble."

But the scene grew stranger. Hannah was startled by the sound of a low moan. At first not certain where it was coming from, her eyes darted around the room until she realized the noise was emanating from Swanson. The moan emerged not from his throat but from deep inside him, increasing in volume and shaping into words, the words building into an incomprehensible tirade about the Lord's vengeance, the blood of Christ, and then something about a weeping stone. He reminded Hannah of a teakettle, first simmering, heating up to a sizzle, and finally to a rolling boil. He shouted about fire and flood, of smiling devils and slaughtered lambs, all of it sounding frightening and threatening. But there was no direct message Hannah could make out, only words strung together, seemingly intended to arouse emotion rather than thought. She had never encountered anything like it.

Swanson's body trembled and his face reddened; sweat streamed from his brow. Hannah could feel perspiration on her own hands, her nerves so rattled by what she was witnessing. Only moments before, this man had seemed normal, perhaps more charismatic than most, but still your basic carbon-based Homo sapiens. But he had transformed into something bizarre. His face and voice had changed, an electric current seemed to shoot through his body as if something had invaded him, causing him to spew words over which he had no control.

Then the torrent stopped as suddenly as it had begun. He stepped down into the left aisle, walked a few paces, then touched the shoulder of a man in the third pew. The man stood, holding on to the back of the pew to brace himself. He looked to be in his eighties, his hair gray and his body bent. Reverend Swanson placed one of the man's gnarled hands on top of the stone and held it there. At first the man stood frozen, his eyes locked with the reverend's.

"What the hell's happening?" Hannah whispered to Lauren, but her niece, eyes wide, just shook her head.

Then the elderly man closed his eyes and began to moan just as Swanson had. If was soft at first, his body swaying.

"Take hold of the weeping stone and feel Christ's tears." The reverend repeated the sentence several times, saying the words rhythmically, the man's moaning layered beneath them, the resulting effect musical and hypnotic. "Feel his pain. Can you see our Lord?"

"Yes . . . yes, I see the Lord," the man said, his voice quavering. His moaning grew louder, stopping only when Swanson placed his hand on his forehead. The man immediately quieted and sat back down.

Reverend Swanson moved farther down the aisle, closer to where Hannah, Lauren, Kiki, and Naomi sat, taking the stone with him. This time he chose a middle-aged woman. Blond, dressed in a designer suit and lots of gold jewelry, she looked frightened when he touched her, but she stood anyway. Swanson pressed her hand against the stone. She stared at him as he asked the same question he had asked the old man.

Hannah felt a gnawing in her stomach as she watched. It took longer this time, but the woman soon let out a muffled exclamation.

"I feel His tears," she cried out. "I feel them." She continued talking, but the words reconfigured into the same incomprehensible jumble Swanson had spoken earlier. Then she shuddered and collapsed back onto the pew.

Leaning forward, Hannah took a closer look at the stone and realized its shiny appearance was due to its being wet.

Swanson headed toward the back of the church.

"Oh, no," Kiki muttered, sinking down in her seat. "I hope he's not coming for me. Hannah, don't let him take me."

"Well, *I'm* ready. I think it's fascinating." Naomi wiggled her fingers in the air, trying to get his attention. But he unexpectedly walked back to the platform. He opened his mouth to speak, but his attention fixed on something in the rear of the room.

Wondering what had grabbed his interest, Hannah twisted around and saw a woman in her late twenties standing in the doorway. Blond, doe-eyed, and petite, she stood uncertainly, her legs wobbly beneath her. A much larger red-haired woman stood protectively by her side, holding on to her arm.

Lauren leaned close to Hannah. "That's Lisa Lempke," she whispered.

"Which one?" Hannah asked.

"The blonde. Except she looks just awful. Poor thing. Losing your mother and then your father all in one year."

Hannah looked more closely at Lisa. It had been years since she had seen her and she barely remembered her. Lisa looked colorless, with pale lips and hair, skin the color of a sun-bleached shell. She had even, pretty features, but at that moment she seemed translucent, a human on the verge of disappearing. Only her eyes had color—large and very dark brown, two bottomless holes bored into her pale face.

Swanson raised his arms. "Christ is with you, Lisa," he called out, his voice filling the room. "He feels your grief. He looks into the black hollows of your soul, sees the depth of your pain. Come to me, Lisa." He reached out his hand in her direction. "Let Christ share your tears as you share His."

Hannah's eyes moved from Swanson to Lisa. Lisa, still standing at the rear door, looked skittish and Hannah thought she might bolt out of the room, but her companion kept a firm grip on her arm. Finally they walked slowly forward. It didn't look like she was forcing Lisa to move down the aisle as much as she was keeping the poor girl from falling down. Step by hesitant step they slowly made their way up the red carpet.

"Share the tears!" Swanson cried out, his voice a bassoon rolling through the chapel and through Hannah's head. She, as well as everyone else in the room, was watching Lisa, but Lisa seemed unaware of anyone except Swanson. Pulling back her shoulders, the girl began to move with more certainty, appearing to grow stronger with each step closer to the platform.

When she neared Reverend Swanson, he reached for her hand and pulled her toward him. Lisa's companion held on to her at first, and for a second Hannah thought she and Swanson might play tug-of-war with the poor girl. But Lisa stepped in the reverend's direction and her friend had no choice but to release her. Lisa belonged to him now, her body relaxing, her chin tilted upward, dark eyes staring into his shining blues. Swanson was in control. Lisa's companion took a seat in the front pew.

Hannah's fist raised to her mouth, her discomfort growing each moment. Who was this man? This was no church service. It was some sort of voodoo.

"We grieve for your father, Lisa. Christ hears your sorrows and cries for you." With this last statement the reverend took Lisa's small white hand and pressed it against the stone. "Touch his tears, Lisa, and you will see him. Touch the weeping stone and Christ will come to you. Can you see him, Lisa?"

He was on a roll now, his voice low and urging, its sound mesmerizing. Lisa, pale as a sick angel, seemed helpless.

At that moment it looked to Hannah as if Lisa tried to pull her hand off the stone. It happened in an instant, but Hannah felt certain she saw the girl's arm pull back, but then Swanson held her fingers in place. Lisa closed her eyes and shook her head, strands of blond hair whipping her cheek.

"Christ will come to you, Lisa," the reverend said, his voice now softened but no less commanding. "You must let him in. Can you see him, Lisa? Look with your soul's eye. You can see him."

Hannah swallowed hard. The room was deadly silent, nobody daring to breathe as they watched the drama. This was why every pew was filled, Hannah thought. They weren't here to worship God. They were part of a cult, participating in this bizarre form of theater where sad, lonely people let themselves believe this pompous little man had the power to heal their emotional pain.

But Lisa wasn't succumbing as quickly as the others.

There was a soundless struggle between her and Swanson, a contest between the weak and the strong.

Run, Lisa. This isn't religion he offers. It's black magic. Save yourself and run from this man. Hannah said the words silently, but it seemed to be another voice Lisa allowed inside her. Suddenly she let out a cry.

"I see him!" Her dark eyes were open wide as she looked, not at Swanson, but at some point behind him.

"Where is he, Lisa? Tell me where you see him?" Swanson asked, egging her on.

She pointed a finger. "There. Right there. He's with me." She strained her hand forward, reaching at nothing.

"Give in to him, Lisa. Let him cleanse your heart. Let him take your pain into his body. Give in to him."

Sobbing, her face twitched, her knees buckled under her. In one leap, the redhead was back at her side, catching her before she hit the floor. Lisa crumpled into her arms, tears streaming, unintelligible mutterings falling from her mouth.

"My God," Hannah said, repelled. What was this craziness where people spoke gibberish, where they held rocks you could find in any garden and hallucinated from them?

But what she found most repugnant was the look on Swanson's face. As he gazed down at Lisa collapsed in the redhead's arms, Hannah felt certain she saw a smile of victory on his face.

Twenty minutes later, when they were back outside on the sidewalk, Hannah turned her face upward into a light breeze. What happened in the church had been so disturbing that she felt she needed to be scrubbed clean. People poured out of the church around her. After Lisa's bout with the stone, the service continued with a few more hymns, then ushers passed bowls for donations. Swanson was especially strident about Christ wanting them to fill the bowls.

Hannah felt a familiar tap on her arm. Turning, she saw Kiki, with Naomi and Lauren right behind. They all looked shell-shocked.

"Hannah, I don't understand what went on in there. I

thought at a funeral the service was supposed to be comforting,'' Kiki said.

"I think the people who choose this church are looking for something more dramatic. They yearn for emotional release,'' Hannah told her. "They've been hurt in their lives. They feel weak and powerless and they want a father figure to take control.''

"Well, I don't want to investigate Arnold's murder anymore,'' Kiki said. "This whole thing is starting to scare me.''

"More than the police?'' Hannah asked.

"The police know I'm innocent. I couldn't hurt a fly. They know that. They have to.''

Hearing this exchange between her two aunts, Lauren stepped in. "Hannah, I wouldn't have brought you here if I had known you were trying to investigate Mr. Lempke's murder. That's a job for the police.''

Hannah faced her, her expression urgent. "I didn't come here to investigate anything. At least that wasn't my direct intention, but I've learned a lot tonight.''

"Like what?'' Kiki asked.

"That this church, which Arnold despised, appears to have a lot of money running through it. That Reverend Swanson has some strange control over Arnold's daughter.'' Hannah paused, these ideas simmering in her head. "Yes,'' she said thoughtfully. "There's definitely information here. It might help us learn more about Arnold, maybe to learn *why* he was murdered, if nothing else.''

"So just tell the police what we saw here tonight, Aunt Hannah. Give them your ideas and let them run with it,'' Lauren suggested. "There's nothing you can do that they can't do better.''

Hannah's attention snapped back to her niece, her eyes keen. "But that's where you're wrong, dear. There are so many things I can do that the police can't.''

They all looked at her quizzically.

"Like what?'' Naomi asked.

"When the police question someone, that person is on guard, on the defensive. But me, I'm a sixty-one-year-old woman and not a threat. Haven't you heard? Women our age are close to invisible."

Naomi crossed her arms. "That's a negative attitude."

"Not at all," Hannah told her. "Being invisible has its advantages. At our age we can snoop around, ask questions, and no one notices us. It can be quite a plus."

Naomi sidled closer to Hannah. "So you're going to investigate the church?"

Hannah glanced at the building next to her. "I must help clear Kiki's name, and the church seems an excellent place to start."

Just then an older Mercedes in mint condition drove past, catching Hannah's eye. She looked around at the cars parked outside the church and noticed that a large portion of them were expensive, even for Marin—several new Porsches, another large classic Mercedes, a Bentley, a Rolls. Yes, there was a lot of money associated with the church. And where there was money there could be a motive for murder, especially since Lempke was threatening to expose the church as a fraudulent operation.

She walked down the sidewalk, her head filled with ideas. Lauren, Naomi, and Kiki looked at each other with resignation then followed her.

"Well, Hannah," Kiki said nervously. "To be honest, I'm relieved that you're still curious. I want to find out who killed my sweet Arnie."

"I'll say one thing," Naomi said. "Swanson is either a master of deception or he's the real thing."

Lauren looked at her with astonishment. "You can't possibly think he's for real? That the rock is for real?" She quickened her pace until she was by Hannah's side. "You don't think the stone is really covered with Jesus' tears, do you?"

But it was Naomi who answered. "It could be," she said.

"There are many phenomena in this world that we can't understand."

"But it's so ridiculous," Lauren said.

"Then what made those people act so strangely?" Kiki asked.

Hannah stopped in her tracks and the rest of them stopped with her. "But don't you see, all of you? That's another reason I'm so concerned about that church. I think that silly rock is covered with some sort of hallucinogenic drug."

$\mathcal{S}$EVEN

LATE THAT NIGHT, IN THE silence of Kiki's bedroom, as she donned her frilly nightgown, cold-creamed her face, and generously slathered Porcelana to the age spots on her hands, Kiki felt less anxious about the police suspicions regarding her involvement in Arnold's murder. After all, the police had begun canvassing the neighborhood and were bound to discover something that would point the finger at someone else.

But more important, Hannah, her protector, was going to help her, and once Hannah set her mind to something, the woman was like a bulldozer. To ease any doubts Kiki might have had, Hannah had announced over that night's dinner that the following day she would begin her investigation by visiting Lisa Lempke as well as Reverend Swanson. This take-charge approach comforted Kiki to no end. She padded off to bed reassured that all would be well. Hannah would never let anything bad happen to her very own sister.

But the morning delivered fresh trauma in the form of a phone call—a simple nagging ring of the machine that turned out to be the start of all hell breaking loose.

Having just finished cleaning up the breakfast dishes, Hannah, drying her hands on a kitchen towel, eyed the ringing phone with distaste but finally answered it. She didn't like the phone and never felt any compulsion to leap for the receiver just because an unidentified someone demanded it, but she picked it up this morning because she was expecting a call from a bulb distributor in North Carolina regarding an upcoming shipment of a Sweet Musette iris.

She frowned when it turned out to be Detective Morgan. A troublesome insistence could be heard in his tone that had been lacking in their previous encounters. He wanted her and Kiki at the police station in an hour and was coldly unreceptive to Hannah's suggestion that the afternoon would be more convenient. They wanted to talk to her and Kiki again, making it a second interview for Hannah and a third for Kiki. Upon hanging up, Hannah glowered at the machine that bore such bad tidings.

After telling her sister the bad news, Kiki erupted into a Vesuvius of hysteria. She flew around the house in her bathrobe, her hair still in hot curlers, ranting and weeping. "You'd think Bedouin marauders were after us," Hannah proclaimed in frustration after Kiki threatened to escape to Mexico. After twenty minutes of cajoling, she accepted the fact that she had to see the police, but this argument was quickly followed by a battle over whether they should call Louis Caufield, a criminal attorney who raised orchids in San Anselmo, to accompany them. Hannah thought it foolhardy to step one foot in the police station without legal counsel, but Kiki wouldn't hear of it.

"Everyone in town will know Louis went with us and they'll all think I'm guilty," she wailed. "You know it's me they're accusing. Not you."

Hannah understood her reasoning. It *was* Kiki they were interested in. Hannah had little connection to Arnold Lempke and an unshakable alibi, having spent the morning of the murder doing her volunteer work in front of a dozen people. There was no doubt the police were after Kiki. But Hannah decided that her sister was at least chronologically an adult, and whether or not to have a lawyer was her decision.

So she gave in and drove them to the Hill Creek police station. A contemporary one-story building, it sat nestled in some eucalyptus trees across from a park a few blocks from Center Avenue. The police offices were attached to the fire department, and Hannah had been to the building once when she planted three rosebushes for the police-and fire-department landscaping project, but she had never seen the inside. It looked pleasant enough, more like a small library branch than the home of local crime fighters, but Kiki still froze up when they reached the double doors at the entrance.

"We are strong women. We are not afraid of people just because they wear uniforms," Hannah said to Kiki, giving the air a punch of confidence and doing her best to squelch her own butterflies. After she gave Kiki a hug, the sisters walked arm in arm inside the building.

It didn't look anything like the police stations she saw in television cop shows. It was small, contemporary, and squeaky-clean with blue carpet, cedar paneling on the walls, and a couple a healthy potted plants scattered around—a crime-fighting station suitable for a town that had little crime. Giving the air a sniff, Hannah felt certain she smelled apple-spice potpourri.

When they got to the reception desk, no one was there, and it took a few minutes for them to be noticed. Eventually a policeman who looked much more like a fresh-faced frat boy than a grizzled cop smiled and asked if he could help them. Hannah wanted to smile back, but she was too nervous, and when this happened, she usually appeared reserved and indifferent. Stiffly, she asked for Detective Morgan. With his smile dimmed, the young man turned and led them through a door and down a short hallway, where, despite her protest, she and Kiki were separated and placed in different rooms. Detective Morgan went with Kiki, which Hannah thought didn't bode well, since he appeared to be in charge of the case.

A lesser gun was saved for Hannah. As young Detective Donald Shea entered the small interrogation room, he bumped his large frame into a table, then lowered himself into a flimsy plastic chair that squeaked ominously under his weight. Even in uniform, he looked out of place in the tiny room. It was about eight-by-eight feet, furnished with only a table and two chairs.

Hannah noticed a small mirrored window in one wall. "Is someone watching us?" she asked.

Dropping his steno pad, Shea bent down to grab it, hitting his head on the edge of the table as he straightened himself. It occurred to Hannah that the poor man must go around constantly bruised.

"No, ma'am," he said. "The window there is so we can film interviews. Our conversation is just being taped."

"I'm not important enough to film?" Hannah asked.

"Well, we only have one camera," Shea said, embarrassed. She assumed the camera was being used for her sister.

At first Hannah was surprised at the detective's fumbling uneasiness but quickly realized he probably had never interrogated anyone in connection with a murder before. He treated her in a manner as polite as a choir boy's, bringing her coffee and replacing her plastic chair with one more comfortable before settling down to business.

He said his name, Hannah's name, the time and date for the benefit of the tape recorder before beginning the questioning. That seemingly insignificant act wrenched Hannah's stomach. Despite Shea's friendliness, being in that tiny interrogation room coupled with the formality of his speaking into the recorder made her comprehend anew how grave the situation was. Even though she had told Kiki it was serious, in the back of her mind she thought that nothing bad could really happen. She now realized she had been wrong.

All the questions Shea delivered centered on Kiki, an additional bad omen about the way things were heading. What time had Kiki arrived home the morning Lempke was murdered? Had she seemed upset? Had Hannah witnessed the argument between her sister and the deceased at the Rose Club cocktail reception?

"There was no argument," she answered firmly. "Arnold had merely decided not to go on the cruise."

"And was your sister upset about that?" Shea asked, his manner growing more assertive as he gained confidence. Still, he was trying hard to be polite, and that touched her. She noticed he wasn't wearing a wedding ring and she would have tried to fix him up with Lauren if she hadn't met him under such despicable circumstances.

"Of course she was upset. But she's just emotional."

Hannah immediately regretted these words. She wouldn't have lied in any case, but people were bound to remember Kiki's tearful dash into the ladies' room after Lempke's pronouncement about the cruise, so there was no point in sugarcoating it.

Shea asked her about the morning they found Lempke. He wanted to know what time Kiki left the house, what time she returned, and how she had behaved. Hannah answered as best she could, struggling not to show her anger that anyone could think for an instant that Kiki could commit any act as vile as murder.

After forty-five minutes of questions she was allowed to leave and she walked the few blocks to the Book Stop, where she and Kiki had arranged to meet. First thing, she used the pay phone and called Lisa Lempke as well as Reverend Swanson's office, but couldn't get appointments with either until the next day.

Two hours later she had read three newspapers, done two crosswords, including most of *The New York Times*'s, and was feeling frantic when Kiki finally straggled in, looking shaken to her shoes. She was all to bits, her hair a mess, her lipstick reapplied with so wobbly a hand it streaked out of the corners of her mouth.

Hannah jumped up from her seat. "What happened?"

Kiki grabbed onto her and Hannah led her to a chair. Hannah tried to keep as low a profile as possible, quickly ordering her sister a cup of Lemon Lift, although, by Kiki's looks, a shot of whiskey would have been more appropriate.

When she first sat down, Kiki was too agitated to speak. She just whimpered and bit her thumbnail, making a nasty dent in her manicure over which she would later curse. Once a few sips of tea were in her, the words spilled forth.

"Fortuna has swished her skirts again, Hannie. Someone saw the Cadillac on Arnold's street. I knew I should have gotten that fender fixed. It sticks out like a sore thumb."

The Cadillac stuck out regardless of whatever dents it possessed, but Hannah didn't mention this.

Kiki pressed her hands against her cheeks. "You should have heard the way they talked to me."

Hannah patted her shoulder. "Relax, dear, and just tell me what happened," she said, trying not to let her apprehension show on her face.

Kiki kept chattering in a frenzied way. "I told one of them, I said, 'Listen, buster, I'll get my sister in here and she'll tell you a thing or two,' but they wouldn't let me get you, and—"

Hannah placed strong hands on her shoulders. "Sweetie, take a deep breath and bottom-line things for me."

Kiki sighed deeply, her chest heaving upward in a manner that would have pleased her during a calmer moment. "They really think I might have killed poor Arnold!"

"Keep your voice down." Hannah looked around the café and saw the young girl working the cappuccino machine looking keenly in their direction. Most people in Hill Creek felt they were on too high a spiritual plane to gossip, yet gossip they did, and at an alarming pace. "What did the police say that makes you think that?"

"It's what they didn't say. The way they looked at me, like I was lying to them."

"You did lie to them."

Inhaling sharply, Kiki pushed her shoulders back. "I didn't lie, not exactly. You're supposed to be on my side. My God, what if they arrest me? I could be raped by prison guards." She paused briefly while she weighed the pros and cons of this possibility, then continued. "You won't let them arrest me? You've never let anything bad happen to me."

Hannah sat mute, thoughts twirling inside her brain. She had protected Kiki from the time they were toddlers. She had fended off bullies, tutored her in math (a grueling and unrewarding experience), counseled her on boyfriends, built up her self-esteem after her divorce, soothed her after the unexpected death of her second husband, Cecil. She had always been there to comfort and assist. But for the first time in their lives the forces working against Kiki were beyond her control, and she was frightened for her sister.

"It will be fine, Kiki. We'll fix this somehow."

But with trepidation Kiki looked in her sister's eyes and saw that Hannah didn't believe what she was saying.

At times like these she wished she still drank. That afternoon, while Kiki rested in her darkened bedroom with a cold compress on her forehead, Hannah sat in the old grape-vine chair on her front porch facing Walnut Avenue, a tree-lined street that curved through Hill Creek's oldest neighborhood. Most of these small houses had been built in the forties as affordable housing for young families. Now they were high-priced real estate, the majority remodeled beyond recognition. Hannah had inherited hers twenty years earlier from a friend, Randall Cummins. He had been an old lover, though she didn't broadcast that fact, because one, it would have annoyed her husband, and two, it didn't seem important anyway. She and Randall had remained friends long after the love affair had ended, and when he became ill Hannah had sat by his bedside at least three evenings a week. Her husband, Paul, hadn't liked it, but she did it anyway, talking with Randall about the past, comforting him with old stories and bad jokes until, after six months, he died. She was surprised when she learned of his will and his generosity. She rented out the house for several years, moving into it when Paul died.

It was one story and brown-shingled, though in the summer the shingles weren't visible from the street, the house's sides covered with climbing red roses that grew so profusely that the structure became a blazing tangle of flowers. Its best feature was a front porch that wrapped around the side, and this was where she sat that afternoon, surrounded by terra-cotta pots of basil and pink geraniums, her sandaled feet propped on the railing, her head conjuring up visions of booze.

She imagined how a sip of an ice-cold Bloody Mary would taste, how the pungent flavor of the vodka mixed with the spiciness of the tomato would blend on her tongue, then slide down her throat, taking the edge off the anxiety that gnawed at her.

But she had stopped all alcohol ten years before. She had never been the fall-down-drunk type but was just getting pleasantly potted every night, waking up each morning feeling fuzzy and slightly nauseous. She didn't go to AA. She just knew she was drinking too much, depending on it to ease life's disappointments, to calm her nerves. Quitting had been hard, and she still thought about liquor frequently. But thinking about it was okay. She just couldn't drink it.

The Bloody Mary image was still firmly in her mind and on her tongue when to her astonishment she saw Perez at the end of her garden path next to the open gate. Oddly, it was his dog she recognized first. The spaniel, tail wagging, held a tattered green tennis ball in his teeth, and he looked at Hannah with playful eyes.

In contrast, his master's expression was not so easy to interpret. Perez stood there looking awkward and surprisingly boyish for a man who had to be in his sixties. He was wearing a denim shirt, blue jeans, and well-worn running shoes. His head was bare and tanned at the temples, but he wore his gray hair long at the nape where it curled softly just above his collar.

She dropped the book she held in her lap. Teresa barked madly from inside the house. They weren't used to unexpected guests other than Lauren, Naomi, and a few neighbors. Clumsily swinging her legs off the railing, she scooped up the book.

As the spaniel tugged him forward Perez headed up the walkway toward the porch. "What are you reading?" he asked. Hannah thought he sounded uncomfortable, although no more so than she felt.

"Allen Ginsberg," she answered, then added, "he's a poet."

He paused. "I don't read any poetry. Seems like all the good poets are dead. I like to read things written by people who are alive. Is Ginsberg still alive?"

She thought about it a moment, her mind temporarily muddled. "It's terrible, but I can't remember. Sometimes I think I've lost too many brain cells."

"It's called CRAFT."

"What's that?"

"Can't remember a friggin' thing."

Hannah laughed and Perez smiled. There was a moment of ponderous silence while she looked at her lap and thumbed the pages of Ginsberg, trying to figure out what this man was doing in her front yard. It was hardly likely that he had just been walking by, but why would he seek her out? Teresa had stopped barking, but she could hear Sylvia snorting just behind the door. The spaniel heard it, too, tugging at his leash, anxious to inspect the source of the sounds.

Perez commanded the dog to sit then rubbed his head to quiet him. "What's that noise?" he asked Hannah. "It's coming from behind the door."

"It's just my pig."

"You have a pig?"

"A Vietnamese pig. She was abandoned. Wonderful pet. A decent watchdog, too. At least sometimes."

Perez smiled. "I guess she'd surprise any burglars."

"I suppose she would," Hannah said, her heart wanting to return his smile but her head forcing herself not to. "I don't mean to be rude, but what are you doing here?"

He didn't balk. "I take Winston to the school yard a few times a week to play ball." Winston wagged his tail at the sound of his name and the word *ball*.

"That's four blocks away."

Perez fixed his eyes on her. "I got your address at the police department. I still have connections. Do you mind?"

"I just don't understand why you'd go to the trouble."

There were a few seconds of dead air. "Mind if I sit? After a few rounds with Winston my knee aches." Without waiting for an answer, he sat on the steps a yard from Hannah's chair.

She shifted in her seat, watching him scratch Winston's head, and it occurred to her that these two creatures were very much alike. The dog sat next to his master receiving his attention gratefully, but his eyes were set on Hannah as determinedly as his master's. They both expected something from her.

Hannah stiffened as it dawned on her why Perez was there. To get information, to wheedle out whatever secrets he and the Hill Creek police thought she was hiding. But she would turn the tables. She would be the one to get information from him.

Thinking she had him figured out, her confidence returned. Casually she rose from her chair and sat on the step next to him, a few feet away, but as long a distance as she could manage without falling off the porch. She wanted to be eye level with him.

"Tell me what's going on with the murder case. Have they found out anything?" she asked.

Picking a twig off the bottom step, he twirled it in his fingers. "I don't know that much, just a few bits of information. I'm retired, so I don't get all the facts I used to, but you can trust me that they're conducting interviews and running all the evidence through the proper tests. I know they don't think it was a burglar. Nothing was stolen or bothered in any way."

There went one theory out the window. "What about random violence?" she asked. "Could it have just been crazy person?"

"Not likely. The killer had to walk across some gravel, so Lempke must have heard him. Yet he felt comfortable enough to turn his back to him."

"What about the murder weapon?"

"They haven't found it yet."

These morsels whetted her appetite. The range of murder suspects had been narrowed down to someone Lempke knew.

"Do they know what the murder weapon was?" she asked, trying not to sound too eager.

Again, he shook his head. "I don't think so."

"Could it have been a knife?"

"Maybe, but apparently the blade had to have been very narrow and jagged at the tip. Not like any knife I know."

Winston chose that moment to lay his ball at Hannah's feet. Perez released the leash, so Hannah threw the ball across her small front yard. Winston bounded after it, catching it in midair and in the process tromping through Hannah's flower bed. Perez jumped up.

"Winston, come back here!" The dog came trotting up with his tail wagging and Perez took hold of his leash before he sat back down. "I'm sorry. He squashed a couple of those little daisies."

Hannah laughed. "They're asters and it's okay."

"Some people get upset about those things."

"Well, I don't. It's a garden, not a work of art."

He glanced around the yard. "I think you're wrong on that one. This place is beautiful."

"Thank you," Hannah said, studying his profile. Kiki was right. He was a very handsome man and she had never trusted handsome men. "Do the police have any good suspects? Other than my sister and me, I mean."

The easy smile dropped from his face. "You're not a suspect. Your alibi checked out."

Hannah blinked. "I thought you said you didn't know much about the case."

"I know your sister is a suspect. She had motive and opportunity."

He said the words gently, his face compassionate, but the words cut into Hannah. She sat up very straight.

"If you think my sister is a murderer, then should you be fraternizing with me, Mr. Perez?" she said, not able to hide the animosity in her voice.

"Listen, I'm not the police anymore. I fraternize wherever I want. And for your information, I don't think your sister did it. She's not the right profile."

"The Hill Creek police think differently."

"Then they're wrong." He took the ball from Winston's mouth and tossed it a few yards, safely away from the flowers, sending the dog scampering after it. "I didn't come here to talk about the murder case."

"Then why did you come?"

He inhaled then let the air out. "To ask you to dinner."

If he had slapped her, she wouldn't have been more surprised. If it was information the man wanted, he was certainly going to any length to obtain it. It took a moment for her to regain her composure. When she didn't say anything, he spoke.

"Would you go? To dinner?" he asked.

"I'm . . . I'm sorry, but I really couldn't." She wished she had come up with something more suave to say, but her stumbling words were all she could manage.

Perez turned pink. He rose from the step.

"I have to go. You have a nice garden," he said, kneeling down and pretending to focus his attention on the hook on Winston's leash. When he stood up again, he looked directly at her, his eyes not straying. His eyes were soft, with a vigorous glimmer.

She wanted to say something to him, explain herself, but her mouth wasn't cooperating. Finally she muttered an "I'm sorry."

"You don't have to be," was all he said before he turned and walked down the pathway and out the gate, Winston running ahead of him, pulling on the leash. Hannah watched them walk up the sidewalk until they disappeared around a corner. Some aspects of life never change regardless of how old you get, she thought. Both she and Perez were in their sixties, yet they stuttered around, as socially inept as if they were in high school.

"Why did I say no?" she whispered out loud, but then quickly admitted to herself that she knew exactly why. It was the same reason she had shrunk from all men for the past five years, the reason she would continue to shrink from them.

But there were some things in life that couldn't be changed.

EIGHT

NAOMI, LAUREN, KIKI, AND HANNAH cleared the
last of the dinner dishes from Hannah's old oak dining table, one of her most prized possessions. It had belonged to
her mother and grandmother, and for the last ten years had
stood in her house, beautiful and solid, its amber wood
glossy from polishing and age.

"In the soul of every woman there dwells an inner wildness," Naomi pronounced theatrically as she wiped a few
stray peas off the table's surface.

Stepping around Naomi, Hannah picked up the wineglasses, smiling thanks for her attempt to stimulate conversation. Dinner had been dreadful, with everyone eating in
grim silence. They were all too preoccupied to engage in
their usual lively exchange of gossip. Kiki was worrying
about jail. Lauren was naturally worried about Kiki, but
Hannah knew she was also nervous about the séance,
having been one of those children who always thought a
big green monster was lurking under her bed. And Hannah's mind was discombobulated on how she was going to

solve Arnold Lempke's murder in order to keep Kiki out of jail.

As for Naomi, she was still strangely agitated, flitting about the room like a nervous flea and eating everything within arm's reach, which she always did when she was upset. But when Hannah asked her if anything was wrong, she protested that she was fine and then immediately asked for brandy.

"What are you talking about, Naomi?" Hannah asked. "There are all kinds of wildness, from the jungle to things sexual."

Kiki, wiping the tabletop with enough vigor to take off the finish, gave her a scolding look. "That's the third time you've mentioned sex tonight. Did you change your women's herbs? We promised to always tell each other if we changed our women's herbs."

Hannah felt color rising in her cheeks. With everything else she had to think about, the dinner invitation from Perez still stuck in her mind, obviously stimulating some long-dormant sex-starved corner of her brain.

"I'm talking about sexuality. It's a normal healthy part of life," she said.

"But I'm not talking sexual wildness, although I could use some," Naomi told them. "I'm talking creative wildness. Red Moon says that every woman has this creative wildness inside her that harmonizes with water and the sky. It's the life force that comes from the womb." With this, she dramatically raised her hands, fingers fanned. "We each have to find a way to express it, for it to be heard, if only by the wind." She said the last part in a lower, throatier voice, reminding Hannah of Reverend Swanson. The comparison seemed natural since, after all, they were in the same business.

"Well, then Lauren definitely expresses her creative wildness through her cooking," Hannah said, turning to her niece. "That pecan-crusted sole you made tonight was better than any restaurant. You should be a chef, not an accountant.''

The chef-versus-accountant issue came up more than occasionally. Hannah felt Lauren was an artist with food, but that she had chained herself to the sterile confines of corporate accounting. Lauren, who had yet to resolve this conflict within herself, usually managed to sidestep it.

''You're lucky, Aunt Hannah,'' she said. ''You're a poet. You're wild with words.''

''*I'm* wild with creative spirit,'' Naomi said proudly. ''Channeling is my art.''

''What about me?'' Kiki asked, not wanting to be left out. ''How do I express my creative wildness?''

By chasing men was the first thing that ran through Hannah's mind. ''Life is your art,'' she said instead, wanting to make her sister happy. ''But you need to work on finding an artistic outlet as well.''

Kiki smiled appreciatively.

''Oh yes, you must find your creative way,'' Naomi said. ''The spirit must seek its own voice.'' She held up one finger. ''Perhaps a drum. Red Moon thinks highly of spiritual percussion, particularly a slow, deep beat mimicking the child's heartbeat in the womb. But let's get started. I feel Red Moon stirring.''

''More likely it's that second helping of fish,'' Hannah told her.

Naomi threw her a dirty look. ''You're rather testy this evening,'' she said. ''I hope you won't bring your negative energy into our talk with Red Moon. He doesn't like it.'' She then raised her chin and held her hands high. She would have looked Christ-like except for her thigh-length, lipstick-red caftan with matching leggings. Her head was wrapped in a red turban and long beaded earrings dangled from her ears.

''It's important to keep the positive energies flowing,'' she said. ''Lauren, if you'll arrange the candles. Hannah and Kiki, sit.''

Lauren took the twelve candles Hannah had dug out of her earthquake-supplies chest and placed them in the center of the table, then lit them. When everyone was seated, Naomi went to the light switch. Kiki let out an impressed "ooh" as the lights switched off and the golden glow of the candles filled the room.

"Now, all hold hands," Naomi said, still standing.

"What are you going to do?" Lauren asked uneasily.

There was the rustle of a paper bag, then the sound of a match striking. The women turned their heads and saw Naomi touch the match to what looked like a clump of weeds tied with string. As the weeds began to smoke she shook them over the table.

Hannah grimaced. "What the hell—"

"It's all right," Kiki said. "It's called a smudge stick. She's only smudging."

The smudge stick glowed and smoked as Naomi waved it around the room, a few smoldering embers dancing up into the darkness before disappearing.

Hannah was not pacified. "She's shaking burning weeds."

"Not weeds, dear." Naomi said the word *dear* with ever so slight a scowl as she continued waving the ignited foliage in the air. "Sage, cedar, and pine. It's used by native healers for cleansing, which this room could use."

"I scrubbed this whole house top to bottom last week," Hannah said, twisting to watch Naomi as she moved around the room, her turban casting an eerie shadow on the walls. "You're going to set off the smoke alarm."

"It's negative energy I'm having to cleanse, Hannah, which is mostly emanating from you." Naomi had begun a second pass around the table, waving the smudge stick around everyone's head. When she reached Hannah she made an additional pass, shaking it with extra vigor near her face.

"Stop it," Hannah said, coughing. "You're blackening my lungs."

"I think we're done now," Naomi said in a sprightly tone. She dunked the smudge stick into a waiting glass of water; it made a hissing sound as it drowned, the burned smell lingering in the air. After a brief foray into the living room she came back with a fat stick about a yard long with white feathers and bells attached to it. She sat down between Kiki and Lauren, facing Hannah. "Someone at the table will need to ask Red Moon questions. It should be Lauren."

"Why her?" Kiki asked. "I want to do it."

"She's the most receptive, I think," Naomi said. "Now, first things first. To help Red Moon communicate about Arnold's murder, I needed something that Arnold had touched."

"How about Kiki's thigh," Hannah muttered, still irritated over the smudge-stick incident.

"You just stop it," Kiki spat.

"Sorry," Hannah replied.

Naomi pursed her lips. "Watch that negative energy. I have another smudge stick in my bag."

Hannah crossed her arms. "No need for threats."

"So, do you have it?" Naomi asked Kiki. Kiki looked sheepish as she handed Naomi a wad of blue-and-white printed cotton. Naomi dropped it in a small heap on the table in front of her.

"What's that?" Lauren asked.

"Undershorts," Naomi answered, as if it were the most natural thing in the world. "They belonged to Arnold."

Hannah cast a dubious look at her sister. "Where did you get them?"

"Arnold left them here," Kiki answered after a pause. "I washed them."

Hannah's eyes narrowed. "He took off his undershorts here in our house?"

Kiki pressed her hand to her chest. "Well, you could say that. Shouldn't we get started?"

But Hannah refused to change the subject. "You had sex with him here, didn't you?"

"You make it sound so crude, when it wasn't anything like that. Arnold and I explored that special magic—"

"Did he have much of a wand?" Hannah asked, interrupting. Her annoyance was justified since she and Kiki had agreed years before that in order to maintain their privacy they wouldn't bring men home. Not that the opportunity arose much for Hannah.

Kiki opened her mouth to protest but was stopped by Naomi pounding her fist on the table. "Stop this bickering or the mood will be destroyed and we'll have to start over."

"Is Red Moon going to speak English?" Lauren asked.

"Certainly," Naomi said. "He melds his mind with mine." She touched her finger to her lips. "I am his vessel."

Kiki emitted a low, approving murmur.

Naomi held up a finger. "We must begin. Join hands."

Hannah took Kiki's hand, giving it an apologetic squeeze. When she reached for Lauren's hand, her niece held back at first, finally slipping her fingers into Hannah's.

"Now close your eyes and clear your minds of everyday thoughts," Naomi ordered, closing her own eyes. "Think of a flame, a flame burning in your mind's eye."

Eyes closed, the women sat silently in the darkened room, the candles throwing yellow light and black shadows that pranced on the dining-room walls. Hannah expected something to happen. She waited for what seemed forever but nothing occurred except that her hand started to hurt because Lauren was gripping it so tightly. In the background the antique clock in the living room ticked away the passing seconds.

"Naomi," Kiki whispered. "When does Red Moon come out?"

"I don't know. I'm feeling blocked. Someone in the room is emitting opposing energy." She opened one eye and aimed it at Hannah.

"Don't look at me," Hannah said. "You had three glasses of wine and enough mashed potatoes for a family of four. That's bound to block something."

Naomi's mouth twisted. "If we're going to communicate with Red Moon successfully, you're going to have to clear your mind, Hannah. Empty your head of all thoughts."

"That's so hard for her," Kiki said. "She's always thinking. She's a thoughtaholic."

"More reason to get rid of them for a few minutes," Naomi replied. "That poor brain must be tired. Empty your head, Hannah. Think only of the flame."

At that moment Naomi began chanting. Hannah recognized the sound because in the past it had often drifted, thin and barely discernible, from Naomi's house into her own backyard. Hannah never minded it, figuring it probably scared off the gophers. But it had more cadence and fullness up close. It definitely sounded like an Indian language, and Hannah wondered where her neighbor had learned it. It reverberated in the small dining room, the sound, mixed with the candlelight and the black shadows, adding an eerie feel to the atmosphere. Hannah felt Lauren and Kiki's hands tighten around hers. It occurred to her that if you believed in this sort of channeling nonsense, you would gladly fork over fifty dollars just to hear Naomi chant.

Wanting to cooperate even if she did think the whole Red Moon act was a scam, Hannah closed her eyes, listened to the chanting, and made her mind as blank as it ever became. She pushed out thoughts of poems she had yet to write, books to read, roses to grow, of Kiki's predicament with the police, images of Lempke lying dead in the middle of his rosebush like so much fertilizer. And what was left was a not unpleasant emptiness, a fuzzy gray nothingness.

But this meditative state was shattered by the sudden, explosive pounding of Naomi's stick, the bells clanging as it hit the floor. Startled, Hannah bolted up in her chair. Kiki let out a yelp and Lauren whimpered.

Then it happened. Hannah opened her mouth to protest

about Naomi scaring everyone half to death with her ridiculous stick, but instead she froze. For at that moment Naomi's voice took on a completely different character—deep and guttural, the chanting seeming to come from her bowels rather than her lips. The change happened slowly and fast at the same time, as if someone else had slipped into her body.

The hairs stood up on Hannah's arm. It was a man's voice, a voice that couldn't possibly have come from Naomi's vocal cords. But it had to.

Hannah opened her eyes to make sure Naomi was still there. She was. Everyone but Hannah had kept their eyes closed. Kiki and Lauren looked frightened, but Hannah wasn't scared as much as simply amazed. Naomi's face looked different, her features distorted into someone else's face, someone larger and more masculine.

"Clouds on fire above yellow grasses." Naomi spoke as Red Moon uttered his first words of English, although the words sounded heavy and were pronounced oddly. "Earth shrieks her warning as crested birds cry. All debts are paid. Paid in blood."

Hannah felt Lauren's hand trembling. Her own skin was prickling. Naomi clutched Lempke's undershorts in one hand, the blue-and-white cotton squeezing out between her fingers.

"Ask Naomi something," Hannah whispered to her niece.

Lauren squeaked with trepidation, but then pressed her lips together, gathering nerve. Finally she said, "Mr. Red Moon, is that you? Are you . . . are you with us?"

This seemingly innocent question provoked Red Moon into earsplitting intonations. "Coyote comes from beneath the ground. Tawa shrieks her warning!" he shouted several times at the top of his ancient lungs.

"Oh, God," Kiki whispered, frightened.

"Lauren, honey, ask him about the murder," Hannah said.

"But he seems to be in such a bad mood right now," she answered, her voice faltering.

"Please, Lauren."

Lauren took a deep, fortifying breath. "Mr. Red Moon, please tell us about . . . about the man. The man who owned the, uh, undershorts. How did he die?"

Red Moon's head fell forward and he began chanting in a low, whispery voice, now holding the undershorts in both hands. Everyone bent forward, eager to hear what he would say next. He was silent a moment, then muttered something that sounded roughly like English but was unintelligible.

Hannah kept waiting for Lauren to press him to speak more clearly, and when she didn't, she decided to seize the mystical reins herself. "Can you repeat that, please?"

Lauren, her eyes now open, gave her a disapproving look since she was the only one who was supposed to communicate with Red Moon. But, his head still hanging forward, Red Moon complied with Hannah's wishes.

"He caused pain. He bad man," he said.

"Now, I really don't think—" Kiki began, but a quick hand squeeze from Hannah stopped her. Still, she looked at Red Moon with supreme annoyance.

Hannah nodded at Lauren, urging her to ask more questions.

How did he die?" Lauren asked.

"Evil ones side by side," Red Moon replied.

"Evil ones side by side?" Hannah whispered to Lauren. "That's awfully oblique."

Lauren shushed her. "He's five hundred years old."

It seemed to Hannah that at that age the Indian could express himself a bit more clearly. "Who killed him?" she asked, deciding to throw séance protocol out the window. "Who killed Arnold Lempke?"

"Coyote come from beneath the earth. Black eagle flies over yellow grass," Red Moon answered.

Darn, Hannah thought. More Sierra Club doublespeak. But Red Moon followed with something more intriguing.

"Out of Tawa, the corpse rose." Red Moon said the words slowly and dramatically. "The corpse rose," he repeated, then his head fell backward. There was a long pause.

"I think you made him angry," Lauren said.

"What will he do?" Kiki asked.

"He won't do anything," Hannah replied. "He's dead." She frowned. "What am I saying? He's not dead. He's not anything. He doesn't—"

But she stopped speaking as Red Moon slowly raised his head. "Han-nah," he intoned.

"Oh, good Lord," Kiki said, alarmed. "He's talking to you, Hannah."

Hannah was a little surprised herself, but she wasn't about to be cowed by anyone, five hundred years old or not. "Yes, I'm listening."

"Seek water," Red Moon said, although in a voice now suspiciously higher than before.

Seek water? The comment sounded wonderfully mysterious until it occurred to Hannah that Red Moon was trying to convince her to take Naomi's dunking-booth duty at the Rose Club festival.

Nine

To ADD MORE FUEL TO Hill Creek's fire of misery, Wanda Backus's little dog Bon Bon unexpectedly died the following morning. Overtaken by a peculiar and unprecedented seizure, Bon Bon fell dead while lifting his leg on Wanda's new Henredon silk-fringed sofa, life brutally wrenched from him in mid-weewee.

Wanda's wails of grief could be heard for blocks. The fact that this tragic event followed so close upon the heels of Arnold Lempke's murder sent her fleeing temporarily back to the folds of her childhood Presbyterian religion, and she tore through the Book of Revelations, certain Bon Bon's untimely demise was one of the Seven Signs.

Hannah felt truly sorry for Wanda when she heard the news from Naomi. She called and expressed her condolences, but the truth was that with a neighbor having been so recently murdered, it was hard to get too worked up over Bon Bon. There were a dozen more important issues running through Hannah's head, and as she hiked up the stone steps to Lisa Lempke's house, it was the previous night's soirée with Red Moon that was uppermost in her mind.

How gullible did Naomi think she was? All that bunk about corpses rising, two numeral ones standing side by side, coyotes, and Tawa, which Naomi later explained was a Hopi word for Mother Earth.

Although Naomi's antique-Indian act had been convincing at moments, Hannah, to her relief, remained a nonbeliever. And if for a few milliseconds she had been sucked in, she had come to her senses as soon as the vaporous Hopi tried to talk her into dunking-booth duty, a deceitful act to which no self-respecting snake shaman, dead or otherwise, would lower himself.

To make things worse, Hannah had awakened that morning with an unpleasant sourness in her stomach. A séance on top of a good meal was obviously an unfortunate and Maalox-neccessitating combination, and one that would not be repeated.

Pausing in her trek, Hannah closed her eyes and took a deep yoga breath. It was time to get all thoughts of her neighbor and that ridiculous Red Moon out of her mind. If she was going to get Kiki off Detective Morgan's murder-suspect list, she had to focus on the task at hand. She had to dig out information from Lisa Lemkpe and dig it out as determinedly as she dug for dahlia tubers in her garden.

The steps to Lisa's house being steep, Hannah began breathing heavily but maintained a steady pace. The San Francisco Bay stretched out in a glorious expanse of blue as she neared the top, and though her lungs burned and her knees ached, she sighed with pleasure. It was views like this that made her love Northern California—vivid blue water framed by pink impatiens and the heavy green branches of a fir tree, the remnants of the morning fog floating in the air as gently as a silk scarf in a breeze. Absolutely delicious.

Lisa Lempke lived in a small, wood-framed house nestled in the hills of Sausalito, the type of house that had no garage, only two bedrooms, thirty steep steps to the front door, and a behemoth of a mortgage payment. Land was expensive in southern Marin County because there was so little of it, and what hadn't been given up long ago to parks had all been built on. Bay-view property was worth whatever exorbitant price one had to pay for it.

Since Kiki had decided that morning to get a pedicure to relax her nerves, Hannah had the luxury of visiting Lisa on her own, which was fortunate: Kiki would have collapsed and shrieked for paramedics by the tenth step. Luckily Hannah walked two miles a day at least five times a week, but even with all her exercise, she was panting.

When she finally reached the small porch, she sat on an iron bench to catch her breath, taking the opportunity to glance around. There were two large stone pots filled with impatiens and lobelia, but Sausalito was too foggy for Lisa to have good roses like her father. On the other hand, maybe Lisa didn't care for roses. Not everyone in the world did, although Hannah couldn't understand it.

The front door was painted a glossy black and bore a tarnished brass lion's-head knocker. The lion's face looked menacing, warning off visitors, but Hannah grabbed the ring in its mouth and firmly rapped it against the front door.

She heard a faint "I'm coming," then footsteps. Within seconds the huge door creaked open about a foot. Lisa Lempke appeared in the gap, looking uncertain about whether or not to open it completely.

Hannah smiled broadly. "I'm Hannah Malloy. I called this morning."

Lisa didn't speak. She simply stared at Hannah with dark, vacant eyes, her thin blond hair falling in uncombed waves around her face. With her loose cotton dress and bare feet, she looked like a child. It occurred to Hannah to ask her if her mommy was home.

"May I come in for a moment?" she asked instead.

The glazed look on Lisa's face didn't alter as she opened the door, motioning Hannah through.

Hannah walked into a cluttered and comfortable-looking living room. It was filled with well-worn furniture, stacks of books, and flea-market odds and ends, the bay glistening behind a wall of glass. She immediately liked the feel of it, preferring an attractive mess to the overdecorated, spotless perfection some of her friends favored.

"This is Crayton." Lisa gestured toward a tall red-haired woman slouched on an aged green velvet sofa by the window, her feet curled up beneath her. "Crayton, this is Hannah Malloy."

Crayton nodded, and Hannah recognized her as the woman who had been by Lisa's side at the Church of Revelations. She was a big-boned woman, everything about her appearing a few sizes larger than Lisa. Looking at the two of them together reminded Hannah of buying shampoo at the grocery. There was always the small attractive bottle, then the larger, more cost-effective economy size. Crayton was like the latter, but there was a refinement to her features, a softness about her eyes and mouth that kept her femininity in evidence.

While Lisa excused herself to go to the kitchen, Crayton stood, shook Hannah's hand, then sat back down, her eyes never leaving the visitor. Hannah felt she was being sized up.

"I like your outfit," Crayton said after a few moments of silence. "Is it by a Japanese designer?"

Hannah looked down self-consciously at her simple jacket and loose pants. "I designed this myself."

"You sew?" Crayton said it with the same incredulity as she would have said, "You rode the Hale-Bopp comet?" Nobody sewed anymore. Not in Marin. They hiked mountains, saved whales, explored their souls. They didn't sew.

Hannah shook her head. "I sketch out the clothes then find the fabric on sale. A woman in Oakland sews them for me."

Crayton nodded approvingly, then, leaning forward, she ran a finger along the fabric of Hannah's jacket. "Nice."

"I like simple things," Hannah said, her voice cracking, her discomfort growing. She was embarrassed to be talking about herself when it was supposed to be the other way around. Now that she was actually inside Lisa's house, her earlier bravado escaped her, and she fought the urge hastily to excuse herself and run down the steps to the safety of the Cadillac. But she had to see this through. It's just like digging in the garden, she reminded herself. You put the spade in, apply some pressure, and remove the soil. You could find interesting things digging in the garden.

There was a lull in the conversation. Hannah heard Lisa's feet padding around the kitchen along with the sound of cabinet doors opening and slamming shut.

"I can't afford the clothes I like in the stores," Hannah said just to keep a dialogue going.

Crayton smiled for the first time. "I know what you mean. Lisa and I are both schoolteachers. We work together."

In the next minute Lisa reentered the room holding an open bag of Pepperidge Farm Mint Milano cookies. "Please sit down," she said, her manner formal.

Hannah took a chair across from the sofa and Lisa placed the bag of cookies on the table beside her. In spite of her youth and petite frame, Lisa moved heavily, her feet shuffling ponderously across the frayed sisal rug. Hannah thought it was as if depression had become a second force of gravity pressing her into the earth.

"Would you like coffee or anything?" Lisa asked before sitting on the sofa near Crayton.

"No, I'm fine. I'm only staying a minute." Hannah inhaled, gathering steam. "I only wanted to express my condolences about your father."

As soon as the words fell out of her mouth, she felt ashamed. They sounded so hollow. And they *were* hollow, she told herself, and at least partially a lie. The main reason she was there was to get information from Lisa. Hannah always prided herself on her honesty and directness, and now here she was visiting under false pretenses a young woman who had just lost her father, invading her privacy.

She considered apologizing and walking out, but the thought of Kiki stopped her. She had to help her sister and she didn't know any other way. Just for something to do with her hands, she reached in the cookie bag. She loved Mint Milano cookies and told herself that the mint might calm her stomach.

As she took the first bite she noticed Lisa staring at her. After a couple of moments of unwieldy silence, the younger women glanced at each other, then back at Hannah.

"We were wondering . . . I mean I was wondering," Lisa said, stammering, "why you asked to come over. I mean, we didn't really know each other. And I don't remember my father mentioning you."

Oh dear, Hannah thought. She took another bite of cookie, using the chewing time to prepare a response.

"You were school friends with my niece Lauren Osborn," she said after she swallowed, cookie crumbs sticking in her throat.

With the mention of Lauren the atmosphere thawed. Lisa brightened. "She's your niece? I always liked her. She was quiet and kind of serious but still fun. We played on the girls' softball team in junior high school," she said, directing the last part to Crayton, then turning her attention back to Hannah. Lisa studied her a moment, the intensity of her gaze making Hannah uncomfortable.

"I think I remember you now." Lisa leaned forward, her hands on her knees. "This is a weird question, but did you ever go to Lauren's softball games?"

Hannah smiled. "Never missed one."

"I played in them. I was always terrible," Lisa said.

Crayton frowned. "You always put yourself down."

"But I was really awful," Lisa insisted. "The point is, one day I struck out every time I went to bat. It was so demoralizing. The last time I struck out I ran behind the bleachers crying."

"How terrible for you," Hannah said with sincerity.

"But don't you remember?" Lisa said with new energy. "You came over. You spoke to me."

The statement surprised Hannah. She had just taken another bite of cookie and hurriedly chewed and swallowed it. "I'm not certain I remember. You're sure it was me?"

Lisa's expression softened. "Yes, I am, now that I've gotten a good look at you. I don't remember what you said exactly. Something about my having a graceful swing, I think. That I was swinging the bat so beautifully that it didn't matter whether or not I hit the ball."

Crayton laughed out loud, and Lisa and Hannah joined in. It was a nice moment, the mood in the room suddenly turning chummy. But then just as quickly Crayton stopped smiling, and as soon as Lisa saw this, she stiffened up, as though she was a child and had done something naughty.

"I haven't seen Lauren in so long," she said to Hannah. "How is she?"

"Fine. Doing very well," Hannah told her. "She wanted to come with me today, but she works in San Francisco and can't visit you until the weekend."

"It still seems odd that you drove all the way over here," Crayton said. "Most people would've just called."

Lisa cast her a scolding look, but the redhead ignored it.

"You're right," Hannah responded. "My sister and I are the ones who found your father's body. I guess it's made me feel closer to the situation than I otherwise would. It's one of the reasons I came in person."

Lisa gulped, her hand moving to her mouth. Reaching over, Crayton slid the back of her hand along her friend's arm. It was a small gesture, but there was an intimacy to it that, along with her protectiveness of Lisa at the church, made Hannah wonder if they were lovers.

"That must have been awful. Seeing him like that," Lisa said. All traces of geniality were replaced with sadness as she wrapped her arms around herself and scooted to the corner of the couch. Once again she shrank into herself, a creature retreating from sunlight back into its cave.

Hannah nodded. "Yes. But better us finding him than you or some other member of your family."

Lisa studied her lap a moment then looked up. "Then your sister is being questioned by the police. They told me."

Hannah's fingers wrapped around the arm of her chair. "I can assure you my sister had nothing to do with your father's death. We just happened to be visiting him and, well, there he was."

"Daddy mentioned Kiki Goldstein to me," Lisa said, her brow knitted. "I knew she was Lauren's aunt, I just didn't make the connection with you at first. I don't think for a minute she had anything to do with Daddy's death."

Crayton looked at Lisa with skepticism. "I don't want to be rude, but, Lisa, the police are questioning the woman. How can you be sure she had nothing to do with it?"

"I just can," Lisa said with a sharpness to her voice. "I've met Lauren's aunt. It was years ago, but I remember her. She's a funny little woman. So sweet and harmless."

"I appreciate your confidence in my sister," Hannah said. "I'm sure this whole thing will be cleared up."

Lisa stood up. She walked around the couch, her gaze directed out the window at the bay. "I can think of a dozen people who held grudges against my father."

Hannah sat up straighter. It was time to poke her spade into the dirt. "What type of grudges?"

Lisa remained facing the window as she answered. "Daddy wasn't exactly Mr. Personality. He had a way of pissing people off."

Hannah couldn't see the young woman's face, but she could hear the hostility in her voice, and it made her think Lisa was one of those people who held a grudge against Arnold Lempke. At last some progress.

"Could he have upset someone at the Church of Revelations?"

At the mention of the church, Lisa spun around, her eyes aimed at Hannah, the little-girl fragility replaced by something tougher. "What does my church have to do with this?"

Lisa's reaction confounded Hannah. Still, she pressed on. "The night before he was murdered, your father said he thought the church was doing something fraudulent," she said.

"Like what?" Arms folded, Lisa spat out the question. Hannah could tell by the tone of her voice and the tension in her face that she was trying hard to control her emotions. There was definitely something about her father and the church that rankled her.

"He didn't say exactly. But he did say he was going to talk to the district attorney's office. I can only suppose he wanted to have the church closed down."

Lisa shrugged with what looked to Hannah like feigned casualness. "Daddy was always going off half-cocked about things. Like I told you, he had a way of pissing people off."

"But that's just it, Lisa," Hannah told her, sliding to the edge of her seat, resting her arms on her legs. "Could he have pissed someone off at the church enough so that they killed him?"

Lisa's upper lip trembled slightly. Hannah's digging was more effective than she had anticipated, and she thought perhaps a big spadeful of dirt was about to come flying.

"No. That's completely impossible. Leave my church out of this." Lisa's voice had grown shrill. "You don't know anything."

"I'm sorry, Lisa. I just think we have to look at all the possibilities—"

"I think you better go, Ms. Malloy." It was Crayton speaking now. She stood up, moving intimidatingly close to Hannah. Hannah stood up also, having received the distinct impression that if she didn't leave of her own accord, she might be thrown out bodily.

She quickly said a polite good-bye. It wasn't returned so

politely, and neither of the young women invited her back again.

As she stood on the porch the front door closed behind her with a thud of finality. It embarrassed her to be practically thrown out of someone's house, but at least she had gotten some information. She had learned that other people might have had grudges against Lempke and she confirmed her suspicion that Lempke's relationship with his daughter was troubled. It wasn't nearly all she needed, but she had made a start.

Feeling newly energized, she started down the stone steps with even more horsepower than she had mounted them. Investigating a murder was almost as fascinating as gardening.

TEN

A FEW HOURS LATER HANNAH walked somewhat jerkily up the walkway to the Church of Revelations, fighting off the urge to grab her own buttocks. She prided herself in no longer owning panty hose, but if she was going to pass herself off as a wealthy Marin County matron, she had to dress the part, which she felt included hosiery. Only she hadn't counted on such discomfort and inconvenience.

After her visit to Lisa, Hannah had gone straight home and changed into a dark suit for her next appointment. Rifling through Kiki's panty hose, she had been able to find only industrial-strength control tops, and now that she had them on, she deeply regretted not buying a pair the correct size. The crotch hovered somewhere around the middle of her thighs and it would have required jumping on a donkey to get the things up any higher. And the panty, obviously constructed from some synthetic rubber suitable for a NASA space flight, gripped her body in places God hadn't meant it to be gripped.

After her pedicure, Kiki had gone on a stress-reducing shopping trip, so, in her absence, Hannah took the liberty of borrowing a few of her sister's other belongings to complete her outfit, choosing a double strand of fake pearls, fake gold earrings and bracelets, as well as a scarf to complete her ensemble. She felt weighted down by all these accessories, but she had a job to do and it required a uniform. After gulping down a tuna sandwich, she headed for the Church of Revelations to continue her investigation.

Hesitating before the church door, she looked around her to make sure she wasn't being observed, then grabbed the back of her panty hose and hitched them upward. Thus temporarily relieved, she opened the door and walked inside.

The church office wasn't as opulent as the sanctuary. The reception area was an eight-by-ten room with wood paneling and minimal decoration, its predominant feature being the Asian woman who sat at a desk in the middle of it. Wearing a perplexed expression and grumbling unintelligibly, she thumbed through a foot-high stack of paper that sat next to the computer in front of her. She looked up at Hannah, squinting her eyes.

"Give me a sec, honey. I'm smack in the middle of something," she said with a slight accent. She seemed to be in her late forties, pretty, with straight chin-length black hair and round red glasses that made her look bookish.

Too antsy to sit, Hannah stood near the door. The woman at the desk ignored her, flipping madly through documents, frequently licking her index finger for enhanced traction. Finally she let go of the papers with a cry of exasperation.

"I can't find it. I swear I can't find it!"

"Find what?" Hannah asked.

The woman started in on the papers once more. "Oh, info on a donation we got."

"You don't keep the records on your computer?"

Hannah had become computer literate toward the end of her career as secretary to the president of a large corporation. Over her twenty-five-year tenure the presidents had changed, but Hannah remained. When she retired with a pension, the company wanted to give her an expensive watch, but she asked to take her computer instead. Now she occasionally surfed the Internet, frequenting a gardening chat group.

"Oh, sure, but I can't find it in the files. That's why I'm looking for the original paper." The woman smiled. "But it's not your worry. I'm Shirley. Shirley Chen. What can I do for you?"

"I have an appointment to see Reverend Swanson."

"Regarding?"

"Joining the church. Perhaps making a donation." Hannah said the words hesitantly. Lying was so difficult.

"Oh, sure, I remember now. Mrs. Malloy, right? Well, take a seat. He's at lunch right now, but he ought to be back in a sec."

Hannah lowered herself into an upholstered chair, hoping to high heaven the process wouldn't send her panty hose sliding to her ankles. Consumed with her own troubles, Shirley sighed and continued her search through the mound of paper. Hannah couldn't help but notice her continuously pained expression.

"Would you like me to help you?" she offered.

Shirley looked up. "Would you?" As soon as Hannah nodded, she eagerly handed her half the stack. "We're looking for the name Schwartz. It'll be right at the top."

Placing the stack of paper in her lap, Hannah began digging through it. Most of the names were of individuals or married couples living in Marin. She also noticed quite a few corporations, although none she had ever heard of. Ten minutes later she was almost through the pile when one page caught her eye. To her surprise, the name of the donor was Walter Backus. She looked at the bottom of the sheet and saw with astonishment that Walter had given the church ten thousand dollars.

"Did you find Schwartz?" Shirley asked hopefully.

Hannah looked up. "Oh, no. Sorry. Just a few more and I'll be done." Moments later she handed the stack back to

Shirley with the bad news that it did not contain a reference to anyone named Schwartz.

"Ah, well, the reverend will be spitting mad, but that's life, isn't it?" Shirley paused, her mind apparently consumed with the import of this philosophy, then her gaze fixed upon Hannah. "You've been to one of the church services?"

"Yes. Only one, but I was very impressed." At least, in one sense, that was the truth. Hannah cleared her throat. "That stone the reverend uses. Where did it come from?"

Shirley's expression turned somber and she lowered her chin so that she looked at Hannah over the top of her red glasses. "The Weeping Stone? It comes straight from Jesus."

This announcement was followed by a brief but pregnant silence. "What exactly do you mean?" Hannah asked.

"The Weeping Stone came from Jesus' grave. It's covered with his tears. It really is." Apparently gifted with unusual fluidity of thought, Shirley suddenly focused on Hannah's neck. "Love your pearls. They real?"

Hannah laughed. "No, unfortunately they're not."

"Mrs. Carson, one of our members, has this big diamond ring with earrings to match, and she had copies made so she wears the fake ones and keeps the real ones in a safe. What do you think of that?"

Hannah thought that, as she had suspected, the church had some very wealthy members.

Shirley pulled a paper bag out of her desk drawer. "You hungry? I have a turkey sandwich here cut right down the middle. We could share."

Hannah declined since she had already eaten but accepted a few potato chips instead, her stomach having fully recovered from the morning's ailment. While they munched, Shirley prattled on about the church members. Hannah asked her as many questions as she dared, but didn't find out anything useful. But chatting with Shirley, so friendly and gregarious, was pleasant in itself.

The door opened and Reverend Swanson rushed into the

room, a gale force assaulting calm seas. He was breathing heavily and looked harried.

"Did you find it?" he asked Shirley without salutation.

Shirley slid down in her chair. "Still looking," she answered, her voice suddenly smaller. "I'm sure I'll have it by the end of the day. This is Mrs. Malloy to see you."

Odd, Hannah thought, that the woman's cozy cheerfulness vanished as soon as Swanson entered the room. Her shoulders hunched up, her hands twisted together. It was hard to tell if she was scared of the man or swooning before him in adoration.

Swanson's expression gave way to a shining smile when he cast his gaze at Hannah. "We can talk in my office," he said smoothly, then turned back to Shirley. "Did you give Mrs. Malloy the form to fill out?"

Shirley's face fell. "No, Reverend, I forgot."

He looked at her like she was some annoying pet who had just chewed a shoe. The look was brief, intended only for her consumption, but Hannah caught it.

"Well, we'll take care of it in my office," he said sweetly to Hannah. "Follow me."

He touched his hand to the small of her back as she walked through the door, which he closed behind them. His private office, though small, was beautifully decorated with an expensive antique desk and oil paintings on the walls. A grand godliness, Hannah mused.

Swanson himself looked considerably less grand under close scrutiny. He was about five-foot-six, impeccably dressed and groomed, the smell of his cologne wafting in Hannah's direction. She could tell that his suit was cut from fine fabric, and his tie looked like an Hermès. He had that style of pert dandiness that only small men seemed to acquire, the total somehow seeming less than the sum of its parts.

Hannah perched on the edge of an upholstered leather chair, and Swanson, rather than sitting behind his desk, sat in the chair next to her, dragging it around so he faced her.

He folded his hands in front of him. They were small and white, the hands of a little boy, and on his left pinkie he wore an ornate ring, a ram's head with emeralds for eyes. A peculiar-looking piece of jewelry, Hannah thought, but then, Swanson seemed like a peculiar man in general.

"So, Mrs. Malloy, you want to join our church?" he asked, sounding genial and caring. He had a wonderful voice, deep and melodic. If the church angle didn't work out for him, Hannah thought he would have career opportunities in radio.

"Uh, yes. I do," she said, shifting in her seat. This was the hard part. "I've attended a couple of services. Well, one service actually, and I found great meaning in it."

Swanson smiled and tilted his head slightly, his eyes tender.

"Our lives are full of trouble and hardship. We struggle along the best we can, feeling so alone. But we're not alone." He was all softness and understanding now, the edge he earlier displayed with Shirley smoothed away. "May I call you Hannah?" he asked. When she nodded, he took her hand and held it, his touch strong and reassuring, his eyes focused on hers.

"Life is hard for you sometimes, Hannah. I can see it in you. I can sense it in your touch. You feel isolated. You worry about that isolation. There've been troubles in your past that you can't forget."

Hannah twisted in her seat. His words were on target, but, like a horoscope, they could have fit most anybody. She pulled her hand away from him, and as she did so he looked down at the spot where her hand had been and softly smiled.

"Did you feel a calling, Hannah?" he asked, his eyes directed at that same spot, his voice reduced to a resonant whisper.

Hannah recrossed her legs, clutching her handbag a little tighter. She had felt more confident at Lisa's, because Lisa and Crayton had been the ones on the defensive. But here

Swanson was in control. He was a master at dealing with people, which made her more determined to keep her wits about her.

"Excuse me?" she said.

His gaze again connected with hers. His eyes had a way of shining and quivering slightly that forced you to look into them. "A calling from the Lord Jesus. Did he speak to you, Hannah?"

She had been temporarily lost in Swanson's eyes, but she snapped to attention. Did Jesus speak to her? Yes or no? To say yes was such a blatant lie, but if she said no, would Swanson realize she was there under false pretenses and throw her out? Under pressure, it was her nature to opt for the truth. She told him no, Jesus had not spoken to her.

It didn't faze him. "He will, Hannah," Swanson assured her. He reached out and gave her hand another squeeze, letting one finger linger a few seconds longer than necessary, the communication clearly sexual. "Just come to our services and He will." He stood up then walked behind his desk, pulling a five-by-seven card from a drawer. "Here's our membership form. We like a little information about our new members." He put it on a clipboard and handed it to her with a silver pen. "If you could take a minute, Hannah, and fill it out."

The card asked for her name and address, any previous religious affiliations—all normal questions, the spaces for answers set in boxes to make it easier for computer entry. At the bottom of the card was a space for *Initial Donation*. There were five boxes to the left of the decimal.

"Regarding my donation, would it be acceptable if I made a transfer directly from my trust account?" Hannah asked. "I never carry checks."

She had no trust account and a fat supply of checks in her handbag, but the last thing she wanted was to give Swanson a donation and could hardly afford it anyway. Lying was getting easier the more lies she told, and this troubled her.

Swanson's eyes lit up at the mention of a trust account. He sat back down. "That will be no problem. Many of our members prefer transactions carried out in that manner. Shirley can give you our account number on the way out." His smile was wider now. "Tell me, Hannah, how you learned of our church."

Regaining some self-assurance, she decided it was high time for her to do some digging. "Lisa Lempke mentioned it to me. She's a close friend of my niece."

Just then she noticed a purple velvet box sitting on the credenza behind Swanson, the same type of box that held the stone she had seen in church.

"Oh yes, Lisa. Poor Lisa." Swanson shook his head. "Terrible about her father. With God's help, they'll find who did it."

"I know you've been supportive of her. That's very kind of you." She took a breath. The spade was poised. "Considering that her father was less than supportive of you."

Swanson stiffened just slightly, a cloud passing over his features. "Yes, Mr. Lempke preferred a more traditional church."

Things were getting interesting. Hannah rested her elbow on the arm of the chair. "From what he said, it was somewhat stronger than that. He threatened to complain about this church to the district attorney's office."

Now Swanson's face visibly tightened and he looked at her with distrust.

"It was awful of him," Hannah quickly added. "Foolish, petty behavior."

Swanson relaxed a little, but he still looked rattled. "Mr. Lempke actually went to the DA's office the morning before he died."

"Really? How terrible. How did you find out?"

"They contacted me yesterday. There was only the one phone call from him. He wanted to meet with them. I don't think they took him too seriously. They just asked me a few questions, that's all." Swanson began to toy with the diamond stud in his tie. "They thought the accusations were groundless, naturally, but they had to follow up. I just hope Mr. Lempke is with our Lord now. He was a mean and hurtful man in life."

Hannah had never liked the man herself, but she felt obligated to defend him, since he was dead. "Not so mean. He must have cared deeply for his wife."

Swanson made a "pfft" sound. "I doubt he cared much for anyone in his family. Lisa had very troubled relations with him."

"But he took care of his wife at home while she was ill. He nursed her himself."

The corners of Swanson's mouth turned down. "Nurses cost money." He stood up. "I'm sorry to say, dear Mrs. Malloy, that as much as I've enjoyed our conversation, my ministry leaves me very busy and I must go out into the world and do God's work."

Standing in front of her, he picked up her hands and held them. "We'll see you this Wednesday night. We'll be talking with Jesus, feeling His presence and His glory."

They exchanged good-byes and Hannah walked out, saying good-bye to Shirley and purposely forgetting to ask for the Church of Revelations' bank-account number.

Walking down the sidewalk toward the Cadillac, she wondered how Walter Backus could justify giving such a large sum of money to such an oddball church. And why hadn't he defended the church when Lempke was bad-mouthing it at the Rose Club cocktail reception? She was busy pondering all this when a shiny black Mercedes sped down the street past her. Looking up, she saw Swanson at the wheel. He stopped at a red light at the corner.

Expensive jewelry, rich furnishings, and a shiny new Mercedes. The reverend had expensive tastes and Hannah wondered if he used church money to support them. Swanson seemed much too savvy to stoop to such an obvious transgression, but perhaps his tastes for finer things were his weakness. If so, he would be quite upset if Lempke had suspected misuse of church funds and taken his suspicions to the DA's office.

A smile crossed Hannah's lips. Her pace quickened. The day had been most productive. It had been a long time since she had anything really goal-directed to do. Of course she had her garden, her poetry, her volunteer work, but those things were less urgent pursuits, activities most anyone could accomplish. But to help find a killer and keep your sister out of jail? Now that was something you could sink your teeth into. She felt happier and more invigorated than she had in months.

The light turned green and Swanson took off, Hannah watching the Mercedes until it disappeared around the corner. Damaging disclosures about the misuse of donations could hurt a church's nonprofit status, she supposed, if there was any truth to them. The fear of them could also provide an excellent motive for murder.

ELEVEN

$\mathcal{B}$ETWEEN STUMBLING UPON CORPSES, PARTIC-
IPATING in séances, performing clandestine detective
work, and keeping Kiki from imbibing too many toddies,
Hannah had found precious little time in the past few days
for her garden, and the neglect nagged at her. Having arrived home from her meeting with Reverend Swanson with
several good hours of daylight left, she jumped at the opportunity to do some pruning in her backyard.

Hannah adjusted her straw hat as she studied the leaves
of her favorite and most prolific rose. One especially large
bud of her Mr. Lincoln was just beginning to open, and if
the ruby petals unfurled as perfectly as she anticipated, it
would have an even chance of taking first prize at the Rose
Club festival.

She sniffed an open blossom, drinking in the perfume
that worked upon her like a tonic. Whenever she became
discouraged her roses always lifted up her spirits. Roses
were enigmatic and provocative, always teasing you with
some new side of themselves, responding in some unexpected way. A rose was seductive in sight and smell and

touch. Naturally a rose had thorns, but thorns were on the surface; there was nothing ambiguous or furtive about them. Not like some people. You knew how to protect yourself. Why couldn't the rest of life be as simple and satisfying as a rose?

With one finger Hannah gently removed the tiny nodules springing up on either side of the central bud, a process that would result in fewer but larger flowers. She struggled to maintain her attention on the rose. Disbudding required some concentration, and she was distracted by Kiki's chattering.

"Hannah, I'm feeling so frail. I'm not sure I could walk if I tried. I miss poor Arnie."

Kiki lay like liquid on the patio recliner positioned in front of a pink hydrangea bush, a floppy purple hat covering her head, a teacup of vodka in one hand and a copy of *Cosmopolitan* in the other.

"I know you didn't like him," she continued, "but you never saw his tender side. He could be so sweet sometimes. And now the police thinking that I, of all people, could have killed him. It makes me feel so sapped. I'm prostate with worry."

"The word is prostrate," Hannah told her, getting a little annoyed with her sister's continuing dramatics.

Kiki paid no attention. Pleased with her sympathy-provoking speech, she, with pinkie outstretched, took a bracing sip from her china teacup, then glanced again at her reading material. Along with the vodka, she was intoxicating herself with an article entitled "Men's Sex Secrets."

The title of this piece of journalism, broadcast across the glossy cover, amused Hannah. She didn't think men *had* any sex secrets. To her, it seemed that most of them wore their sexuality directly on the outside of their pants.

She picked up her pruning shears and snipped off a wilting blossom. "You were well enough today to get a pedicure and do three hours of shopping." Squatting, she inspected the underside of a leaf for spider mites. "I know what you're up to. You have to go to Lempke's funeral tomorrow morning, and pretending to be sick won't get you out of it." She clipped off a dead blossom for emphasis. "You used to do this in high school. Pretending to be sick to miss a test you hadn't studied for."

Kiki eyed her over the top of *Cosmo*. "I just don't think I could stand to see poor Arnie's cold corpse."

Putting on her reading glasses, Hannah closely studied the undersides of a few more leaves, finding a whitish substance she considered suspicious. "Most likely the casket won't be open."

"How can you know?"

Eyes still glued to the leaf, Hannah scratched at it with her fingernail, then pulled her head back a few inches. It was difficult to see an object so close, which meant it was time for stronger glasses. The aging process could be so inconvenient. "Because they probably did an autopsy on him, which means most of him was chopped up and put in Ziploc freezer bags."

Kiki cast away her *Cosmo* in despair. "Oh, Gawd! How can you talk that way?"

"Sorry. That was insensitive." Yes, there were tiny webs underneath two of the lower leaves. She would have to get her miticide from the gardening shed and send the little spiders to their Maker. She wished them a pleasant afterlife.

Kiki was sitting up now, her face filled with worry. "But, Hannah, what if they stare at me or call me a murderer behind my back?"

Hannah stopped studying her roses and looked her sister. "It will be worse if you don't show up. People will think you have something to hide."

Kiki bit her lip, took an especially bracing gulp from her teacup, then returned to a reclining position, reburying her face in the magazine.

Hannah began working with a new florabunda she had found dirt cheap at the chain drugstore by the freeway.

Although this was the wrong time of year for planting roses, she couldn't resist its unusual scalloped pink petals and intoxicating fragrance. It hadn't been properly pruned, poor thing, and she began making a few well-considered snips here and there. As she worked, finally placing the newcomer in its new hole with a base of bonemeal, she tried mentally to sort out her meeting with Reverend Swanson. She definitely didn't trust the man. He was duplicitous, she had no doubt. Then there was the puzzling issue of the ten-thousand-dollar donation by Walter Backus. She was absolutely dying to question him about it, but also wanted to be careful in case he had made the contribution without Wanda's knowledge. She wouldn't want to be responsible for making trouble for him. Being married to Wanda was trouble enough for any man.

"Hannah!"

The voice that interrupted her ruminations belonged to Naomi, who was peering over the redwood lattice fence. Hannah said hello then refocused on getting her rosebush properly positioned.

"Hannah, I think we need another session with Red Moon. I feel him rising in me."

"Take an antacid," Hannah joked as she scooped fresh dirt into the hole.

The fence was five feet high, and she could barely see Naomi's nostrils flare at the remark. "Your gastrointestinal jokes are no longer amusing," her neighbor said. Hannah felt that this was probably true, but she couldn't help herself. Teasing Naomi was too enjoyable.

Kiki looked at her over the top of her rhinestoned sunglasses. "Is that uncomfortable? Red Moon rising in you like that?"

At that moment Hannah heard some rustling of azaleas followed by the sound of Naomi mounting an upturned plastic bucket so she could see better. "Of course not," she replied, her face now fully visible, though somewhat wobbly due to the bucket's unsteadiness. "It's more like a pressure. Hannah, stop playing in the dirt and pay attention. We must consult Red Moon again.''

Hannah paused in her shoveling and eyed her neighbor. Something was definitely up. Naomi had never tried to push Red Moon on her before, and now she had done it twice in one week. On the other hand, they had never before had a neighbor murdered.

''I have to get this rose watered, then we'll talk.''

After carefully packing the dirt around the plant with her hand, she picked up the hose with the rain sprayer attached. ''Kiki, could you turn on the water, please?''

Kiki languidly waved a hand. ''Can't move, Hannie. Too weak.''

With a disgusted sigh, Hannah went to the faucet and turned on the water herself, making sure she gave Kiki an accidental sprinkling.

Kiki sat up with a yelp. ''Hannah, you can be so exasperating!''

''She certainly can,'' Naomi chimed in. ''What about Red Moon, Hannah?''

The rose watered, Hannah laid the hose in the flower bed to soak the lilies, then approached the fence. ''Yes, we could do it tonight.''

Naomi frowned. ''Can't. I have two channeling sessions and I need the money. Tomorrow, then?''

Hannah agreed. While Naomi chatted over the fence with Kiki she returned to her chores. Her garden was laid out in a curved bed in what she called controlled chaos, with over twenty varieties of hybrid teas, floribundas, and grandifloras, including several antique roses she especially prized.

As Kiki went over for Naomi's benefit her laundry list of stress-induced physical and emotional ailments, Hannah continued scrutinizing her plants, pruning shears in hand, looking for canes that needed shaping. As she inspected them one by one she reached a favorite and knelt in front of it, touching its petals of pale pink edged with red. The metal marker beneath it read SUMMER LOVE.

A knot formed in her throat. The marker and the name written on it reminded her of Arnold Lempke's Summer Surprise, his beloved hybrid of white with red streaks, the bush he had fallen into after having some strange jagged knife shoved in his neck.

Hannah tried to get the image out of her mind, but it remained firmly entrenched. Then something curious occurred to her.

"Hannah, are you all right?" Kiki asked. "You're staring at that plant like it was talking to you."

"Oh. Yes, I'm fine." She took off her hat and wiped the sweat from her brow. There was something about Lempke's rose garden that day she and Kiki had found him, something unusual, although she couldn't put her finger on precisely what it was.

The rosebush *was* talking to her. If only she could figure out what it was trying to say.

Moonlight streamed in through the window blinds, streaking Hannah's white bedspread with horizontal bars of silvery blue, making the bed look like a cage.

Lying in the darkness before she fell asleep was when she felt the most alone and the only time she really minded it. She had been married for sixteen years, and when her husband died so unexpectedly, she realized she had never known him that well. There was less love or intimacy between them than a need for companionship. Love, she felt, was something that came rarely. Most relationships were just attempts to fill imagined voids.

It was impossible to sleep. Hannah sat up, her white silk nightgown rustling against the cotton sheets. She raised the blind and the bed was bathed in pure moonlight; then she opened the window and breathed in the cool air. Leaning her elbows on the sill, she looked out at the stars and a wisp of a cloud passing over the moon.

By sticking her head out a few inches, she was able to see her rear neighbor Blair Epstein in her kitchen doing a late-night cleanup. Naturally nosy, Hannah loved to look in windows. Not that she was a Peeping Tom, but she relished brief glimpses into other people's inner sanctums. And she enjoyed this secret peek at Blair busily scrubbing her stove. She liked Blair. Her husband wasn't home much because of his job, but they seemed to be a close couple in spite of the frequent separations. There was a unity, a silent tether between them that Hannah envied.

She thought she had recognized the same closeness in Lisa and Crayton. She saw it in the way they looked at each other, the way Crayton had run her hand along Lisa's arm. Hannah would never judge the rightness of such an intimacy. People were lucky to find love wherever it came upon them. Love between two people of the same sex was just as poignant, just as important, although she realized that some people wouldn't share this view.

Go to sleep, she commanded herself, slipping back down under the sheet.

She closed her eyes and saw the face of John Perez. It was time to confess that she liked him. She wouldn't have allowed herself that admission in the light of day, but somehow in the dark it seemed safe to own up to it, at least to herself. It had been years since she had been so attracted to a man. It wasn't just that he was good-looking, although Lord knows he was. John Perez had intelligence and depth. When he spoke one got the impression that there were many layers to him. Yes, she was definitely interested. Maybe she could call him and say she had changed her mind about dinner. Maybe it was possible.

But then she opened her eyes, rolling onto her side, pushing her face into the pillow. It wasn't possible. And it never could be.

TWELVE

THE WESTMORELAND FUNERAL HOME WAS quintessentially Marin. A low, redwood-sided, contemporary building, it provided the open-minded Bay Area bereaved with a menu of services. These included not only your everyday Protestant, Catholic, and Jewish varieties but an exotic array of funerary festivities ranging from *Egyptian Book of the Dead* rites and Zen Buddhist ash ceremonies all the way to Druid rituals, the latter being held atop Mt. Tamalpais with all participants, including the deceased, wearing nothing but garlands of indigenous, drought-tolerant flowers.

But Arnold Lempke, as dull in death as he had been in life, specified in his will—which he damn well didn't intend to be implemented so quickly—that he receive the basic no-frills Protestant rendition.

It was a typically sun-drenched Marin day, the sky an effulgent blue with a cap of fog veiling the hilltops, like fluffy icing on a cupcake. But in the midst of nature's grace, a microcosm of angst thrived at the funeral home, for just inside its threshold Kiki had, by her own diagnosis, experienced a complete nervous breakdown.

Hannah, Lauren, and Naomi, dressed in their Sunday best, observed her with a mix of annoyance and concern. What had started with only moist eyes and a slowing of pace as she walked from the car toward the funeral home erupted into a rigid-limbed, owl-eyed state of trauma by the time they made it into the lobby. All attempts to coax her into the sanctuary had proved fruitless.

"I can't do this. I'm not strong enough," Kiki declared, gripping a Greek column in a side hallway hidden from the other guests. Her companions had each taken turns talking to her, but all reasoning had been ignored.

The organ music began. In a fit of exasperation, Hannah put her hands around her sister's waist and gave her a gentle tug, then a stronger one, but with no success.

"Not strong enough?" she said. "You're hanging on with the strength of Hercules."

Kiki's expression grew steely. "Insult me all you want. I'm still not going in."

Hannah tried another path. "Fine. You're an adult and entitled to make your own decisions. If you choose to go to jail, that's your business."

Kiki's eyes darted to her sister. "What do you mean?"

"I mean that this funeral is an excellent opportunity to have the people who knew Lempke all in one room. The murderer could very well be in there. We can ask people questions, monitor their reactions. But I need you with me," Hannah told her.

Lauren's brow furrowed. "You're not still thinking of chasing after his murderer, are you?"

"I'm not thinking of it. I'm doing it," Hannah replied. "The police suspect Kiki. They're on the wrong track and we have to get them on the right one. Don't you remember reading a few years ago about that mother in Oregon who found her daughter's killer when the police couldn't?"

"Are you saying our Hill Creek police can't do the job?" Naomi asked.

"Nothing of the sort," Hannah answered. "Our police are fine men and doing their best, but we can't leave everything up to the powers that be." Increasingly losing patience, she turned to Kiki. "What do I have to do to get you in there? Dangle a Moon Pie on a stick? I've always told you that when strong women get knocked down—"

"They pick themselves up and keep going. I know, I know," Kiki said, sniffling. Lauren smiled. It was one of Hannah's favorite maxims. "But it's easier to say it than to do it."

"Most of life falls into that category," Hannah told her.

Her reasoning worked. Kiki let go of the column and the four women at last entered the sanctuary. They found only half the pews filled, most people milling around and chatting in hushed tones. Hannah paraded their small group down the aisle to the front, making everyone aware that Kiki was in attendance. She knew that the gossip about her sister was flying, and she wanted all to see that Kiki had nothing to be ashamed of, which was the real reason she insisted on her being there.

"The mood in here is awfully depressing," Naomi observed.

"It's a funeral," Lauren replied. "It's supposed to be depressing, isn't it?"

Naomi emitted a knowing chuckle. "Quite the opposite. Arnold Lempke has been reincarnated into another life. We should rejoice."

"If karma has anything to do with it, Lempke's been reincarnated into a dung beetle," Hannah whispered.

Kiki slapped her arm. "Don't speak ill of the dead."

"He's not dead if he's currently a dung beetle," Hannah replied. Lauren laughed until Kiki shushed her.

"I'm so jittery. I have to go to the ladies' room. Wait for me." As Kiki took off, the other women went back up the aisle and waited behind the last pew.

The sanctuary was a simple room with plain wooden pews and a low platform at the front. There on a table sat a brass urn filled presumably with Lempke's ashes.

Hannah perused the pews to see who was there, spotting Lisa and Crayton in the front with some older people who must have been relatives. There was a fair showing of Rose Club members, including Wanda and Walter Backus in the third pew on the right. Hannah was musing over whether or not Wanda knew that Walter was forking over huge sums of money to the Church of Revelations when, to her surprise, she saw Shirley Chen sitting a few rows behind him. What was she doing at Lempke's funeral?

Kiki came trotting back looking flushed. "I'm better now."

Hannah sniffed the air. "There's liquor on your breath."

"No, there's not."

Hannah grabbed Kiki's shoulder bag, opened it, and found two canned margaritas nestled among her hair spray and makeup bags. She gave her sister a reproachful look. "How many did you drink in the rest room?"

"Just one."

"One drink and you're off to the races. Shame on you. This is hardly the place."

"I won't have another one, I promise."

Hannah considered taking the remaining cans from her, but they wouldn't fit in her own small purse, so she let the issue rest.

"Let's find a seat. I feel conspicuous standing here. People are staring at me," Kiki said.

"No one's staring," Lauren told her. "It's your imagination. Even if they are, you look very nice."

Even though Kiki hated the color, she'd bought a new black suit just for the funeral, thinking that as a suspected murderess she would be the center of attention. But the truth was, no one was paying attention to her at all. It was worse than that. They seemed to be avoiding her. There were a few strained acknowledgments from people, but no one had come over to chat.

Naomi nodded toward the front of the room. "There's the urn. Come, let's say our farewells to Arnold's physical manifestation."

Hannah shivered. She had already seen Arnold dead once and wasn't interested in greeting his ashes. "You go."

Lauren also showed no enthusiasm. She and Hannah slid into a pew while Naomi and Kiki went to look at what was left of Lempke. Seeing Naomi approach the front, Wanda jumped up and hustled toward her, probably to discuss some petty issue she needed Red Moon to resolve, Hannah thought.

Just then she saw John Perez standing in the next aisle, this sighting followed by a small but distinct fluttering in her stomach. He was wearing a black sport coat, a tie, and gray pants that needed ironing. Rather than hide from him, she chose to tackle her fear directly.

"How are you?" she asked. He turned, and when he saw her, he tensed. After a moment's hesitation he replied stiffly that he was fine, and asked her how she was. She replied stiffly she was fine, and then he headed up the aisle, where he took a seat in the far right corner of the room, as far from her as possible.

"That's a nice-looking man. Who is he?" Lauren asked.

"Just someone I met," Hannah replied, turning back toward the front. She studied the back of Perez's head while Lauren chatted about reincarnation and the possibilities of Lempke actually being a dung beetle. Hannah tried to pay attention but all she could think about was Perez.

Finally Kiki and Naomi returned. Lauren and Hannah slid over to make room for them.

Once seated, Kiki, who was now in the aisle seat, leaned over Naomi and said loudly, "Arnie looks good."

Naomi made a face. "He's in an urn for God sake."

"I'm sure Kiki meant that Mr. Lempke looks good considering his condition,'' Lauren said, always trying to be conciliatory.

Kiki nudged Hannah's knee. "I said hello to Wanda and she barely spoke to me."

"Funerals have strange effects on people. She's probably grieving for Bon Bon," Hannah said, though she knew it was more than that.

Wanda was back in her pew and Hannah noticed her turn around to look at Kiki. After a good long glare she leaned over to Walter and the two Rose Club members on the other side of him, and they all began whispering. Ridiculous, small-minded people, Hannah thought. She didn't want Kiki to see what was going on.

"Kiki probably still wants to take Arnold on the cruise. Set his urn on a deck chair. Maybe put some sunglasses and a hat on it," Hannah said, hoping the statement would annoy her sister enough to keep her attention off Wanda.

"You're so terrible," Kiki said. Hannah muttered a "sorry."

"Personally, I think Arnold was only midway on his spiritual path. He had many incarnations to go," Naomi said with a trace of hostility. But before anyone could comment on this possibility, a contralto voice boomed from behind, followed by a conspicuous rattle.

"Well, Kiki," the voice said, sounding like an oboe on steroids.

The women turned and saw Bertha Malone, Wanda's best friend and the Rose Club treasurer, in the pew behind them. Tall and loud, Bertha had run an art gallery in chic Santa Fe before moving to Hill Creek, a fact she liked to remind everyone of by always wearing several pounds of silver-and-turquoise Indian jewelry. Her bracelets clattered as she shoved her fist onto her hip.

Hannah said a silent "ugh." She always avoided Bertha, finding her not only overbearing but incredibly noisy, both in voice and jewelry.

"I'm surprised to see you here," Bertha said.

"Why should you be surprised?" Hannah asked.

Bertha made a small "hummpa" sound, the heaving of her chest making her necklace jingle. "The police are questioning you, Kiki. Two times they've interrogated you, I heard. You're a murder suspect. There's no point in denying it."

The color drained from Kiki's face. Her mouth opened to defend herself but no words came out.

Hannah had no such difficulty. "She is *not* a murder suspect. She and I found Mr. Lempke's body, so naturally we were both questioned. I'm getting tired of this ridiculous gossip."

"Gossip?" Bertha looked offended. "I have no idea what you're talking about."

"You know exactly. I advise you and Wanda to keep your ill-found opinions to yourself."

Bertha's face puckered as she rearranged herself in her seat. "It's admirable for you to attempt to protect your sister, but everyone knows the truth here. And the truth is that the police think she could very well be the one who killed Arnold. And for her to show up here, to flaunt herself in front of the family, is in questionable taste."

After dropping that little turd of malice in the punch bowl, Bertha grabbed her leather-fringed handbag, slid out of the pew, and marched up the aisle, plopping herself behind Wanda and Walter. Immediately she tapped Wanda's shoulder and they began whispering.

Kiki's lips quivered, her eyes filled with tears. She jumped up and hurried toward the door.

"Poor Kiki," Lauren said. "I'll go after her."

"Better let me." Hannah headed out just as Dr. John Westmoreland began talking to Lisa and the rest of the Lempke family. As she suspected, Kiki made a beeline for the back of the sanctuary and the ladies' room, the latch on the stall clicking as Hannah entered. Hannah tapped on the door.

"Kiki, come out of there. You can't pay any attention

to Bertha.'' She heard the toilet-paper roll spin.

"Oh, Hannah, I was right,'' Kiki said, her voice muffled through a wad of tissue. "Everyone thinks I killed Arnie.''

"They don't. I told you, Lisa Lempke herself doesn't think you did it.'' Hannah heard sniffles. "Honey, you have to come out and face these people. I'll be with you.''

"I know, Hannah. I know you're right. Just give me a minute.''

Again, Hannah tapped lightly on the door. "Don't touch those margaritas.''

"I won't.''

"I'll be waiting outside.'' She exited the ladies' room and leaned against the wall, arms crossed, to wait for her sister. Minutes passed. She noticed a group of four women, positioned near a potted palm, busily signing the guest book, the palm concealing her from them. The music in the sanctuary grew louder and Hannah was just about to retrieve Kiki from the ladies' room when she heard the women mention Perez. She froze behind the palm. Eavesdropping on their conversation, she heard something that twisted her stomach into a knot.

"I'm back.''

Startled, Hannah jumped, then saw Kiki next to her with a lopsided smile on her face. Together they walked through the sanctuary, where the service had already begun. Fortunately everyone's attention was directed toward the front of the room so they didn't notice Kiki trip twice. Hannah gripped her sister's arm firmly to prevent her from falling flat on her face.

"Kiki, you drank those other margaritas, didn't you?'' she said in an accusatory whisper when they were halfway down the aisle.

"I had to. I'm feeling so much better.''

"How many?'' Kiki didn't reply. "One?'' Hannah asked. Kiki nodded. "Two?'' Kiki nodded again. Hannah whispered a curse.

They slid back in the pew just as Dr. Westmoreland began talking about everlasting life.

Lauren glanced over at Kiki, her forehead knitting up when she saw the smile on her aunt's face. "Is Kiki okay?" she whispered to Hannah.

"Sort of," Hannah replied. "Help me keep an eye on her."

Hannah had difficulty listening to the service between shushing Kiki, who was giggling inappropriately, and ruminating on the disturbing tale she had overheard outside the ladies' room. In the middle of an especially loud oration on sin and God's will, she felt a jab in her side.

"That Bertha," Kiki said, her voice husky as she leaned over Naomi to reach her sister. "What right does she have to talk to me that way?" Hannah's eyebrows rose as Kiki's plump fingers clenched into a fist. "I could knock her on her big butt. Big Butt Bertha. That's what they should call her."

Naomi looked at her with disapproval.

"Kiki, be quiet," Hannah said sternly.

"Bertha had plastic surgery, you know," Kiki continued, and Naomi's expression sharpened into keen interest. "Had it last summer. Said she was going to Mexico to celebrate the equinox, but she really had a butt lift."

"Must have required a construction crane," Naomi said softly but audibly, sending Kiki into giggles that Hannah had to stop by clamping her hand over Kiki's mouth.

After an ominous reprimand Hannah communicated mostly with her eyes, Kiki was silent the rest of the service. As soon as it was over Hannah, Lauren, and Naomi hustled her to the exit. Although she was behaving better, she was still threatening a fistfight with Bertha and they didn't want to risk a fracas.

"Hannah, could I talk to you?"

Turning, Hannah found herself facing John Perez. For an instant the earth stopped spinning as four sets of eyes belonging to women in various stages of singleness fixed upon the handsome male in front of them. Even though Lauren saw him as a silver-haired father figure rather than a sex object, she was impressed.

A pretzel was less twisted than Hannah's tongue at that moment. It was only when Kiki lurched toward him, Naomi grabbing the back of her jacket to keep her out of fondling distance, that Hannah regained her senses enough to garble out a yes.

Leaving the others waiting in the entry, she followed him outside, her eyes squinting in the sunshine. They stopped at the corner of the building near a tall eucalyptus tree, its leaves rustling in a suddenly strong breeze.

Hands folded, Hannah leaned against the trunk of the tree, trying to look casual when she felt anything but that. Perez's eyes met hers without wavering until she looked away. She saw Wanda and Walter Backus walking in a huddle with Bertha.

"I wanted to let you know," he began, "that Lisa Lempke is also being investigated. Looks like she and her dad had a big fight two weeks ago."

Hannah's eyes snapped back to him. "How do the police know?"

"A neighbor heard the argument. And Lisa doesn't have a great alibi for the time of the murder." He paused. "I thought you'd want to know. It might take some heat off your sister."

"I don't see why."

Her remark obviously surprised him. "Because now there's another suspect."

"Then that makes three," Hannah said. He looked puzzled. "I overheard a conversation today. Six months ago you accused Lempke of poisoning one of your dogs."

There were several moments of silence as the expectant expression on Perez's face collapsed into anger. Hannah could see the memory of the painful event settling on his features.

"It was a justified accusation," he finally said.

"How so?"

Perez reddened. "I had two spaniels. One got into Lempke's precious damn garden. It only happened once, but afterward he claimed the dog was wrecking his flowers every day. He threatened several times to get rid of my dog. So when the dog was poisoned, I knew it was him. He put arsenic in a piece of meat and fed it to him."

"That's despicable. You love your dog like a child. I'm sure you felt the same way about the other one."

"So what if I did?"

"It makes you a suspect in Lempke's murder."

He opened his mouth to argue, thought better of it, and just looked at her a moment. "I suppose it does," Perez finally blurted out, then he turned and left.

Hannah stood there, staring after him as he walked with long angry strides down the sidewalk, his jacket flapping. If he weren't so attractive, it would have been easier to accept the possibility that the man was a killer.

$\mathcal{T}$HIRTEEN

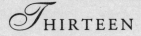

$\mathcal{H}$ALF THE PEOPLE WHO ATTENDED the funeral, around thirty in all, showed up at Lisa Lempke's afterward for a buffet lunch. Lisa felt that some sort of commemorative gathering for her father was appropriate, but what she originally intended as a lunch for a few friends and relatives was quickly commandeered by Wanda and transformed into a larger function. In spite of her grief over the loss of Bon Bon, Wanda personally handled all the food and donated the services of her own housekeeper since she didn't feel that poor Lisa would be up to the task.

A suitably somber work of Tchaikovsky drifted from Lisa's CD player, and Wanda had her housekeeper bring extra chairs into the living room, though they remained empty. Most people preferred crowding onto Lisa's deck to admire the bay view. A few huddled in the living room and the remainder chatted quietly near the dining table, nibbling on salmon pâté and brown-rice salad. The party's atmosphere was understandably subdued, at least on the surface, but beneath this politely bereaved ambience a cauldron of excitement bubbled.

The amply funded, cushioned lives of most Rose Club members provided few crises as dramatic as an unsolved murder in the neighborhood. In the past few days attendance at tai chi, yoga, and foot reflexology classes had dropped off, everyone preferring to gather in the coffee shops or on the plaza where they could swap theories.

So far, everybody's favorite suspect was Kiki, her particular scenario including the juicy combination of sex and revenge. Naomi had briefly been runner-up since Lempke had ridiculed her the night before he was murdered, but because she had been with a client at the time of the killing, Kiki's position remained unchallenged.

In fact, Kiki had been such a hot topic of conversation that when put in close confines with her in Lisa's house, everyone remained at a discreet distance, preferring to watch her from afar, like she was an animal in a zoo. One or two took her aside and chatted with her about the weather in hopes she would choose that moment to crack and spew out a confession, but for the most part Kiki was left alone by all but her family. The only outsider who showed any kindness to her was Lisa, who greeted her warmly as soon as she arrived.

Noticing the appalling way most people were treating her sister, Hannah was more determined than ever to nail somebody else in the room as Lempke's killer. Standing in a corner, crunching a carrot stick drenched in spinach tofu dip, she planned her strategy. She would circulate through the room and talk to as many guests as possible in hopes of getting information. Special attention would be paid to Walter in order to find out more about his donation to the church, as well as to Shirley, to find out what she was doing at the funeral in the first place. It was a shame that no liquor was being served, since that would loosen people's tongues, but it was, after all, a funeral and therefore a highly inappropriate time for frozen margaritas, though probably not in Kiki's view. Still, a little white wine would have taken the edge off people and made Hannah's job easier.

As she schemed she couldn't help taking note of the chic bereavement fashions in the room. Wanda was wearing a dark gray Nehru jacket with matching cigarette pants, and the woman next to her was in a black two-piece wrap-around outfit that made her look like an expert in some especially lethal form of karate. There was at least one black Chanel suit and two black Armanis, and Hannah was fairly certain she had seen one of the those at the consignment shop the week before. Naomi naturally dressed idiosyncratically, swathed in yards of green silk with a matching beret. Green was the color of life, she told everyone who would listen plus a few who wouldn't. Hannah wore a loose brown jacket she had designed herself and a long brown skirt with black boots.

Her heart fluttered when Perez walked in, but as soon as he saw her he moved toward the kitchen, obviously avoiding her. She couldn't blame him.

Hannah stood there alone, watching the door through which he had just passed, her thoughts about him all jumbled. Perez had a motive for wanting revenge against Lempke, but if he did kill him, why did he return so quickly to the murder scene? Maybe he remembered evidence he had left and came back to remove it, only to find Hannah and Kiki there. But despite their presence, Perez could easily have hidden or destroyed evidence since she and Kiki weren't watching him the whole time. Regardless, Hannah intended to head for the police station right after lunch and tell them what she had learned about Lempke allegedly poisoning Perez's dog.

Interrupting these thoughts, Naomi swept toward her, the green caftan flapping and giving the appearance of a tent being blown off its stakes. "Save me, Hannah," she whispered frantically. "Pretend we're deep in conversation."

"What's wrong?"

"Wanda won't leave me alone. She wants Red Moon to communicate to that dead dog of hers. I told her quite emphatically that Red Moon does not speak to dead pets, but she won't take no for an answer."

"Did you check on Kiki for me?"

"She's fine." Naomi peered anxiously around the room for Wanda. "She's in the kitchen helping cut cheese."

"Behaving herself?"

"As much as her karma and genetic coding permit."

"Is she drinking anything?"

"Only coffee, which is a drug, of course." Naomi leaned close to Hannah. "Our dear Kiki isn't becoming a closet boozer, is she?"

"Of course not. It's only this situation, with people avoiding her like she was cholesterol. It would bother anybody."

Naomi nodded. "And she's not good with liquor."

"Never has been. She was famous in high school for taking off her blouse after two beers."

"Perhaps she was an early feminist and it was a gesture of liberation," Naomi suggested. "Oops. Gotta go."

She ducked into the hallway. Glancing around to her left, Hannah saw that Wanda had entered the living room with Walter at her side. She decided to wait and catch Walter alone. It was then that she noticed Shirley sitting in a chair in a corner eating a finger sandwich and looking lost. Hannah approached her.

After she said hello, Shirley looked startled a second but then smiled gratefully. She wore an unfashionable shirt-waist dress in a red synthetic that was supposed to look like silk, and her lack of Marin chic made Hannah like her that much more.

"I'm so glad you came over," she said, standing up. "I don't really know anyone here except Lisa and Crayton, and they're busy with the guests. It's nice to see a friend. Well, not really a friend, I guess, but at least I know you."

"I'd say we're friends. We shared a bag of potato chips, didn't we?" Hannah said with a smile.

Shirley smiled back. She was taller than Hannah had expected, since she had only seen Shirley sitting. "Are you going ahead and joining the church?" she asked.

At first stumbling on her response, Hannah said she was perhaps going to do so, but had some family responsibilities that would keep her from attending in the very near future. Once through that minor trial, she asked Shirley a few benign questions about how many members belonged to the church, how long it had been in its current building, then finally got to the question she really wanted to ask, which was where the church's money came from.

"Donations," Shirley replied. "The church has big contributors."

"Who are some of the biggest?" Hannah asked. "If I'm going to join an organization, I like to know how it's funded."

Just then, out of the corner of her eye, she noticed John Perez speaking to Lisa. He clasped her hand, then headed for the door, casting Hannah a quick glance before he left. Squelching a pang, she returned her full attention to Shirley, who was studying something in her sandwich.

"I can't tell you much about the funding," she said.

"But you have all the information on your computer."

She looked up. "I mean I don't think I'm supposed to. So, how do you know Arnold Lempke?" she asked, trying to change the subject.

"From the Rose Club," Hannah told her. For the time being she wanted to leave Kiki's name out of it.

Shirley nodded. "Yeah, he talked about that club sometimes. I used to visit his wife, Mary, when she was sick and he and I talked a lot. He and Mary went to the Baptist church I belonged to before the Church of Revelations."

A woman walked by with a platter of appetizers and offered them to Hannah and Shirley. Hannah took a stuffed mushroom.

"How long did you know Arnold?" she asked.

"A couple of years. I saw Mary at least twice a week until she died, so I got to know Arnold and Lisa pretty well. I'm the one who told Lisa about the Church of Revelations." She stopped, chewed the last bite of sandwich, then continued. "I don't think Arnold much appreciated that, but it was her life, right?"

"Arnold was upset with you over it?" Hannah asked.

"You kidding? He had a hissy fit. I think that's why he dumped me." As soon as the words came out, her eyes grew wide and she covered her mouth with her fingers. Hannah almost choked on her mushroom. "Shoot. I shouldn't have said anything," Shirley said fretfully.

"You dated Arnold?" Hannah tried not to sound as keenly interested as she was.

Shirley worriedly looked around the room before pulling Hannah closer to the corner. "Not until after Mary died," she said, her voice low. "It didn't last long. He spent the night a few times, then I never saw him again. I like to tell myself it was because of the church thing and Lisa, but I don't know. Men stink sometimes." She shook her head, her eyes drifting off. "Still, we've got to be Christian about these things."

Watching Shirley's dark expression, Hannah guessed that she was more complex than her easygoing demeanor suggested. Shirley must have been working the prayer list for widowers at the Baptist church just as Kiki had done, only Shirley had begun long before. She had put two years into courting Lempke, only to have him sleep with her then reject her. That sort of thing could make a woman angry. Hannah popped the rest of the mushroom in her mouth. Another murder suspect, she thought. Such a fruitful day.

Soon Shirley took her leave, saying she needed to go home, making some excuse about her cat and Hannah returned to circulating about the room, checked on Kiki in the kitchen, then searched for Walter. She found him on the deck. He stood by himself at one end, sipping what looked like a gin and tonic.

Buttoning her jacket to protect against the cool air caused by the incoming fog, she walked outside. She called Walter's name and he turned, smiling slightly when he recognized her. He was wearing his usual outfit—double-breasted blue sport coat, khaki pants, a boozy smile, and the same look in his eyes you see on animals that have been stuffed and mounted. Walter wasn't a bad-looking man. He was in fact attractive if you took the time to study his features, but there was something insubstantial about him that would never allow him to be handsome.

He looked around to make certain Wanda wasn't watching before approaching Hannah. "Hi. Have you tried the guacamole? It looks excellent. Of course, I never eat anything that particular shade of green." He chuckled.

"Walter, I have to ask you about something. Something private."

"Sounds painful," he said, his tone mocking.

"I wanted to talk to you when Wanda wasn't around."

He raised his eyebrows lasciviously. "Good. Just because I'm married doesn't mean I don't date."

"That's not what I had in mind."

"Too bad. You're still a hot woman, you know, and of course you do. Mr. Gravity's been very kind to you. I, for one, have always liked women a little older—"

She cut him off. "Walter, I know that you donated ten thousand dollars to the Church of Revelations."

His smile evaporated. He looked at her a few seconds then took a gulp of his drink. "How?"

"It doesn't matter."

"It does," he said, his tone low and close to threatening.

"It was a fluke. No one else could probably find out. The thing is, I *did* find out."

"I made a donation. Wanda doesn't know."

"And I won't tell her. But how could you donate that much money and have her not know?" The import of this question was clear, since everyone knew Wanda had all the money and Walter had zero.

"It wasn't actually money. I transferred some stock from an IRA account I had before I married her. The only money

I had that wasn't hers. Stupid of me. Huge mistake.''

"Why did you get involved in the first place?''

He took another gulp of his drink. "I was going through a bad time. A friend got me into it." Leaning on the railing, Walter directed his gaze out at the bay, fixing on a large sailboat that glided closer to shore than was prudent, its white sails gleaming. "Old Swanson has a way of sucking you in, you know? Making you believe that there's this big, omnipotent something out there that's going to save your ass," he said with a sweep of his arm, his drink sloshing over the side of the glass. He turned to her. "But you see, Hannah. There's nothing. Nothing to save you or me.''

Just then they heard Wanda calling his name. He closed his eyes, opened them, then downed the rest of his drink and went to her. Hannah couldn't help feeling sorry for the man, but she didn't understand people who stayed in bad marriages. How could money or some ultimately groundless sense of security be worth more than self-respect?

Ready to go home, she walked inside to look for the bathroom. After passing through the living room, she turned a corner that looked like it might lead to what she wanted, but she stopped in her tracks, a loud "my God!" involuntarily escaping from her. There at her feet was little Bon Bon, Wanda's supposedly dead poodle, his leg lifted stiffly on an antique chest, his countenance unusually serene.

Hannah heard feet behind her, then a shriek she recognized as coming from Wanda. Hannah spun around.

"I thought he died," Hannah said to her, stupefied.

Unable to speak, Wanda just gurgled in shock and rage until she finally blurted, "He did.''

Hannah looked down at the dog then back at Wanda, her mouth open, her expression questioning.

"I had him stuffed," Wanda said, her tone sharp, as if any intelligent person would have assumed it.

"In that position?''

Wanda scooped up the rigid remains of Bon Bon into

her arms. "Of course not. I thought it would be nice for Bon Bon to come to the party so it could be a wake for him as well, but look what happened. Somebody twisted his little leg up that way." She sniffled. "Who could have done such a thing?"

Hannah put a consoling hand on her arm. "Maybe it was an accident. Someone could have bumped into him."

"An accident? No, it was done on purpose, I'm sure of it." Her eyes narrowed into slits of furious concentration. "Walter!" she bellowed, then stomped off in search of him.

$\mathcal{F}$OURTEEN

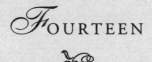

$\mathcal{S}$TEELING HERSELF, HANNAH TOOK A deep breath, letting it out in a frustrated rush. Sometimes there was nothing more annoying than politeness.

"Well, ma'am, again, let me say that we appreciate you trying to be helpful," Detective Morgan said.

I know he means well, but if he calls me "ma'am" one more time I'll slug him, Hannah said silently, sitting in front of Morgan's desk in an uncomfortable wooden chair that was probably meant for about-to-be-grilled suspects.

"Detective Morgan, I don't understand your lack of interest. Maybe Shirley Chen's motive for killing Arnold Lempke is a bit of a stretch, but certainly not John Perez's." With this last statement she gave his desktop a small rap with her fist for emphasis. "If you saw him with his dog, you'd realize that he treats it with the same love he would a child. I'm sure he thought of the other dog the same way, and for Lempke to have poisoned it was a motive for—"

"Mrs. Malloy." Morgan interrupted her. "You see, we know all about John's dog and about its being poisoned.

He reported it to us when it happened. We investigated Mr. Lempke and couldn't prove anything.''

"Even more of a motive for murder. Perez was frustrated. He wanted justice.''

Morgan gave her a patient, although somewhat labored smile. "But even though we had the information about Daisy—''

"Daisy?''

"That was the dog's name. The poisoned one. Even though that information was in our records, John reminded us of it that day we found Lempke. He was very up-front.''

Hannah turned up one palm. "Of course he would be. He knew you'd find out anyway. Did you check out an alibi for him?''

"I don't have to tell you this, but I'm going to because I know you're upset and I want you to calm down. Perez was at the Book Stop at the time Lempke was murdered.''

"And who vouched for him?''

"A college kid who works the espresso machine.''

Hannah stood, throwing up her hands in frustration. "I've had coffee at the Book Stop several times a week for fifteen years and I can assure you that no one behind the café counter has a clue about what day of the week it is, much less who's there and what time they arrived and left.''

Morgan stood up, too, pushing his chair back noisily. "First of all, Mrs. Malloy, I worked behind that café counter when I was in high school.''

"Oh. Sorry.''

"Secondly, John Perez was chief of the Tri-City Police Department for twenty years. He's a well-respected man around here. We checked his alibi and it's solid.''

"What about the Church of Revelations? Have you looked into Reverend Swanson? You know that Mr. Lempke was doing his best to ruin him. He called the DA's office and complained about him.''

"We've checked that out. They think Lempke was just irate because he didn't like his daughter going to that kind of church. As far as anybody knows, Swanson hasn't done a thing wrong.''

"But has anyone looked into his finances or anything else that might indicate if the church was doing something fraudulent? Lempke acted like he had information, and if he did, Swanson had a motive for murder.''

"No offense, ma'am, but we have other people with motives that we're looking into first.'' There was a pause. Hannah glared at him. "Now I have to ask you to leave. I'm very busy.''

"Busy trying to nail my sister for murder,'' Hannah said, then turned and walked out.

"I've been thinking about going to church, Hannah.''

Hannah looked up from that day's *New York Times* crossword puzzle. They had just finished the dinner dishes and were sitting in the living room listening to a recording of *La Bohème*. The kitchen was her favorite room in the house, but the living room was a close second. It was painted a deep dusty rose with comfy chairs and a plump sofa, all perfect for dropping into with a good book. And the cool nights made a fire in the fireplace almost always a worthwhile proposition, even in summer.

"But you've been going to the Baptist church every Sunday for the past year.''

Kiki put down her *People* magazine, her face all seriousness. "I mean *really* go to church. Listen to the sermons, close my eyes during the praying. The whole ball of wax.''

Hannah now knew why her sister had been singing "Bringing in the Sheaves'' all afternoon. "I have my doubts about God saving you from this mess merely because you start closing your eyes during church prayers, but I guess it's worth a shot.''

The doorbell rang.

"Who could that be?'' Kiki asked anxiously, afraid that

the police were going to haul her off to central lockup at any moment.

Hannah went to the door, looked through the peephole, and saw Shirley Chen.

"Surprised, aren't you?" Shirley said as soon as Hannah opened the door. There was an edge to her normally friendly voice.

"It's a pleasant surprise," Hannah said, meaning it. She led Shirley into the living room, where Kiki was waiting expectantly. Hannah introduced them, hoping to high heaven they wouldn't discover that they had both enjoyed the loins of Arnold Lempke. Kiki was the jealous type, and for all Hannah knew, Shirley had murdered Lempke as a result of him dropping her. What would Shirley do if she suspected that Lempke had dropped her for Kiki?

But Hannah didn't have to worry because Shirley immediately asked if she could talk to her alone. Hannah and Kiki exchanged a meaningful glance, then Kiki excused herself and scooted out, taking her magazine with her.

Hannah invited Shirley to sit down, but she remained standing.

"You weren't ever thinking about joining the Church of Revelations, were you?" Shirley said as soon as felt secure that Kiki was out of earshot. Hannah knew her sister well enough to realize Kiki would be listening through the door.

"No, I wasn't," she answered, fighting the tinge of fear nestled in her stomach. Shirley's black eyes fixed on her.

"You were there to snoop. When Lisa told me that the cops were questioning your sister, it made me think. I got your address out of the phone book and drove by this house. You're no rich lady. But the reverend thinks you are. You wanted him to think it."

"I'm guilty of that, yes. My sister is no murderer and I'm trying to get any information that can convince the police of that."

Shirley opened her purse, and frightened, Hannah gripped the back of a chair, bracing herself for God knew what. But all Shirley pulled out was a piece of white notepaper. She handed it to Hannah, who opened it. Five names were written on it.

"What is this?" she asked.

"Some of the church's big donors. That's what you want, isn't it? You think something funny is going on at the church. I don't think there is, but you can check those people out if it makes you happy."

"Why are you giving this to me?"

Shirley bit her lip, and her hands clenched. "Because the reverend is low-life scum. He's a womanizer. A sex maniac." A bump came from the other side of the living-room door. "I'd like nothing better than if his church got in trouble."

Her eyes not leaving Shirley, Hannah folded the paper and slipped it in the pocket of her sweater. "He womanized you?"

The rims of Shirley's eyes grew pink and she shrank down into Kiki's favorite chair. Even on the verge of tears, she had a certain toughness.

"I'm not too good with the men. First Arnold, then the reverend, and a string of them before that. They think because my parents came to this country on a boat, they can abuse me. Men think that's what Asian women are for."

"I'm sure not all men are like that. Only the bad ones," Hannah said.

Shirley stood up. "You may have lied, but you're still an okay lady." She headed for the door, stopped, and turned back. "Check out those names if you want. I hope you find something." Then she left.

"What a little tramp!" Kiki exclaimed, bouncing into the room, hands on hips, as soon as Shirley was gone. "Sleeps with anything in pants."

"Stop it, Kiki," Hannah said. "Just because a woman wants a little companionship—even if it's just sex she wants—it doesn't mean she's a tramp. You should know that." Kiki opened her mouth to protest, but nothing came out. "I hate that word," Hannah continued. "It's sexist. Men are never called tramps, are they?" She picked up the phone.

"Who are you calling?"

"Lauren. I'm going to give her these names and see if she can use her accounting connections and know-how to figure out who they are."

Kiki sighed and collapsed back into her chair, the cushion gasping under the impact. "How did Shirley manage to get both those men in bed with her? That's what I want to know," she said. Her previous irritation had been replaced with wistfulness. "It took me two months, a Wonder Bra, and a bottle of Boodles Gin to just get the shorts off of Arnold. And even at that, it hardly lasted long enough to notice."

Fifteen

" '*S*TABLE, SEXY SENIOR SWM LOOKING for fun and frolic with lusty SWF, age forty to fifty,' " Hannah read out loud as she sat alone in her kitchen over toast and a third cup of coffee. Kiki had rushed off early that morning for Nordstrom's annual sale, the doors opening at seven-thirty, and she had left her breakfast reading along with her dirty dishes on the kitchen table.

Most people, having been shunned the way Kiki had been the previous day at Lisa Lempke's, would have been deep in depression. Instead Kiki hurled herself into total denial, and she popped out of bed at dawn, frisky as a colt, eager to search both for love and a good bargain.

Kiki had obviously spent breakfast busily searching for a new cruise companion, and this particular classified ad, located next to ads for penile enlargement and colon hydrotherapy, had been circled and underlined with purple ink.

Rereading the ad, Hannah considered its real import. The writer actually admitting he was a senior probably meant he was at least ninety, and *stable* could only mean that his seizure medication was starting to kick in. Having recently eaten, Hannah didn't dare contemplate what the writer meant by *sexy*. She couldn't understand why Kiki had circled the ad in the first place, since she was outside the gentleman's requested age range by a decade. Was she going to lie about it and hope his eyesight was failing?

The phone rang; it was Lauren. Hannah had been anxiously waiting for her call all morning. The news was disappointing. She told Hannah that she had done research on the five Church of Revelations contributors on Shirley's list, and as far as she could tell, they were all established and moneyed Marin residents.

Hannah thanked her for going to all the trouble and hung up. Giving large sums of money to the Church of Revelations may have shown bad judgment by some people's standards, but in all likelihood it showed no wrongdoing, ethical or legal. If Arnold Lempke had discovered something about the church, something so damaging that Swanson would have murdered to keep it a secret, then he had taken it with him to the grave. Unless Shirley, by intent or accident, had given Hannah the names only of those people of whose integrity she was certain.

Having spent enough of the morning waiting for Lauren's call, Hannah was all afire to tackle the problem anew. She got out the phone book and rang up Shirley at the church office.

"No, I've given you all the information I can," Shirley told her curtly.

"But I know there are corporations that donated money. I remember seeing some names when I helped you go through your files. I need those companies' names and addresses."

"I can't help you. If he found out I'd given you what I did, he'd . . ." She let the sentence hang.

"He'd do what?" Hannah pressed. "Are you afraid of him?

"No." There was a pause. "Well, maybe. A little. He

can get so worked up. And I need this job. If you want more, you'll have to ask the reverend yourself.''

"He would never give me any information.''

"I haven't told him you're not rich. He might do anything for you if he thinks he's going to get a big enough check for it.''

If Hannah wanted to see the reverend, he would be in that morning after eleven, Shirley said, but she refused to provide any more information. Then she hung up.

Sitting at the kitchen table, Hannah was pondering the situation when Kiki flounced in carrying a stuffed shopping bag. She was wearing a white Liz Claiborne jogging suit, her hair swept up into a tuft sprouting frothily from her scalp, but through her layer of makeup Hannah could see the fatigue around her eyes. Denial took a great deal of effort.

"I'm going back down there,'' Hannah said before her sister even had a chance to say hello.

Kiki put the bag on the kitchen table. "Where?''

"The Church of Revelations.''

Kiki's face screwed up. "What for?''

"To somehow get a complete list of donors. If Shirley won't help me anymore, I'll just have to get the information myself.''

Surprisingly, Kiki offered no protest, and after she had spent twenty minutes primping, the two women headed out. Kiki had insisted on going along, which was the first glimmer of investigative zeal she had shown. She claimed to be motivated by a desire to participate in her own defense, but Hannah knew she was really hoping to be womanized by the supposed sex-maniac reverend.

"Personally I don't understand what a man could see in Shirley Chen,'' Kiki opined as she checked her face in her compact mirror and clomped up the church walkway on wedged cork-soled shoes that *Cosmopolitan* claimed were especially flattering to thick legs. "I'm sure Arnold was just using her. She was a plaything until he met the right woman.''

Hannah cast her a sidewise look. ''Jealousy is a waste of energy.''

Ignoring Hannah's remark and remaining glued to her mirror while she smoothed out her lipstick with her pinkie, Kiki tripped on a crack in the sidewalk and stumbled into Hannah. Hannah caught her by the elbow.

''Besides, I don't see why it matters since—'' Hannah was about to say ''since he's dead anyway,'' but instead paused and finished the sentence with, ''Since the incident.''

Any mention of Lempke's murder sent Kiki into tear-soaked wails, so they now referred to his unfortunate demise as ''the incident.'' Despite the euphemism, Kiki still had to stop and shake off the negative image before continuing on.

On the first of the steps that led to the double front doors of the Church of Revelations, Kiki halted, taking hold of Hannah's arm. ''How do I look?'' she asked.

''Button up two buttons or we're not going in.''

Kiki had dug into the bowels of her closet and found one of her more sedate flowered dresses, spicing it up by unbuttoning it to an indecent degree.

Kiki folded her arms. ''I won't. I'm hot. I need the breeze.'' But one good look at Hannah told her that arguing was useless, so she buttoned the offending two buttons. Since ''the incident'' and her subsequent woes, she had been so grateful for Hannah's sisterly support that she was giving in on small issues, including switching the television the night before from *Melrose Place* to a PBS *Nova* program on ancient architecture. She had dozed off in the middle but later lied and said she enjoyed it.

Shirley was sitting at her desk staring intently at her computer when they walked in. She looked up expectantly. Upon seeing them, her face fell. It was plain that she was expecting someone else.

"Oh, hi," she said.

Kiki gave her rival a chilly hello, which was immediately followed by a warm greeting from Hannah.

"We're here to see Reverend Swanson," Hannah said.

The mention of the name sent a cloud across Shirley's face. "He's not here. To tell you the truth, I'm worried. He's always here by eleven. He does his mission work between eleven and two."

"What's mission work?" Hannah asked.

"He calls the church members who've been generous in the past to drum up new donations, usually for a specific project."

Like paying off his Mercedes, Hannah thought.

Shirley continued. "He never misses a day. That's why I'm worried."

"Have you called him?"

Shirley nodded. "Three or four times." She paused, pressing her lips together. "What if he had an accident?"

Shirley hadn't been too concerned with the reverend's health when she had called him scum the night before, but Hannah had the good taste not to mention it.

Shirley glanced down at her lap and then raised her eyes to Hannah. "What if he's sick or hurt?"

Wanting to be included in the conversation, Kiki pushed closer to Shirley's desk. "Maybe someone should go by his house."

Shirley nodded eagerly. "I want to. He doesn't live far from here. But, you see, I can't. We have painters arriving any minute and the reverend would be spitting mad if they didn't finish his office because I wasn't here. He wants his office robin's-egg blue."

"Then why not let Kiki and me go?" Hannah suggested. "If he doesn't answer his door, we'll at least know if his car is there. Maybe the neighbors will know where he is."

Shirley stood up and walked around the desk. "Would you? I don't like the fact that he hasn't even called."

Hannah didn't like the sound of it either.

• • •

Swanson resided in a quaint bay-front community across the freeway from Hill Creek proper and down a small peninsula. The area was known for its fabulous water views and the occasional snobbishness of its residents. To live there was a statement of exalted status, usually based on one's bank balance, either earned or inherited, the latter referred to by Hannah as membership in the Lucky Sperm Club.

"I feel so sorry for Shirley," Kiki said as she ran the Cadillac up the curb in front of the reverend's house. Shifting into reverse, she backed it off onto the street.

Hannah eyed the house. It was on the small side but had a direct view of the Golden Gate Bridge. Expensive real estate.

"Why do you feel sorry for Shirley?" Hannah asked.

"Because Arnie obviously preferred me to her. And her having to face me this morning."

"Yes, it must have been hell," Hannah said in a tone dripping with irony, then focused her attention on the project at hand. "Swanson's car is in the driveway. He's home."

"Ooh, good."

They walked up to the front door, rang the bell, but nothing happened. Hannah rang again. Still no reply.

Kiki groaned. "Drat. He's not home."

"We don't know for sure," Hannah told her, giving the door a knock. "Like Shirley said, he might be hurt, had an accident or something." She peered in a window to the right of the door but didn't see anything. "Let's find another window and take a peek inside."

Kiki looked doubtful. "Do you think we should? What if he sees us staring in?"

"What if he does? We're trying to help him."

They walked around the right side of the house, Kiki muttering expletives as her shoes dug into the damp ground. The house was two stories high and built on a slope, and the only reachable window Hannah found was on the west side, but she wasn't tall enough to see in.

"Kiki, I'm going to give you a boost. You look in and tell me if you see anything."

Kiki looked at her as if she had asked her to strip naked. "A boost? What do you mean?"

"I mean you put your foot here." Hannah laced her fingers together to make a foothold. "Take off those shoes first, then I'll hoist you up."

Kiki winced at the word *hoist*. "I don't think so."

"Listen, I have the hard part. I have to do the hoisting. Now be a sport."

After removing her shoes, Kiki gingerly put one foot in Hannah's hands. Hannah counted to three, then, with a groan, lifted her sister up to the window.

"Have you put on a few pounds?" she asked, panting under Kiki's weight.

Kiki glared down at her. "I most certainly have not." Just then she began wobbling precariously. "You must not be balanced right. If you'd hold me steady . . ." She braced her hands on the window ledge and peered inside. "I can't see anything unless—"

Kiki let out a terrified scream.

Frightened, Hannah jumped backward. Kiki's foot slipped out of her hands, and within seconds Hannah was on the ground, with Kiki sprawled next to her.

"Are you okay?" Hannah asked, panicked and breathing hard. Kiki nodded, eyes scared. "What was in there?"

Kiki pointed a trembling finger at the window. "He's . . . he's in there. I saw blood."

Pulling herself up, Hannah raced to the front porch and grabbed a rock, one of many used to line the front walkway. She had never broken a window before, but didn't see an alternative. She took a breath, then shoved the rock through, the glass shattering with a crash. After reaching in and unlatching the window, she raised it, and she and Kiki managed to remove enough glass from the sill so she could crawl inside without cutting herself too badly.

Kiki looked downward, covering her mouth with her hand. "Hannah, you're bleeding!"

Hannah hadn't noticed the blood dripping from her hand. "It's okay," she said shakily, feeling anything but okay. "I'll find something inside to wrap it. You go knock on doors. Find somebody home and call an ambulance." Kiki looked at her wide-eyed, scared, but she took off, still barefoot, down the walkway.

Hannah braced herself with her hands against the window's upper casement and carefully lifted one leg, then the other through the window, cutting herself on some jagged shards of glass.

She found herself in Swanson's living room. The furniture was sleek and contemporary, the carpet a clean cottony white, but she didn't take the time to admire it. Moving quickly, she passed through a dining area before reaching the kitchen. That's where she found Swanson.

She gasped, her stomach twisting in revulsion. He was facedown on the floor, his legs strangely twisted, his arms at his sides, palms turned upward. But the most striking thing about him was his back. It was covered with blood. A bloody knife lay in the corner of the kitchen floor.

It was then that she noticed his right hand sitting in a puddle of red. Hannah looked closer at that hand, then felt bile rising in her throat. Grabbing the edge of the counter to brace herself, she made it to the sink and threw up.

Swanson's pinkie finger, the finger on which he wore his garish ring, had been chopped off.

$\mathcal{S}$IXTEEN

$\mathcal{F}$INDING TWO CORPSES IN ONE week was two too many, and it was all beginning to have a dampening effect on Hannah's normally unruffled demeanor.

From the moment she and Kiki discovered Swanson, events began happening so fast that Hannah couldn't remember their chronological order. As far as she could recall, the first thing she did was check Swanson's pulse, which was sadly nonexistent. That grim deed accomplished, she called 911. When she went back outside and told her sister what had happened, including the absence of the reverend's pinkie, Kiki swirled into a tornado of hysteria, crying and babbling, hanging on to Hannah's arm. Having clutched at her head a few times during this conniption, Kiki had destroyed her hairdo, resulting in erratic tufts of hair standing upright from her scalp.

Hannah felt like succumbing to hysterics herself, but she remained calm by focusing on Kiki. She spoke to her soothingly, made her take deep breaths, and helped her get her wedgie shoes back on her feet.

Detective Morgan didn't come with the other police,

which Hannah regretted. At a time like this she didn't like dealing with strangers, although she recognized a couple of the policemen from the Lempke crime scene. After a paramedic bandaged her hand, she and Kiki told their story to the police while they stood in Swanson's front yard. Unlike the central part of Hill Creek, the neighbors in this upper-crust area didn't come out and stare. They sent out their housekeepers and nannies to stare for them, and Hannah noticed women of various immigrant groups carrying brooms or babies popping in and out of houses so they could provide their employers with minute-by-minute updates.

Both Hannah and Kiki were asked to go to the police station. When Hannah asked why this was necessary, the officer explained that he wanted them to give their descriptions where they could be taped. He then insisted on driving them to the station, suggesting that the women might be too upset to drive themselves. It all sounded reasonable enough, but Hannah became suspicious when the policeman requested firmly that they go in separate squad cars.

"Don't say anything more to the police until Caufield arrives," Hannah said to Kiki as a young female officer arrived to steer her away. "I'll call him as soon as I get to the police station."

Kiki gulped. Her eyes darted to the officer then back to Hannah. "You don't think *they* think that I had anything to do with what happened to Reverend Swanson?"

"Of course not," Hannah said with a confidence in her voice she didn't feel in her heart. "I just feel it's time we involved Louis. If they ask you questions, just tell them you want to wait for Louis. Do you understand?"

Kiki nodded.

"We need to go," the officer said to Kiki, her manner kind. "You feeling all right?"

It was obvious to Hannah that Kiki was far from all right. Her eyes were the size of salad plates and the rest of her was shaking. But she nodded and followed the woman to the squad car.

Once at the police station, Hannah was again taken to the tiny room with the small mirrored window. When she asked to make a phone call, the officer immediately obliged, bringing a phone in for her. She called Louis Caufield's office and told his assistant that Kiki needed him immediately. As for herself, she didn't feel she required an attorney since she couldn't imagine how the police could possibly suspect her of any wrongdoing. She had received at least four phone calls that morning that would prove she had been at home and not traipsing around town wielding a knife.

Her next call was much more difficult. When Hannah told Shirley that Reverend Swanson was dead, there was a long silence.

"Are you going to be all right? Can I call someone for you?" Hannah asked. Shirley assured her that she would be fine, although she didn't sound it. At Hannah's urging, she agreed to go stay with a female cousin, at least for the night.

Later, sitting anxiously in the small interrogation room, Hannah told her story to the police three times. Each time she told it—fighting to keep her voice steady—the events seemed to grow less and less clear, which only increased her nervousness.

The lead detective was a woman named Louann Dawson. She was about forty, with short, prematurely gray hair, a pretty face, and a surly attitude Hannah felt certain she worked at. It occurred to her that in her black slacks and simple white shirt, Dawson could have used a little color, perhaps a scarf or a touch of lipstick, but she chose not to mention it. Her male partner, Joe Brattain, was in uniform.

There was barely enough space in the room for three people. Hannah sat in a plastic chair at a table, with Brattain across from her. Dawson remained standing. He remained silent while his partners shot the questions.

Why were she and Kiki at Swanson's house? How could they see his body through so high a window? How did they get in the house? What rooms did Hannah walk through and in what order? Hannah answered every question the best she could. Halfway through, the cut on her hand began to hurt, the gauze growing damp from perspiration.

When they photographed the soles of Hannah's shoes as well as her hand, she realized with indignation that Dawson suspected her of murder. Hannah explained about the phone calls she had received that morning that would establish her alibi, but Dawson's accusatory attitude didn't alter until there was a knock at the door and a male officer asked to speak with her. When the detective returned, her questions centered on Kiki's whereabouts that morning.

"Shopping," Hannah said. Her mouth dry, she took a sip of water from a glass brought to her by Officer Brattain. "Nordstrom's annual sale. It's a big thing. Excellent prices. Half of Marin was probably there."

Leaning against the wall with her arms crossed, Dawson studied Hannah. Hannah wished she wouldn't look at her in that manner, so remote and suspicious. She found herself missing nice Detective Morgan.

"Did anyone go with her?" Dawson asked.

"No. She went alone. She's normally very sociable, but she likes to go to the big sales alone. She has this theory about getting there when the doors open, then being able to move quickly from rack to rack. She even wears her running shoes."

Apparently not a shopper, Dawson looked at Hannah with a stony face.

"I want to see my sister," Hannah said, the fourth time she had made the request. The answer was the same. No.

Unfolding her arms, Dawson moved toward the door. "You can go now. Thanks for your time."

With that, she walked out, but Brattain lagged behind.

"Does the Nordstrom's sale include menswear?" he asked, his voice lowered. Puzzled, Hannah assured him that it did. Having given him that bit of vital information, she asked him if he would see if Caufield had arrived, and if he had, to tell him that she would be in the waiting room. Brattain agreed.

Hannah went to the waiting room near the station's front door, where she took a seat on a hard chair, clutching her handbag in her lap. She couldn't remember ever being so tense, as if an electric current were shooting through her. Everything in her gut seemed to have knotted up. Her hand still hurt and there was a gnawing in her stomach that she couldn't distinguish as hunger or raw nerves. Now she knew why people took Valium.

In the past week her life with her sister had careened out of control, their pleasant, safe existence now a distant memory. And two people were dead. For the first time since Lempke's death, Hannah realized the depth of the evil that was at work in Hill Creek. The two murders had to be connected. And what if the killer wasn't finished? It was hard to imagine that this person could be someone she knew. Surely it had to be a stranger from the outside and not someone she saw at the grocery store. But whoever it was, he or she had to be brought to justice.

"Hannah?"

She looked up and saw Louis Caufield, looking very lawyerish in a gray suit. He stayed only briefly, telling Hannah he didn't know yet where things stood with Kiki. Hannah felt certain Caufield was privy to more information than he was revealing, but she didn't know him well enough to be able to read him, being only moderately acquainted with him from the Rose Club. He seemed like an intelligent man and he had an excellent reputation as a lawyer, but other than that she knew little.

After Caufield left, Hannah was soon joined by a group of rough-looking men with pierced ears and noses. They grimly stared at her, causing her to hold her purse even more tightly. Was it possible to be mugged at the police station? That event would have capped off the day.

After another hour of waiting, Caufield returned. His expression didn't bode well. As soon as she saw him, Hannah stood up.

"What's going on? Where's my sister?"

The young men, still sitting across from her, looked on with vague interest.

Caufield took her elbow. "Let's talk in here." He ushered her back into a brown hallway that led, among other unsavory places, to the room where Hannah had been questioned.

Caufield closed the door behind them and pulled out a chair for her. "You better sit down, Hannah." Normally she might have objected to such a cliché, but at that moment she had an ominous feeling that sitting would be a very good idea. She lowered herself into the chair.

"Kiki's been arrested," he said.

At first it didn't register. He could have said, "Kiki's at the hairdresser's," and it wouldn't have affected her any differently. Reality took a few moments to hit her, but when it did it smacked her squarely. The color drained from her face.

"Arrested?" she blurted when she was finally able to speak. "Arrested for what?"

"For Swanson's murder. They found the weapon on the kitchen floor."

She raised her hand to her forehead. "I saw the knife in the corner by the cabinets. I don't understand."

Caufield rubbed his temple, as if not quite understanding it all himself. "The knife had Kiki's fingerprints on it."

Being struck by a blunt object would have been less of a blow. Hannah's throat turned dry. It was impossible. Kiki's prints couldn't have been on that knife.

"I can't believe . . ." she said, her voice trailing off.

"It's true. And they won't talk bail. Kiki has an international plane ticket."

"Of course she does," Hannah told him, her voice edged

with panic. "She's supposed to go to Acapulco in a few days for a cruise."

"That's enough to consider her a flight risk."

Hannah stood up, walked a yard, then spun around. "This is all absurd. My sister can't possibly stay in jail."

"Listen, Hannah. I'll get in front of a judge as soon as I can and try to get her home. But for now she has to stay here."

Hannah fought tears. "Poor Kiki. What will happen to her?"

Caufield came closer, resting his hands on Hannah's shoulders. "This is Hill Creek, not South Central L.A. She'll be okay."

"Can I talk to her?"

He nodded. "I already asked them. You can't stay long."

Hannah followed him through double doors into another dingy hallway. Caufield stopped at a small office and began to speak to the officer behind the desk until Hannah shoved herself between the two men.

"Your arresting Kiki Goldstein is ridiculous," she said to the surprised officer. "She was obviously framed."

The officer looked confused.

Caufield gave him a tight-lipped smile. "Hannah, leave this to me," he told her politely but firmly.

She pretended she didn't hear him. "Furthermore, that religious rock Swanson used in his church. Don't you realize it's drugged?" She didn't intend to raise her voice and slap the man's desk the way she did, but she wasn't in full control of herself. "It has to be drugged. People wailing and seeing things. That's where you should be spending your time."

"Hannah, I'm going to insist," Caufield said, his voice now even firmer, giving her a little push. He made a quick apology to the officer and they exchanged a few words before he took Hannah's arm.

"A couple of things, Hannah," the lawyer said as he led

her down the hallway. "One, leave the talking to me. Two, that gentleman handles parking tickets. If you had taken the time to look at the sign on his desk, you would have known that. I parked in a thirty-minute zone and I wanted to make sure my car wasn't going to get towed." He stopped in front of a closed door. "Here she is."

Hannah didn't apologize. She faced the door, taking a moment to pull herself together. It wouldn't be good to let Kiki see her so frazzled.

Caufield opened the door, following Hannah inside. There was a policewoman sitting across a table from Kiki. She stood as they entered, and stepped outside the door, closing it.

Hannah had expected Kiki to explode into tears as soon as she walked in. Instead she just sat at a table looking shrunken, pale, and very afraid. Hannah knew she had been crying because of the black streak running down her cheek, but Kiki was doing her best to put on a brave front, her thin facade of courage patched together with spit and Scotch tape. Hannah sat down opposite her. Kiki clasped her hand.

"They're arresting me, Hannah. I have to stay here. I don't even know why." The words came out in a high-pitched warble.

Hannah pressed her hand more tightly. "Your fingerprints were on the knife that killed Swanson." Kiki opened her mouth to protest, but Hannah beat her to it. "I know you didn't do it. All of this will be cleared up."

Kiki didn't say anything. She just nodded, giant tears forming in her eyes.

"Kiki, I want to ask you some questions," Hannah said, her voice low. Hearing this, Caufield moved closer. "Did you use a knife to cut anything, any food when you were in Lisa's kitchen yesterday?"

Kiki's brow furrowed. "I don't know. Maybe. Yes, I cut some cheese."

"Was it a big knife?"

"I'm not sure. Why does it matter?"

Hannah squeezed her hand again. "Think, Kiki. What kind of knife was it? A small knife, like a paring knife? Or a big knife?"

"A big knife. Yes, that's right," she said, nodding. "I opened a kitchen drawer and it was right there, so I used it."

Hannah turned to Caufield. "The bloody knife I saw near Swanson's body could have been a kitchen knife. Half the people at Lempke's funeral turned up at his daughter's house afterward for lunch. Anyone there could have seen Kiki use the knife. And everyone in town knows the police questioned her about Lempke's murder. The killer could have stolen the knife then used it to kill Swanson, wearing gloves or something, knowing that Kiki's prints were on the handle."

Caufield turned to Kiki. "When you were through using the knife, what did you do with it?"

Kiki thought a moment. "I'd been cutting cheese. I rinsed the knife, dried it off, and put it back in the drawer.

Caufield leaned back in his chair. "I'll talk to the detective about this. It should be checked out."

There was a knock at the door. "Excuse me," said the policewoman. "We have to go now."

Kiki's gaze moved frantically to the policewoman and back to Hannah.

"Don't worry, Kiki. We'll get you out of here," Hannah said.

"I know," she answered shakily. "I didn't do anything wrong."

Hannah stroked her sister's cheek with one finger. "What do strong women do when they get knocked down?"

"They pick themselves up and keep going," Kiki said shakily. "I'll be okay, Hannah. I'm just going to think of jail as a really, really strict spa. Maybe I'll lose a few pounds."

With her flowered dress and fluffy blond hair, Kiki looked out of place in her grim surroundings. Her eyes as startled as a frightened animal, she wouldn't let go of Hannah's hand until the policewoman gently nudged her toward the door.

Before walking out, Kiki turned and, looking at Hannah with teary eyes, wiggled her fingers at her, then left.

Hannah fought back tears.

"I'll drive you back to your car," Caufield said. Hannah then felt his hand on her shoulder. "She'll be all right."

She wasn't sure she believed him. But Kiki's show of strength in the last few minutes had won her wholehearted admiration. After so many years of living in the world with men and women, Hannah suspected that while men often put on a strong front, they had a weaker core than women. Women, however delicate on the outside, seemed to have a vein of iron, the kind of strength that Kiki had just displayed. Hannah was glad of it. For the first time in her life Kiki was facing real trouble.

$\mathcal{S}$EVENTEEN

$\mathcal{B}$Y THREE THAT AFTERNOON KIKI was in the slammer. It took a good hour for the horrible reality to sink into Hannah's brain, but once it did, she catapulted into action as ferociously as a battalion charging into enemy territory, with the certainty of Kiki's innocence her shield and the phone her sword. And wield her sword she did.

By four that afternoon she was in her kitchen—command central for the Save Kiki Operation—on her kitchen phone calling Detective Morgan, the Hill Creek mayor, and the chief of police. But the enemy had bivoauced. No one was available to talk to her. She then started dialing her congressmen, but all she got was voice mail. She left everyone urgent messages that her sister had been wrongly incarcerated, with the longest one left for Detective Morgan.

"There are probably dozens of people with motives to kill Reverend Swanson. I don't mean to speak ill of the dead, but the man was slimy as squid. And there's too much money floating around that church for it to all be on the up-and-up. As for that rock he forced on people, it had to be drugged," she said to Morgan's answering machine.

"That could be what Lempke meant when he said the church was a fraud. Which gives Swanson an excellent motive for murdering Lempke and probably lots of people motives for murdering Swanson. But are you looking at that? No, you prefer to jail an innocent woman who—"

But there's a limit to what even a machine can take, and at that moment Hannah heard a scolding beep followed by an electronic voice saying she had run out of time.

Slamming down the receiver, she paced the tile floor, thirsting for a Bloody Mary more than she had in years. But herb tea would have to do, and Hannah sat at her table gulping Red Zinger while she busily outlined her plan of attack, jotting down ideas on the back of her electric bill. Step one, question Lisa Lempke about a knife missing from her kitchen. Hannah immediately called Lisa but again got an answering machine. Taking some yoga breaths so she wouldn't sound crazed, she left an urgent message for Lisa to call her.

She had just hung up from telling Lauren about Kiki's arrest and assuring her, with no substance to back it up, that everything would be fine, when there was a horrendous banging at the back door. Hannah said a quick good-bye, hung up, and rushed to see who was causing the racket.

"Great Buddha, I've heard the news," Naomi announced, pushing past Hannah into the kitchen, uninterested in an invitation. She was wearing a billowing white caftan covered with brown blotches that made her look like a dairy cow overdue for a milking. "She'll never last in jail. She didn't even do well during our bus trip last year to Reno." She eyed the teapot. "I could use some tea. I hope it's herbal."

"How do you know Kiki's in jail?" Hannah asked. "I've only told Lauren."

Naomi gave her a disbelieving look accompanied by a *tsk-tsk* sound. "Dear, you're so naive. I heard it from Bertha in the tofu section at the grocery and she heard it from Aurora at the Book Stop. Apparently Aurora's spiritual guide from last year's feng shui seminar has a cousin whose girlfriend is dating a policeman she met at a Sufi camp in Mendocino. Point is, Hannah, the word's on the street.''

Hannah turned on the burner of her aging Wolf Range, blue flames sprouting beneath the teakettle. ''Somebody framed her.''

''Unarguably, but the question is who?''

As Hannah made tea she explained about the knife and how she planned to question Lisa regarding it.

''Do you think that's wise?'' Naomi said as she sat down at the kitchen table, cup in hand.

Hannah remained standing by the stove. ''I don't know what you're getting at.''

Naomi took a strengthening swallow of Red Zinger, grimacing when she burned her tongue. ''What I'm getting at is that Lisa may have as good a motive as anyone for killing Swanson and framing Kiki for it.''

Hannah put her cup down on the countertop. ''You've lost me.''

Naomi leaned forward. ''You have to admit that Lisa could have had a motive for killing her father. They fought constantly,'' she said. ''I used to hear them when I was channeling for Mary. What if somehow Swanson found out Lisa did it and she killed him to keep him quiet?''

The idea sat in Hannah's mind at a cockeyed angle. ''But, Naomi, it's her father who was murdered. Not some lover who jilted her. Why would she kill her own father?''

Naomi raised an eyebrow. ''Happens all the time. Lizzie Borden. The Menendez brothers. Oedipus.''

Hannah took a moment to absorb this, then shook her head. ''I just don't see Lisa as a killer. She's too passive.''

Naomi pointed a ringed finger. ''That's the type with all the suppressed rage.'' She paused, then resumed speaking in a low, very serious voice. ''I think we should consult Red Moon. I can feel him in here.'' She pressed her hand against her heart. ''He needs to speak. It'll be no charge, naturally.''

Hannah took another sip of tea and contemplated her
friend with cynicism. Something was swimming in the
brackish waters of Naomi's brain. This was the third time
in a week her neighbor had pushed her psychic services on
her at no charge. It was well known that Red Moon never
spit out one ancient Hopi syllable without money crossing
his channeler's palm. Now all of a sudden he was just a-
bustin' to chat gratis. There had to be a reason.

Naomi raced home and retrieved her Hopi war stick and
the two women sat at the dining table, the room dark as a
crypt. Naomi had insisted that Hannah close all the drapes
and light the earthquake candles, giving the room an especially spooky look for late afternoon. The general pro-
cedure was the same as they had done a few days earlier,
only with just the two of them.

"What about the smudge thing? Don't you need to wave
it around the room?" Hannah asked.

"We'll have to go without it," Naomi said hurriedly.

"Am I supposed to ask Red Moon questions?"

"Only if he seems reticent."

"I could always offer him a ballpark wiener."

Naomi's mouth pinched up with irritation. "I have a
feeling he's going to talk."

Hannah had a sneaking suspicion that Red Moon was
going to sing like a canary. They sat down at the table. She
held on to Naomi's hand.

"Now close your eyes and clear your mind of everyday
thoughts. Think of a flame, a flame burning in your mind's
eye."

Both she and Hannah closed their eyes and Naomi began
to chant. Hannah had forgotten to close up the pets in the
bedroom and suddenly she was aware of Sylvia's snout
nuzzling her ankle. Naomi's chanting grew deeper, slower,
her hand squeezing Hannah's until it hurt. Then the deep,
rough voice of Red Moon filled the small room. Strange
the way she can make her voice so different, Hannah
thought.

"Earth womb gives forth grain. Thunder in the north. Coyote trembles," Red Moon said.

Here we go, Hannah complained silently. Apparently unaware of her negative attitude, the snake shaman continued. "High clouds speak to God's soil. The sky weeps tears—"

"Mr. Moon," Hannah interrupted. In a foul mood to begin with, she didn't have the patience for any shaman mumbo jumbo. "What can you tell me about the murders of Arnold Lempke and Reverend Swanson?"

There was more chanting and some pounding of the war stick, which sent Sylvia squealing into the kitchen. Hannah heard the slapping of the flap on the pet door.

"The murders?" Hannah politely reminded Red Moon of her question. Five-hundred-year-old spirits could be so forgetful.

"The earth bears wheat and wheat rots in fields," Red Moon said.

Hannah gave Naomi's hand a small jerk. "Could you please be more specific?"

"Look to God's soil. Look to God's soil," was all Red Moon would say. He repeated it several times before Naomi slumped over.

Naomi immediately asked for water, which Hannah got for her. She took a couple of big sips. "Did Red Moon give any information?" she asked in a weakened voice.

"Nothing but a few gardening tips." Hannah sat back down at the table. "Naomi, you know something about this murder, and it's time to stop hiding behind Red Moon."

Naomi's lips pursed. "I'm offended to hear you say such a thing."

"If you know something, you have to tell the police."

"I know nothing. Did Red Moon say something I should be aware of?"

"Oh, stop this Red Moon charade. This is too important."

"Charade?" Naomi stood up, her eyes throwing daggers. "I've never been more blasphemed in my life." Grabbing her war stick, she flounced out of the room without a good-bye.

"Naomi, you come back here and talk to me," Hannah demanded, but Naomi was already out the back door. As soon as she left, Sylvia and Teresa trotted in, nuzzling Hannah's legs for attention. Still sitting at the dining table, Hannah reached down and petted each one in turn, her thoughts reeling about Naomi. Her friend had some information about these murders and she had to find out what it was.

She doused the candles, opened the drapes, then called Lisa again. Crayton answered and said Lisa was working at school until five-thirty.

"Well, I'll just call back later, then," Hannah said sweetly, though she had no intention of doing so. "You know, I have a good friend who's looking for a good private school. What school do you and Lisa teach at?"

"Wesley. But enrollment's booked solid for several years," Crayton answered. Hannah thanked her then got out the phone book and looked up the address of Wesley. Within ten minutes she was in the Cadillac headed north on Highway 101.

Bright colors pelted her as she walked through the Wesley School hallway. The walls were covered with the children's art—reds, purples, pinks, and yellows in colored ink and construction paper. She glanced at each one with curiosity as she passed. Like ancient cave paintings, this art was the visual language of a world she had never known. Even after all these years she wasn't sure how she felt about being childless. She had never been the type to fawn over babies, and though sometimes she felt a pang when she came across an adorable one, she just as often felt glad she had never had them when she read in the newspaper all the problems people had with their kids, including drugs and sex when they were barely out of diapers.

These days most public schools in California were in various stages of shabbiness, but this school, being private, was well maintained, its stucco walls freshly painted, its grounds landscaped. Wesley was very exclusive, the type that upwardly mobile parents fought to get their children into. Many parents in Marin would pay anything to get their little Heather or Jason into the best schools, and Hannah had heard from others besides Crayton that there was a long waiting list for Wesley. She wondered if children were admitted strictly on a first-come-first-served basis or if there were other criteria for entrance. Maybe they took the kids out into the parking lot and saw which ones could pick out the BMWs.

Hannah walked into the school office and was amused to see a prim looking-little girl of about ten sitting behind the desk. She had long blond hair and was wearing a hand-knit sweater that probably cost more than most of Hannah's dresses. She eyed Hannah with suspicion.

"I need to find one of the teachers," Hannah said.

"Who are you?" the little girl asked, her tone snotty.

"A visitor from another solar system. I need to see an adult, please," Hannah replied, in no mood for childish antics.

The little girl just looked at her. Although her body was that of a ten-year-old, she wore the expression of a forty-year-old with a couple of ex-husbands and some nasty habits. "I think you're stupid."

Hannah raised an eyebrow. "Really? For your information, I'm here to annihilate your planet. I'm taking out the female children first."

The child shifted in her seat, swinging one leg beneath her and turning her lips inward. "You're lying."

"Do you want to take the chance?"

They locked eyes and it was a standoff until the door opened and a woman in a suit walked in.

"Off my chair, Sandra. I told you to wait for your mother in there." The woman pointed to a side office. Sandra pouted but made a quick exit, looking glad for the excuse.

Hannah asked the woman where she could find Lisa Lempke and was directed down the hallway to the library.

It was a large open room with book-crammed shelves lining all four walls and more shelves lined up at right angles. Above the shelves the walls were painted different colors and held brightly hued letters about a foot high that spelled READING IS THE DOOR TO IMAGINATION.

Just being there made Hannah smile, it was so cheerful. It smelled of dust and paste, reminding her of her own days in grammar school. She could still remember the smell and the taste of the thick white paste that came in those little glass jars. She used to eat it when she was eight years old, and for the moment it didn't seem so long ago.

The sound of a woman talking followed by children's laughter drew her farther into the room. Peering around a bank of shelves, she saw Lisa standing by a table covered with large picture books. A group of about ten children sat cross-legged on the floor in front of her, their faces rapt.

For the first time Lisa seemed relaxed and comfortable. With these children sitting at her feet, she was in her element, her gestures animated, her eyes joyful as she read to them from a shiny-covered book, using a squeaky voice for one of the characters, a gruff tone for another. She certainly didn't look or sound like a killer.

Just as the children broke out into laughter Lisa looked up, her face registering concern when she caught sight of Hannah. After saying something to the kids, she walked over.

"I'm sorry to bother you when you're working. I need to talk to you. It's urgent," Hannah said.

Lisa seemed to weigh her options before answering. "Okay. Wait over there." She pointed to some chairs near the bookshelves.

Hannah took a seat, folding her hands on top of her purse, drumming her fingers against the leather. She wasn't in the mood for waiting. She was in the mood for taking action, for asking questions and getting answers, for grabbing someone by the scruff of the neck if necessary and wringing the truth out of them. But she reasoned that Lisa had her job to do, and she was, after all, interrupting. Five minutes later Lisa came back.

"Lisa, I need to ask you about whether or not you're missing a—"

"A kitchen knife," Lisa said wearily. "I know all about it. The police already called me and I told them I wasn't missing any knives."

Hannah's heart sank. "You're sure?"

"I'm sure."

"But if you haven't gone home to look, how can you be certain?"

"Because I would have noticed it when I cleaned up after the lunch. I *would* have noticed."

This was the moment when Hannah was supposed to thank her politely for her trouble, wish her a lovely day, and walk out the door. But she couldn't do it. She just stood there, her eyes locked on Lisa's. Lisa fiddled with the top button of her blouse, her expression strained, quite different than she had been only a few moments before.

"You act like you don't believe me," she said. "If it will make you feel better, I'll look tonight to make sure, but I have to tell you that I don't like having my veracity questioned."

"I'm questioning everything right now. I'm ashamed to say that I'm even questioning my friends."

"That must be sad for you."

All softness was gone. Lisa sounded cold, imperious, and quite like Arnold, Hannah thought.

"Someone ruthlessly killed your father, Lisa, and very likely the murderer is someone I know," Hannah said. "Someone I may have passed in the grocery store or said hello to in the plaza. This person is not only a murderer but is trying to make people believe my sister is one."

Lisa ran her hand through her blond hair. "You don't think I realize all that?" she said loudly, then stopped, glancing worriedly at the children. She lowered her voice.

"That I'm thinking the same things? But I won't be accused."

"I haven't accused you of anything."

She let out a small, cheerless laugh. "You've been accusing me since the first day you walked into my house pretending to be grieved over my father." Lisa looked at her with venom. "I think that in a weird way this is fun for you. A little excitement for a woman with nothing much to do. I want you to leave. Now. Or I'll call security and have you removed."

EIGHTEEN

WITH THE NIGHT CAME DARK images that scratched inside Hannah's brain, rodents scratching unseen in an attic. That evening, all alone in the house, as she performed the most ordinary tasks—when she changed her clothes, prepared her dinner—she wondered what Kiki was doing, what she was thinking and feeling during her horrendous first night in jail. She did her best not to dwell on it, for what good would that do? But it occupied her mind so completely she might as well have been in jail with her. And in fact she wished she was.

Late that afternoon Hannah had gone to the Hill Creek police station to see her sister, only to learn that she had been transferred to the Marin County jail. Hannah rushed over, but by the time she fought through the commute traffic, visiting hours were over. Desperate over Kiki's predicament, she felt powerless to help her. Again and again, she went over in her mind all the events related to the murder, but she came up with nothing useful.

That evening, sitting at her kitchen table, she toyed with her microwaved dinner while she narrowed the list of suspects for Lempke's murder down to four people—Lisa, Shirley, Swanson, and, unfortunately, Perez. All had motives and none of them really had an alibi as far as she knew. Even if they did, alibis could be concocted.

Other than this, she had little to go on, and she had even less for Swanson's murderer. The only bright light was that the killer had made one mistake. Hannah felt certain that whoever had framed Kiki for Swanson's murder had to have stolen the knife Kiki had used at Lisa's, and by doing so, he or she had identified themselves as someone who had attended Lisa's lunch after the funeral.

After dinner Hannah rambled around her small house straightening up the clutter, scrubbing the bathroom sink, organizing plant catalogs, anything to keep herself occupied. She attempted a crossword puzzle but couldn't keep her mind focused. She tried television but nothing interested her.

Not only was she worried about Kiki. She missed her. They hadn't spent an entire night apart in so long. Hannah hadn't realized how much her sister's constant chatter and absurd scheming livened up her evenings. All alone and filled with worry, she felt tired and old for the first time in her life. She was famous around town for her boundless energy. Now suddenly she felt drained. Was this what it was like to be elderly?

During the few moments when her focus shifted from her sister, she was mulling over Lisa Lempke's accusation that she was using the murders to provide excitement in her life. But it was natural that she would want to help her sister, and she had always been a proactive person. On the other hand, it was true that she had felt a void since her retirement. Perhaps her useful life was behind her.

Feeling sorry for herself, she headed for the small laundry room next to the kitchen and began sorting through the basket of dirty clothes, taking out the lingerie and blouses that needed hand washing, but Lisa's last words stayed with her as she performed her tasks.

There was a theory that Hannah cogitated upon in her darker moments. According to it, after a woman passes her mid-forties and the end of her childbearing years, society considers her expendable. The world viewed women like herself, who never had children in the first place, with a special brand of polite disregard, Hannah thought as she pulled out three of the imitation silk nighties Kiki had bought from Victoria's Secret.

Once the laundry was done, she decided to go to bed early and distract herself with a spicy novel she had found on Kiki's nightstand, and she was in her bedroom finishing buttoning up her flannel pajamas when she heard a sound in the backyard—a distinct rustling of bushes, the chilling sound of something unfamiliar brushing against the side of the house.

Both Sylvia and Teresa lay asleep in their beds near the door, unaware of any noises. Maybe Hannah had only imagined the sound, but then, neither Sylvia nor Teresa was the greatest watchdog.

She had lived in the house for over fifteen years. She knew every creak in its old wood frame, every natural rustle in the garden. The hairs stood up on her arm, her personal radar telling her that something was definitely wrong. If she hadn't seen two murder victims in the past week, maybe her breath wouldn't have stopped, her hands wouldn't have clenched so tightly that her fingernails dug into her palms. But death had recently come too close. She stood frozen.

"Get your wits about you," she said out loud. At the sound of her voice, both pets awakened, but she commanded them to stay in their beds. She walked into the kitchen and dialed 911, told the dispatcher she had a prowler. Next she went into her bedroom and pulled a baseball bat out from under the bed.

Holding her breath, she moved into the living room, heart pounding, bat raised over her shoulder. She stopped. Gravel crunched outside. Lowering her bat, she exhaled with relief. It sounded like a dog's feet.

Chuckling at herself, she opened the front door. It was probably Oscar, the Epsteins' Labrador, digging up her tomatoes. Taking the bat so she could shake it threateningly at the dog, although he knew quite well she would never consider using it, she walked barefoot out onto the porch, then down the steps into the garden. The porch light had burned out the previous week. With everything going on she had forgotten to replace it, and the front garden was lit only by the moon, the shrubbery and Japanese maple casting black shadows on the lawn.

"Oscar?" she called out as she made her way around the corner of the house toward the vegetable patch, the gravel cold and rough beneath her feet. She wished she had thought to put on her shoes. "If you're in my tomatoes—" But she didn't finish the sentence.

She felt a presence behind her. Her skin prickled with fear. She raised the bat, spinning around and emitting a karate yell she had learned in self-defense class.

"Whoa!" said a deep voice in the darkness as a hand grabbed the top of the bat. She found herself facing John Perez.

"What the hell are you doing?" he said angrily, grabbing the bat out of her hand.

Flustered, Hannah fumbled for words. "I thought there was a dog—"

"And you were going to hit a dog with this?" He sounded more unhappy at that prospect than of her bashing him. Winston, his instincts apparently assuring him how harmless Hannah really was, whimpered happily at seeing her.

"No, of course not. At first I thought there was an intruder, so—"

"There *was* an intruder," he said, interrupting. "As I walked up I saw someone coming up from the back of the house. I ran after him." He paused. "I should say I tried to run after him. With my bad knee I didn't get very far.''

Winston gave another friendly whine. Perez released enough of the leash so the dog could lick Hannah's hand.

Hannah knelt down to stroke the spaniel's head, using the time to collect herself.

''I like your outfit,'' Perez said, his irritation subsiding. With embarrassment, Hannah remembered she was in her pajamas, but there wasn't much she could do about it. After Winston seemed satisfied that she adored him, she drew herself up with as much dignity as she could manage in pajamas and bare feet.

''You'll have to pardon my clothing, but I thought I was coming out to see a dog. Now, what are you doing in my yard?''

Perez took a breath, inflated his cheeks, then let out the air. ''I want to talk to you. It's important.'' He paused, waiting for her reaction, but didn't get one immediately. ''Can we sit somewhere?''

She hesitated, then nodded. They were headed toward the porch when she heard tires. Blinking red-and-yellow lights bounced off the house.

''The police,'' Hannah said, startled. ''I forgot that I called them.''

She and Perez hurried to the curb and explained to the two officers what had happened. Perez told them he hadn't seen enough of the prowler to give a description. While they were talking Naomi ran over in her bathrobe to see what was happening, but Hannah quickly sent her home without telling her much, irking her to no end. After agreeing to cruise the neighborhood, the police drove off.

Once they were gone, Hannah went inside and put on her raincoat, then she and Perez sat in the two grapevine chairs on the porch, with Winston settled near their feet. Without the light, the porch was dark, but there was enough moonlight so Hannah could see Perez's face.

He opened his mouth to speak, but Hannah beat him to it.

"My sister's in jail," she said.

"I heard. I'm sorry." He sounded like he meant it.

"John, you know what's going on with the investigation. The police talk to you. Tell me what's happening."

"I don't know that much, Hannah."

"You know more than I do."

He had been looking straight ahead at the garden, and when he turned and saw the worry on her face, his expression softened.

"Okay, I'll tell you what little I know. They did a test on that rock used by Swanson."

Hannah let out a small gasp of excitement. "How did they get it?"

"The secretary turned it over when Larry Morgan asked for it. The test was negative. There's nothing on that rock except traces of dog urine. It must have come from someone's yard."

Hannah's hopes took a nosedive. "I find that hard to believe."

Turning in his chair, he leaned closer. "Hannah, listen to me. You're the one who pressed the police about testing that rock. You've been asking Swanson's secretary lots of questions. She told Larry—I mean Detective Morgan—about it. And Lisa Lempke called and complained about you."

"You think I care if I've ruffled a few feathers? I'm trying to help my sister."

"It's not ruffled feathers I'm worried about. Two people have been murdered. Your snooping around could get you more than you're bargaining for."

The remark astonished her at first, but she quickly grasped the truth of it. Digging around this murder investigation could indeed be dangerous, although she hadn't really considered this until now. Was snooping what had gotten Swanson murdered?

Hannah rubbed her arms, suddenly feeling chilly.

"You need a coat?" Perez offered, starting to remove his wool jacket.

"No, thank you. Listen, I appreciate what you've told me. I know you're trying to be a friend."

"That's where you're wrong."

"Excuse me?"

He raised his finger as if to make an emphatic point, but then lowered it and sighed. "Hannah, I don't want to be your friend. I mean, I want to be more than that." He paused, looking down and chuckling at himself. He returned his eyes to her. "Don't look at me like you don't know what I'm talking about. You like me. I can tell."

"How? I've half accused you of being a murderer. I just tried to hit you with a baseball bat."

Perez grinned. "See what strong emotions I arouse in you?"

They sat quietly a few seconds, Hannah too flustered to speak. Perez broke the silence. "I looked through a couple of back issues of the *Marin Sun* and found one of your poems."

Hannah laughed, feeling self-conscious. "I don't know if I believe you. No one reads my poems. They just say they do."

With a sly smile he closed his eyes and began to speak, the sound low and soft. " 'We built a house where no one lives, hearts full, eyes hollow.' "

Her breath caught in her throat. It was one of her poems from months back. It amazed her that he had found it. He continued.

" 'Angrily we walk from room to room, the space empty, windows shut tight.' "

Hannah watched him as he repeated the stanzas she had written. He didn't miss a word. His recitation made her feel oddly embarrassed. No one had quoted one of her poems to her before, certainly no man. She found herself deeply moved by it, but at the same time it made her feel inexplicably uneasy. Sitting there in the dark with him as he recited her poetry felt so intimate, as if he were physically touching her. Part of her wanted to kiss him, the other part wanted to run into the house and not ever come back out again.

Perez finished the last line. " 'We speak of leaving, but never leave, preferring to imagine a life in this house where no one lives.' "

When he was done she just looked at him dumbly. Having heard her own words come back at her so unexpectedly, she couldn't think of any to say herself.

"What was that poem about?" he finally asked.

"An old relationship."

"Your husband?"

"No. Does it matter?"

He smiled. "No." He kicked at an invisible object on the porch. Winston raised his head expectantly, then laid it back down. "Could we try dinner?"

Hannah's eyes darted toward him, then away again. "I, well, you see . . ." She stumbled on the words.

"See what, Hannah?"

"I don't go out anymore," she said hurriedly.

"Why not? I've asked around. Your husband died a long time ago."

"It has nothing to do with that."

"Then what does it have to do with?"

"Do you have to push me for information? Can't you just take a simple no?" she said with frustration.

"Number one, you haven't actually said no. Number two, you're the last person on earth to criticize anyone for being pushy about asking questions."

Closing her eyes a second, she smiled inwardly, amused at herself, but the humor quickly died away. "Okay, I don't normally tell this to people, but here it is. I had cancer eight years ago. I had a double mastectomy. There. Happy now?"

He waited a few beats. "That's it?"

"That's it."

That said, Hannah's eyes fixed on the outlines of her rose bushes, their foliage gray and muted in the garden's darkness. She had revealed herself to this man who wasn't much more than an acquaintance, and she immediately regretted it. It wasn't that she was ashamed of her mastectomy. There was no reason to be, and she hadn't kept the surgery a secret. She spoke about it weekly with other female cancer patients at the center where she volunteered. But in those conversations there was always a part of her that remained private. She had so many feelings about her sadly altered body that she didn't reveal to others, not even to Kiki or Lauren or any of her friends. She kept the feelings secret, stored them in a box hidden away in her heart. And bringing up her surgery with a man, especially a man she found so attractive, frightened her.

She was about to say good night and go in the house when she felt his fingers close around her hand. Her breath stopped. His skin felt warm, his touch reassuring.

"My wife, Nancy, died twelve years ago from breast cancer. She had both breasts removed. It didn't matter. I just wanted her to live." His fingers increased their pressure. Hannah released her breath, her heart thumping, her feelings chaotic. She couldn't look at him. "I promise you, Hannah, my wife's surgery never made her less attractive to me."

Her eyes started to fill. "I have to go in," she said quickly, then stood up.

Perez stood with her, Winston hopping upward to his side. "Fine." He looked dejected. He turned to go down the steps, but halfway down, he stopped and faced her. "One more thing. You need to stop interfering in this murder case. That's what I came to tell you. That you should stop. You're dealing with murderers. That's a dangerous thing to do."

Hannah watched Perez as he walked through the garden

and pushed open the gate, the old hinges creaking a farewell into the cool night. And when he was gone, she went into her bedroom, turned off the lights, and allowed herself the luxury of crying.

NINETEEN

SHE SLEPT LIKE HELL, TOSSING and turning in an agitated stupor. And waking up wasn't an improvement.

When Hannah opened her eyes to greet the dawn, she found herself smacked with all the symptoms of a hangover—head pounding, body aching, her mouth so dry she felt like she had been licking ashtrays. But it was only an overdose of emotion that plagued her, a fizzy cocktail of anxiety, anger, and confusion. To make it worse, she had an ominous feeling that not only had it been a rotten night, it was going to be a rotten day. She just didn't realize at the time how rotten.

After rolling out of bed with a curse and a groan, she drank coffee, showered, then called the Marin County jail. They told her she could visit Kiki between two and three that afternoon.

Feeling better at the thought of seeing her sister, Hannah dressed and went to retrieve the three newspapers she received every day. She opened the front door, shivering at the dense fog blanketing the neighborhood, a typical occurrence in the summer.

Naomi was in her front yard, dressed in a loose cotton tunic and pants, her knees deeply bent, her arms slowly but dramatically sweeping. She always performed her tai chi exercises in her front yard where everyone could see her, a sort of living psychic advertisement to the neighbors, some of whom were among her best clients. She swore up and down to all of them that she went into a deep trance during her tai chi regimen, a mystical oblivion that rendered her incapable of seeing or hearing anything except for a purple light that supposedly buzzed above one of her chakras.

Hannah watched from the doorway as her neighbor moved into a mantis pose, balancing precariously on one foot, her other leg hoisted high and bent at the knee, her arms lifted and bent at the wrists and elbows. She had always marveled at Naomi's flexibility and balance, especially for a woman her age, but at that moment she couldn't help but notice Naomi wobbling. She suspected that Naomi had heard the front door open, the hinges being so squeaky, and knew her friend well enough to be certain that she was dying to find out what had happened the night before with Perez and the police.

The corners of Hannah's mouth turned up in wicked pleasure as Naomi completely lost her equilibrium, having to hop on one foot in order to remain upright as every pore in her body lusted to race over to Hannah and get the juicy news. But if she broke the pose, she probably knew it would give Hannah the satisfaction of confirming her vocalized doubts about her alleged tai chi trances and could potentially hurt business if any of the neighbors saw.

Hannah spotted the newspapers scattered by the front gate, but when she stepped out the door, her foot hit a small cardboard box. She bent down, picked it up, and found her name printed in large letters on the lid.

Holding the box to her ear, she gave it a little shake. Something rolled around inside. Lifting the lid, she gasped in horror, everything inside her contracting with revulsion.

Lying on a bed of cotton was a severed finger.

Detective Morgan made a heartfelt *ugh* when he saw the whitish, somewhat shriveled amputated digit. That display of emotion seemed unpolicemanlike to Hannah, which made her like him better.

"I've heard of giving someone the finger," his coworker officer Mike Angeletti said with a chuckle. Angeletti was a large burly man with thick black hair that needed combing and perspiration sprouting from his forehead. Morgan gave him an admonishing look followed by a glance at Hannah, who was sitting in a chair sipping the cup of tea Morgan had made for her.

"It's all right," she said. "The bad jokes have already started occurring to me."

"Feeling better now?" Morgan asked. "Need a second round on that tea?"

"I'm fine," she replied with a dim smile, the only kind she could currently manage. When she walked into the police station, the box in her hand, she had been badly shaken. Morgan had been kind to her during the inevitable questioning, but it hadn't calmed her much, especially when she had to tell him that Perez had been walking around her house the night before. She explained that Perez claimed to have seen a prowler, but she had no proof that the prowler had been anyone but himself. Detective Morgan hadn't liked the idea any more than she did.

Hannah put her empty mug on the floor next to her chair. "Whoever left that box on my porch has to be the killer. You realize that the finger is Swanson's?"

Sitting on the edge of a wooden desk, Morgan crossed his arms. "Naturally that's our first guess, but why are you so sure?"

"She's already fingered the culprit," Angeletti muttered.

Morgan shot him a look. "Go find something to do."

Angeletti shrugged and left the room, closing the door behind him.

"I recognized the ring," Hannah said to Morgan as soon as they were alone. "It belonged to Swanson."

"Fingerprints will confirm it."

"The point is that Swanson's killer had to have left that finger on my front porch, which means the killer couldn't have been my sister. She was in jail last night."

Morgan nodded. "I've thought of that. But why would the killer leave the finger, knowing that it would take suspicion away from her?"

Hannah paused before answering. "Maybe the killer has decided that frightening me off my investigation is more important."

Morgan stood up. "No offense, but I don't see where you've gotten enough information to frighten anyone."

"Unless I've gotten it and just don't realize it." Hannah turned up her palms. "So? When does my sister get out of jail?"

"She doesn't. Her fingerprints are still on that knife," Morgan answered, looking sorry to be saying it.

Hannah left the station as frustrated as when she entered, although she was feeling somewhat calmer now that she had gotten rid of the horrible finger.

When she stepped outside, the fog still hadn't lifted. Normally she liked the fog, feeling that at her age she could use the moisture, but that day it seemed suffocating. Using the pay phone at the corner, she called Caufield and told him about the new development, and he said he would use the information to try to get Kiki out on bail. Hannah then checked her voice mail, finding a message from Shirley asking her to stop by the church. Curious about what the woman could want, she got in the Cadillac, the car sputtering and jerking as she pulled out of the police station parking lot. Her first thought was that it needed a tune-up, but then she decided maybe the old car simply missed Kiki as much as she did.

Fifteen minutes later Hannah grabbed the doorknob of the Church of Revelations office and gave it a twist, but the door was locked. She pulled, pushed, and jiggled, but it remained immovable. Finally she knocked, and within seconds it opened. There stood Shirley looking as if a small tornado had swept her up, tossed her about, then set her back down again. Her hair was mussed and her blouse misbuttoned and pulled halfway out of her shirt.

"Sorry," she said hastily, quickly focusing on a security keypad on the wall near the door, making little inhalations of distress as she punched in numbers. "Pull the door shut for me, would you please? Otherwise it takes forever to close. It's on a stupid spring."

"What are you doing?" Hannah asked, closing the door.

"I've got ten seconds to put in the security code, otherwise the alarm goes off," she said, her tone agitated. "With the reverend being killed and all, I don't feel safe, even though everyone at the door is just bringing flowers." After pressing four numbers, Shirley stared at the keypad. When no alarm blasted she sighed with relief and turned to Hannah.

"I noticed a keypad outside as well," Hannah said. "Why two of them?"

"Well, that one on the outside opens the door. Very high technology. You see, you don't need a key. The one on the inside is the burglar alarm." She frowned. "It's so complicated. They're supposed to have different combinations but I told the reverend—" She closed her eyes for a second, then continued. "I told the reverend that I could hardly remember one code, much less two. After I set off the alarm a few times and made the neighbors hopping mad, he had it changed to just the one, which works both for outside and in."

"It was nice that he did that," Hannah said, trying to say something pleasant about the man, feeling guilty for calling him "slimy as a squid" the day before.

A pained smile spread across Shirley's face. "He wasn't

an especially nice man, even though he was a reverend and all.''

Hannah followed her back into the church office. Swanson's death must have weighed heavily on Shirley, she decided, because she walked sluggishly, her shoulders slightly stooped. Perhaps she was worried about her job. She might even miss him.

Shirley sat down at her desk. "Want some coffee? I'm having some." She pointed to a cup in front of her. Hannah's no made her brow furrow. "You sure? You could use some perking up. You look terrible."

"No offense, but you don't look much better."

The two women smiled. "I guess it's been rough for both of us," Shirley said. "Thanks for coming by. I can't leave the office, not with so many people calling."

Hannah sat down in the chair across from the desk. "I don't have much time, because I need to see Kiki."

"That's what I want to talk to you about. I know all about Kiki being arrested."

"Kiki didn't do anything. She's completely innocent."

Shirley leaned forward eagerly. "She doesn't seem like she could do a thing like that. So sweet," she said, unaware of all the nasty things Kiki had said about her. "That's why I think I should tell you something."

Hannah sat up, attentive as a terrier. "What?"

Shirley took a strengthening breath. "I heard Lisa and Reverend Swanson have an argument."

"When?"

"The day before he was killed. They were in his office. I wasn't prying, mind you. I could just hear it, they were so loud."

"What did they say?" Hannah asked, trying to maintain her composure when her stomach was filling with butterflies.

"I couldn't hear the words. I could just tell that Lisa's voice was angry. But I knew something was going on between them, because a few days before that Lisa started acting funny."

"Funny in what way?"

Shirley's eyes narrowed in concentration. "Tense sort of, all worked up about something."

"But her father had just been murdered."

"This was different. Right after her father was killed Lisa was more attached than ever to the reverend. Then all of a sudden her attitude changed."

"How?"

Shirley hesitated before answering. "Like she didn't like him anymore."

Hannah let the information settle in a moment, then leaned toward the desk, resting her fingers on its edge. "You have to tell this to the police. It could help my sister."

"I can't." Shirley leaned backward, increasing the distance between them. "I don't want to be the one to get Lisa in trouble. That's why I asked you over. I thought maybe you could tell the police."

"I'd have to tell them where I got the information, then they'd come to you anyway."

Shirley frowned. She obviously hadn't thought about that. "What about calling in an anonymous tip?"

"No. You have to call them and tell them what you know. It's the right thing to do."

Shirley bit her thumbnail as she batted about the moral issues. "I just don't want to get involved. I mean, I like Lisa. I feel so sorry for her." She paused. "But I guess you're right. Okay, I'll do it after work." She said it with resignation, staring down at the desktop like a child forced to go to the principal's office and tattle on a friend.

"Do it now," Hannah said forcefully.

"No, I have to wait. I've got so many calls coming in." She looked at Hannah. "Okay. I'll do it this morning, I promise."

"There are other things we need the truth about, Shirley."

"Like what?"

"We need to take a closer look at the church's corporate contributors. There could be information there that could help the police catch Swanson's murderer."

"But the police haven't asked to do that."

"But they should. We can help them along, just like you're helping by telling them about the argument you heard between Lisa and Swanson."

Shirley's eyes suddenly turned sharp and her cheeks flushed. "Don't push me. I'm just—" She was so befuddled she knocked over the coffee in front of her, the brown rivulets flowing into her lap. "Dammit!"

Hannah jumped out of her chair. "Let me help you."

Shirley waved her away. "No. I've just got to wash this off my skirt." Just then the front doorbell rang. "Darn. Probably more flowers. Hannah, could you see who it is? Just punch three-two-four-two into the security system if you need to let them in." She turned and headed for the ladies' room, leaving Hannah behind.

Hannah went to the front door, looked through the peephole, and saw a man holding a basket of white gladiolas. She opened the door, heard an ominous beeping sound, and hurriedly pressed the numbers into the security keypad, her mind racing as the deliveryman entered and proceeded to place the basket on a credenza.

If Shirley wouldn't get her a list of the church's corporate contributors, she would get it herself, and now she knew how she would do it.

Kiki's bleached hair lay limp against her scalp, a once-cheery balloon deflated, a soufflé gone despairingly flat. The previous day's eye makeup was smudged around her eyelids giving her the look of a depressed raccoon, and her faded blue, jail-issued jumpsuit hung off her shoulders as if it, too, were gloomy under the weight of penal servitude.

Only one visitor was allowed at a time, so Hannah had let Lauren go in first. Now it was her turn and she was surprised to find her sister sitting behind a glass and Formica booth, only able to communicate through a telephone. Hannah reached for the phone, but her hand stopped in midair. The phone was green and greasy, the mouthpiece encrusted with something she dared not identify. Quickly she took a cloth handkerchief out of her purse and placed it in her hand before picking up the handset.

"How are you doing, sweetie?" She used this term only under the most dire of circumstances.

Kiki forced a smile. "Oh, okay. The food here's awful, which is a plus. I think I've lost a pound."

"You have to be strong."

Kiki's smile dimmed a second, but she put it back on again. "When I start to get upset, I just close my eyes and pretend I'm in a really cut-rate room at Rancho La Puerta. Only I can't leave. And of course there's no gift shop."

"It won't be for long."

"I guess Fortuna swished her skirts good and hard this time, didn't she, Hannah?"

Fortuna was doing the cancan, Hannah thought. "Are they treating you okay? Is anyone—" She paused. "Is anyone being abusive toward you?"

Kiki wrinkled her brow. "Heavens no. All the guards went to sensitivity training week before last. You can be more abused at Macy's than around here. At least that's what Chantal says."

"Chantal?"

"My roomie," Kiki said with a glimmer of a smile. "She's really nice once you get past the external things. She's going to fix my hair for me tomorrow." She paused. "Hopefully I won't be here tomorrow." She gripped the edge of the countertop and anxiously leaned forward. "Tell me I won't be here tomorrow," she said, her eyes turning pink around the rims, tears beginning to well. The very sight of her in this condition broke Hannah's heart.

"I promise I'm doing my best, sweetie. Listen, we only have ten minutes and I've got to make them count if I'm going to get you out of here. Kiki, have you done any thinking? Have you thought of anything about Lempke, about why someone would want to kill him, any idea that could help me figure this thing out?"

Kiki sniffled. "Of course I've thought about it. I've thought about it so much my head's about to bust, but there's nothing except what we already know about him hating the church. He was a good man. I don't care what anybody says about him. How many men would nurse their wives at home the way he did? He was a saint."

She started crying now, each tear cutting into Hannah's heart.

"I'll get you out of here, Kiki. Louis Caufield is working on bail. There's already another suspect for Swanson's murder."

Kiki stopped in mid-sniffle. "Who is it?"

"I'll tell you more tomorrow." Hannah didn't want to let on that she didn't even have a name for this suspect. Besides, the fact that a severed finger had wound up on their front porch might propel Kiki into a state even "sweetie" usage couldn't calm.

"Thank you, Hannah," Kiki said softly, reaching out her index finger and pressing it affectionately against the streaked and grimy glass. "I appreciate so much your trying to help. I'm sure something good's going to come from this. Chantal thinks something will."

"Kiki, what is Chantal in jail for? What did she do?"

"She didn't do anything," Kiki replied, suddenly more animated. "She's a spiritual healer. It was the most unfair thing. She was working with this poor man who had pulled a groin muscle. He was in such pain. And the next thing Chantal knew the police burst in, accusing her of horrible things."

Hannah's eyes widened. Kiki had enough problems

keeping her hands off men without getting chummy with prostitutes.

"You'll get me out of here, right, Hannah?" Kiki's voice, rose to a babyish pitch.

"Yes, of course I will." Just then the guard told her she had to leave. Hannah rose from her chair, the phone still in her hand. "And Kiki, dear, don't get too close to Chantal. These prison friendships probably don't last."

"We hope," she muttered as she left.

TWENTY

THERE ARE THINGS IN LIFE you know you shouldn't do, yet you do them anyway. Though every brain cell shouts out the ludicrousness, the sheer insanity of what you're contemplating, the heart propels the body forward, disregarding the consequences.

And that night at midnight, as Hannah slipped out her back door into the chilling air to embark upon her mission of breaking into the Church of Revelations, as she tiptoed to her car in the driveway and unlocked it, a dozen internal voices commanded her to cease this rash behavior, but she happily managed to ignore every one of them.

With her sister still in jail, she had decided it was high time for the Save Kiki Operation to get more aggressive, and she felt certain there was something suspicious about Swanson's list of contributors. Why else would Shirley be so hesitant about releasing it? And if that wacko church was engaged in some type of fraud, it would be an excellent motive for murder. If Lempke had discovered it, perhaps Swanson killed him to keep it quiet. Then someone found out what Swanson had done, killing him to eliminate the possibility of the truth ever coming out. Perhaps a contributor had killed Swanson, Hannah thought. The image of Walter Backus floated through her mind, but she immediately erased it. Impossible. The point was, no one would know the answer until the entire list of church contributors could be reviewed, and the police were being too lackadaisical about getting it. Someone had to secure that list before it could be destroyed, if it hadn't been already.

To create a "stealth" fashion ensemble, Hannah wore black slacks, a black sweater, and red tennis shoes. The red shoes seemed flashy, but her only other pair of tennis shoes were white and those would show up in the dark.

As she opened the car door she froze. A small thud came from the around the back of the house. She stood perfectly still, listening. "Nerves," she muttered to herself.

All was serene in Hannah's neighborhood at midnight. She could hear nothing but the lonely chirping of a bird and the low thunder of cars on the distant freeway. As quietly as possible she slid into the driver's seat, not daring to close the car door for fear of making noise. The previous evening she had parked the Cadillac on the peak of her driveway's gentle slope. She couldn't risk starting the engine and waking up Naomi, who was a light sleeper. Her neighbor would open her bedroom window in a shot and want to know where Hannah was going and what she was doing.

Now Hannah released the emergency brake and allowed the car to roll into the street. As she closed the car door her heart soared, the initial phase of her plan proceeding perfectly.

Later, from a freeway overpass, she saw San Francisco in the distance, the city's lights turning the blanket of mist to a glowing amber. A stream of cars whizzed past her and she was amazed at how many people were still on the roads after midnight. She had forgotten that a world existed after eleven, though it wasn't all that long ago that at this hour she had been carousing the city with friends or nursing a

drink in some café. Being out late like this made her feel
so much younger. And although she tried to maintain a
serious attitude, she couldn't help but feel a thrill of excitement. Here she was, out on a midnight adventure.

She parked a block from the church and walked the rest
of the way, her pulse increasing with each risky step. A
foggy haze had settled in the air, and shivering in the cold,
Hannah quickened her step, her tennis shoes padding
soundlessly against the cracked sidewalk. She heard a car.
Headlights turned the corner, sending her dashing into an
alley. When the car passed she returned to the sidewalk,
not certain why she had hidden in the first place. But the
fact that she had hidden at all sent a current of titillation
through her.

As she reached the church's front door, looking right
then left, she took a deep breath for courage, then entered
the code three-two-four-two into the outside keypad. She
heard a couple of beeps followed by the sound of the door
clicking open. Bingo.

Exhilaration swept through her as she entered the church
office. Breaking and entering was surprisingly easy if you
did your homework, and as far as lifting one's spirits was
concerned, it was better than a double dose of estrogen. It
reminded her of her days in San Francisco in the sixties,
flaunting authority, feeling free to do exactly as you pleased
whenever you felt like it. At that memory of freedom Hannah bumped into something sharp. Rubbing her hip, she
muttered a curse.

Maneuvering through unfamiliar rooms through pitch
darkness was proving more difficult than she had anticipated, and she stopped and spelunked through her handbag.
In case of an earthquake and an electrical failure, she kept
a matchbook-sized flashlight on her key chain. Held out in
front of her, its silver beam sliced through the blackness,
falling pale and narrow on the dark carpet. With the light
to guide her, she headed straight for Shirley's desk.

Sitting down in the chair, she switched on the computer.

It hummed to life, the screen's vivid blue light bursting into the dark room and casting an icy glow on her face. Her objective was to get a complete list of contributors. She flexed her fingers and poised them over the keyboard, tension building with each second. But her hopes were dashed by the screen rudely demanding a password.

"Poop," Hannah muttered. If she knew Shirley better, she could have guessed her password—her birthday, a child's name, a pet's name. But the woman's life was largely a mystery. The letdown, however, was only momentary. Not to be daunted, Hannah opened the top desk drawer to look for a notebook that might contain the password. Shirley seemed the nervous type who would write the password down in case she forgot it.

The top drawer proved fruitless, but when she opened a side drawer, she found something more interesting. Reaching in with a single finger, she pushed a scarf away from a baseball-sized rock she recognized as the Weeping Stone. Her pulse quickened. Maybe Shirley had purposely given the police a bogus stone, one that hadn't been treated with drugs. Why else wrap this one in a cloth and conceal it?

After pushing the scarf back around the stone, she placed a piece a paper over the whole thing, gingerly lifted it, and stuffed it in her purse. Her handbag was now quite heavy, so she braced it underneath with her arm, affectionately patting the leather. She had discovered a prize. Not the one she was looking for, but a prize nonetheless. It was then that she noticed a plastic case on the desk that held computer disks. How could she have been so stupid? If Shirley had a brain at all, she would certainly keep a backup of the contributor list. Hannah flipped through it, found a disk labeled DONATIONS, and slipped it in her pocket. All in all a wonderful night.

She found herself feeling rather giddy. In fact, she felt so good about things, she would have whistled if she hadn't been committing what was probably a felony. After a quick check to make sure she left everything the way she had found it, *sans* stone and diskette, she walked quietly out of the office toward the front door.

Her hand was on the doorknob when something solid hit her. The blow fell hard on her left shoulder. A flash of pain and astonishment cut through her as she fell to her knees. Then she felt legs pressing against her back. Her head cleared enough for her to realize another blow was imminent. She pushed backward sharply, sending her attacker sprawling.

For a second there seemed to be a dozen arms and legs on top of her. She felt the person scrambling up, and instinctively kicked hard with her left foot. It was too dark and she was too frantic to aim at anything, but she felt her foot land squarely on something firm. She heard a groan followed by a plop against the floor.

It was at that precise moment that something in the situation changed. Hannah sensed the anger rising in this anonymous human sitting only a couple of feet from her. She could hear rapid breathing. A hand grabbed her throat. She tried to cry out but managed only a choking sound. Strong fingers pressed against her windpipe, cutting off her air. In desperation, she grabbed her purse strap and swung it upward. Normally her handbag wasn't heavy enough to hurt anyone, but tonight it had a rock in it. Her strength surprised her. Adrenaline combined with muscles strong from years of heavy gardening sent the purse hurling. It landed solidly. She heard another groan as her attacker reeled backward. Finally free, she scrambled up, lunged for the door and escaped outside.

She didn't stop running until she reached her car. Gasping for air, fumbling with the keys, she finally inserted the right one in the car door, opened it, and threw herself inside. She slammed the door shut, started the engine, and roared off in the Cadillac with a screech of tires.

Hannah wasn't sure who looked worse, she or Detective Morgan. Despite an apparent application of water, his hair lay flat against his scalp on one side and stuck up on the other. His shirttail flopped out the back of his pants and he wore a bleary-eyed look. But what did you expect when a man was dragged out of bed at two in the morning?

After her altercation at the church, she had driven straight to the police station, running inside panicked, demanding to see Detective Morgan. It was only after she told them she had been assaulted and had evidence pertaining to the murder cases that a call was put into Morgan's home.

"He's not going to like this," the officer on duty muttered, shaking his head. "He had a date with Lana. I'm sure he got in late."

If he got in at all, Hannah worried, but fortunately he arrived at the police station a half hour later.

"Let me get this straight," he said, rubbing the bridge of his nose with his thumb and index finger. They were sitting in his small office, his desk cluttered with papers. A large black-and-white photograph of a whale hung on one wall. "You're confessing to a crime?"

Hannah wanted to nod, but couldn't because her neck hurt. She was definitely too old for brawls, although she felt surprisingly good, considering. When she first arrived at the police station, she had been shaking, on the verge of unraveling completely. But now that she had gotten a hold of herself, she realized that she had to be getting close to identifying the killers, or at least one of them, if she was being so actively threatened. Even though part of her—the reasonable, cautious part—wanted to shrink away, she knew that now was not the time for cowardice. Whoever was threatening her had made that abundantly clear.

"Yes," she answered. "Breaking and entering the Church of Revelations."

Morgan's mouth hung open in an unattractive manner. Hannah hoped he didn't display that particular mannerism with Lana.

"And you're telling me this why?"

"Two reasons," Hannah explained. "First, while committing the crime I uncovered two pieces of evidence that should be important to you. A diskette that I believe will have information on the church's contributors." She pointed to the diskette she had put on this desk next to the rock. "This must be checked out. Arnold Lempke said he had evidence that the church was a fraud. It could very well be in here," she said, tapping her finger on the diskette's plastic casing. "I also discovered another Weeping Stone. I think Shirley Chen gave you the wrong one. I believe this one could be covered with drugs. Probably some sort of fast-acting hallucinogen that can be absorbed through the skin."

"Then why didn't Swanson succumb to the drugs?"

Hannah thought about it. "If I remember correctly, Swanson always held the rock with the flat part down. The drugs would be on the top, where he held someone's hand to it."

Morgan looked at the rock then back at Hannah. "You said there were two reasons for confessing."

"Don't rush me. It's very late," she said.

He gave her a wry look. "Tell me about it."

"Someone attacked me in the church."

This got his attention. He stood up from his slouched position and walked around the desk so he could get a good look at her.

"Are you okay?"

"I think so."

"Who was it?"

Hannah shook her head. "I don't know. Whoever it was, I think they followed me from my house, because I thought I heard a noise when I was leaving. Maybe they were going to attack me at home and then saw me leaving and changed their plan."

"And whoever it was followed you inside?"

"He must have. The door is on one of those springs, so it closes slowly. Shirley, Swanson's secretary, mentioned it this morning. Someone following me could have caught the door before it closed."

"You said 'he.' It was a man?"

Hannah thought a moment. "I think so. It was so dark, you see. Everything happened very fast and he was behind me almost all the time."

"Then why do you say it was a man?"

She stared at her lap while she considered this. She wasn't sure until then why she *had* assumed it was a man.

"His cologne. I smelled it. Very expensive and light, but definitely a man's scent. Women wear florals." She paused. "Are you going to arrest me? Because if you are, I'd like to be in the same cell as my sister."

Morgan laughed. "No, ma'am, I'm not."

"How come?" Hannah asked, relieved but a little insulted.

"Because, for one thing, I'm just too tired. Leave the evidence here and go home and take care of yourself. From the look of it, you may have a shiner tomorrow."

"But I committed a crime."

"No one caught you doing anything and no one has called in a complaint. Things may change tomorrow." When he put a hand on her shoulder, she winced with pain. He looked at her with new intensity.

"Do you want to go to the emergency room? I'll drive you."

"No, thank you. I'll be fine. I wrenched my shoulder once hauling some manure for my garden. It sorted itself out in a few days. This feels very similar."

His mouth spread into the beginnings of a smile that he quickly repressed. "I want you to stay away from that church, Ms. Malloy. Do you hear what I'm saying to you? There's a connection between that church and both of the murders."

"My thoughts as well," Hannah said. "The Swanson connection is obvious, of course. But Arnold publicly complained about the church the night before he died. That connection can't be just a coincidence.''

"Exactly." Morgan pointed his finger at her. "You were lucky tonight. You stay away from that church and the investigation.'' He said it politely, but it was a warning nonetheless.

She stood up. "Don't worry. I won't go near the church again. I'm done with it. There are other avenues to explore.''

"Mrs. Malloy, you better . . .'' he began to say, but out of fatigue or frustration, he let the statement hang.

"Good night.'' Hannah gave his hand a pat. She was starting to like him quite a lot. "Thank you for not arresting me. By the way, I have a very attractive niece you might enjoy meeting. When this is all over, maybe you could come over for dinner. She's a fabulous cook.''

At 3:30 A.M. Hannah was up to her chin in hot water and bubbles, her thoughts percolating about the night's events. There was something about the attack that bothered her. Now that she had time to review it, she couldn't shake the feeling that her attacker hadn't really wanted to hurt her. He had hit her hard but only hard enough to knock her down. When his fingers were around her throat, he could easily have killed her, she was in such a vulnerable position, but he didn't. It was as if he wanted to frighten her and frighten her badly, the way she was supposed to have been frightened by the severed finger.

There was something else nagging at her, but it was all in her shoulder, face, and joints. The aches were worsening and Morgan was right. She was going to have a shiner.

TWENTY-ONE

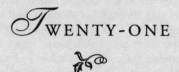

"YOU'RE TOO OLD A BROAD for fistfights," Hannah mumbled the next morning. The sun streamed in her window with a gentle scolding that she had slept late. Opening one eye, she looked at her clock. Eight. Half the morning was gone, and she could hear Sylvia and Teresa scratching the side of the bed, anxious for their breakfasts.

"In a minute," she told them, her voice muffled by the pillow. "Mummy had a rough night."

While still lying in a tangle of sheets, she rolled a little to the right, groaned, rolled to the left, and groaned again, identifying at least six different body parts that were throbbing.

"Oh, yes, Mummy had a very rough night."

She couldn't remember ever being really "physical" before, and with guilty pleasure she admitted that in the previous night's tussle she had given as good as she had received. She wondered if her attacker had any bruises. She certainly hoped so. Hugging her pillow, she smiled with satisfaction. Yes, she might be sixty-one years old, but she was still frisky. There was milk in the old cow yet. And

even at her age life was offering up fresh and exciting encounters. Last night's brawl could have been chalked up as
an energizing new experience if it just didn't hurt so darn
much.

Lifting herself up on her elbows, she let out an *ouch*. A
whopping pain shot through her shoulder, and suddenly the
idea of staying in bed took on substantial appeal. But the
Save Kiki Operation could not pause in its struggle for
justice. She couldn't allow a few aches and pains to slow
her down. Although it took longer than usual and certainly
felt worse than usual, she hauled herself out of bed and got
herself properly bathed and dressed.

The phone rang several times, but she didn't answer it.
She wasn't in the mood to talk to anyone, though she
needed to make two calls, one to the jail to get her name
on the visitors' list, and the other to Naomi to find out what
nursing home Mary Lempke had been in before her husband had taken over her care. She would have asked Shirley, but since she had ransacked the woman's desk only
the night before, she couldn't bring herself to call her. Later
she wished she had, since Naomi grilled her on why she
was asking for the information, but Hannah craftily managed to avoid giving her an answer.

Truth was, the idea had sneaked up on her. As she fed
the pets, watered her houseplants, and cleaned up after her
breakfast, she found something nagging at her in addition
to her aches and pains. It was a fixation on something Kiki
had mentioned umpteen times and had repeated the day
before—how Lempke had been such a saint, how he had
taken care of his ailing wife at home. Remembering it that
morning suddenly jogged Hannah's memory about what
Swanson had said about Lempke nursing his wife simply
because he was too cheap to pay for a nurse. Lempke had
seemed like such a selfish and petty man, and he apparently
hadn't had a decent relationship with his daughter. The idea
of him as a self-sacrificing saint just didn't ring true. She
decided to do a little digging at the nursing home. Maybe

someone there knew something about Mary that could shed more light on the real state of affairs.

It wasn't a lot to go on, but she decided to pursue it, the alternative being sitting around the house focusing on her aches and pains or worrying her head off about Kiki. Better to take any action than no action at all.

After popping a couple of Advils, she set off in the Cadillac, stopping just long enough for a peach muffin from the Sweet Nook bakery before arriving at the address she had looked up in the phone book.

Located in a neighborhood of condominiums and medical offices, the nursing home was a one-story white stucco building with wheelchair ramps glistening on its drab front like braces on teeth. Hannah opened the glass door and halted, inhaling the heavy aroma of disinfectant. She detested that smell. It was a reminder of her mother's death, and of her own mortality as well. She had never considered being in a nursing home herself until reaching her sixties; then the prospect of such a life encouraged her to eat her broccoli, get exercise, and take her calcium twice a day.

Hannah steeled herself and marched inside. After a minute of wandering she found the main office, where she asked a girl in a nurse's uniform, and a badge that read MITZI about Mary Lempke. The girl was red-haired, with plump lips and a wide-eyed innocence about her. Mitzi looked up Mary Lempke on her computer, but didn't find any information she could release.

"It's important I talk to someone about her. I was a friend and I'm doing a history of her for her family. An album with photographs, comments from people who knew her," Hannah said, the lie rolling easily off her tongue. Desperate times, she rationalized.

Tilting her head, Mitzi surveyed Hannah, oozing admiration. "That's so sweet."

"Thank you," Hannah said with a twinge of guilt.

"Listen, I'm pretty new here, but try Sue Olsen. She's the administrator and she's been here for years. She probably remembers your friend.'' She stood up in a sprightly way. ''Come on. I'll take you to her.''

Hannah followed her down a long hallway, Mitzi's white shoes squeaking on the linoleum. Everything was spotless, the walls a cheery pink, the floors polished to a gloss, yet the place had the aura of illness. Patients, all elderly, sat in wheelchairs in the hall, some smiling at Hannah, others sitting listlessly, mouths open and eyes vacant. Hannah and Mitzi passed a woman strapped into a wheelchair. As they walked by she reached out a withered, blue-veined hand, her gnarled fingers grasping at air, her eyes pleading as she muttered something unintelligible.

''Good morning, Mrs. Thompson,'' Mitzi said cheerfully, quickening her pace. Hannah felt a knot growing in her stomach.

Maybe Lempke took his wife out of this place because it was too depressing, she thought. If so, she thought better of him, though she knew that nursing homes were frequently well-run, caring places, and this one seemed to fit that category. But you couldn't disguise the fact that they were places where people went to die.

They reached a nurses' station where two women were examining a chart. Mitzi whispered to the taller of the two, a dark-haired woman in a navy pantsuit, and the woman walked over.

''You have questions about Mary Lempke,'' she said briskly without polite introductions. Hannah said yes. She nodded. ''Let's go into my office.''

They walked down another hallway and into an office with a desk and a small conference table. She gestured to a chair by the table and Hannah sat.

''My name's Sue,'' she said, sitting across from her. She crossed her legs and leaned back, her arm draped casually on the back of her chair as she regarded Hannah with curiosity.

Hannah introduced herself. ''I'd like to find out some things about Mary Lempke's stay here.''

"You're doing a family album?"

"In a way. I'm trying to get some specific information about Mary."

A pause. "Like what?"

"For one thing, how long was she here?"

Olsen eyed her with suspicion.

"Let's just say not long enough."

Hannah's radar switched to "alert." "What do you mean?"

Olsen sat up straighter. "I mean she never should have been taken out of here. I told her husband as much. Mary needed daily nursing care regardless of what the Medicare guidelines allowed. He wasn't capable of handling it."

"I suppose he just wanted her home. He must have loved her."

A look of distaste crossed Olsen's face. "Loved her? I doubt that man cared for his wife at all." She paused, then sighed, her chest heaving. "I'm sorry. That's harsh, especially since the man recently died, but I felt very strongly about it at the time. I still do."

"But if that's the way he felt, why did he go to all the trouble of taking her home?"

Olsen laughed softly but without humor. "To save the money. Mary was in her seventies and Medicare was picking up her costs for the allotted number of weeks. But that ran out and her husband was going to have to pick up the bills himself. Granted, it was several thousand dollars a month to keep her here, but from what I heard, he could afford it."

Hannah let this information stew in her head a moment, then she asked, "Was he taking good care of her? Did anybody check?"

"I did. I was concerned about her, so I dropped by. She was in terrible shape. She was having repeated strokes, I'm sure of it, and she had terrible bedsores, which can be very painful. He had her loaded up with sedatives so she would be less trouble. She was barely conscious. I was going to file a complaint to force him to bring her back here or at least hire a nurse, but then she died.'' Olsen stopped talking, her expression pained. "As far as I'm concerned, her husband helped kill her. Put that in your family album.''

Her words startled Hannah. "You think he purposely harmed her?''

"Do I think he poured drugs down her throat and killed her? No. But she would have lived months, maybe even years longer if she had skilled nursing. So is that murder? You tell me.''

Hannah shifted uneasily in her chair. She asked a few more questions, but didn't learn much else. After thanking Olsen for her time, she started to leave but was stopped before she reached the door.

"It's my turn to ask a question. How'd you get that black eye?'' she asked.

Hannah's hand instinctively moved to her face. She hadn't been aware that the bruise was noticeable. Embarrassed, she took a moment before answering. "I had an accident.''

Olsen frowned. "Are you sure?''

With a shake of her head, Hannah smiled. "I'm a little old to get knocked around by a jealous lover.''

"You'd be surprised. And women your age get physically abused by their children more often than you want to think about.''

"It's nothing like that, I promise. But thanks for asking.''

The women said good-bye. Hannah walked out of the building feeling slightly ill. If what Olsen said was true, for all practical purposes Arnold Lempke had killed his wife.

That afternoon Hannah entered the visitors' room at the jail with her handkerchief out and ready to wrap around the grimy phone receiver. As soon as she saw Kiki, her eyes popped open wide. Penal servitude had provoked a major change in her sister's coiffure.

Kiki's hair had been slicked down on the sides and teased on top until her head resembled an exploded Q-Tip. As Hannah sat on her side of the glass booth, her sister plopped down into the chair and picked up the phone. "My God, Hannah, your face looks awful. Did you run into a door or something?"

"Sort of," Hannah answered, her eyes drifting involuntarily upward.

Kiki patted the rat's nest perched on her skull. "You're noticing my new 'do. Chantal did it for me. Like it?"

A dozen words came to Hannah's mind, none of them utterable. "It's . . . it's intriguing." Two-headed cows were intriguing, Hannah thought. Kiki's hairdo was something beyond than that.

"Thanks. Chantal says it takes ten years off. By the way, I told Chantal about your secret tattoo you won't show anybody. She says that if it took you a couple of trips to get it done, that it must be a big one."

"I wish you wouldn't tell people about that."

"You know, Chantal has a very interesting tattoo in a place you'd never—"

"Yes, well, Kiki, they don't give us much time to visit, and I wanted you to know that I'm running down a couple of leads. It's possible I'll have you out of here in a few days."

"That's so sweet of you, but there's no huge rush." As Hannah's jaw dropped Kiki leaned her head closer to the glass partition. "You see, I think I've lost another pound. That's a pound a day. A few more days and I could be a size eight."

"Kiki, you're in jail, charged with murder. You want out. Trust me on this."

Kiki waggled her hand. "Chantal and a few of the other girls and me have been doing leg lifts together in the rec room. And I've been catching up on all the soaps." She smiled and gave her eyebrows a lascivious lift. "Though the stories the girls tell are better than television, let me tell you. Besides, hon, I'm innocent and you told me not to worry, so . . ." She cast a hand back in a carefree gesture. "I'm not worrying."

It crossed Hannah's mind that Kiki's faith in her abilities was a trifle too confident, but it was nice to see her so upbeat.

"Another thing, Hannah. Do you think you could bring me that jumpsuit I bought for the cruise? I was telling Chantal about it and she wants to see it."

"The guards will let you do that?" Hannah asked.

Kiki looked at her as if she'd just asked a very silly question. "One of the girl guards wants to see it, too," she said, as if they were discussing a sorority and not the county lockup.

As Hannah left the jail she decided that Kiki's fall off a swing set when she was six must have done more damage than previously imagined. Today she had acted as if she didn't have a care in the world, her trust so complete that she actually thought Hannah could pop her out of the jail as soon as she could squeeze into a smaller dress size.

What she didn't realize was that Hannah was running out of ideas. She had pursued the Church of Revelations as well as the nursing home and had come up with some leads, but she wasn't sure what they were worth. Despite the timing of the finger showing up on her front porch, Kiki was still not cleared of murder. Her fingerprints were on the knife that killed Swanson. And the information from the nursing home was interesting but not much more than that. There was a missing piece to the puzzle of the murders, and unless Hannah found it, her sister was going to stay in jail until she was a size two. It didn't matter how thin you were when all you could wear was a prison uniform.

Hannah was lost in thought, practically stomping down the jail's steps, when she looked up and saw John Perez bounding up toward her. He came to a halt two steps below her, blocking her path. He looked anxious, his brows drawn together. Hannah's heart did some definite flip-flopping at the sight of him, but she steeled herself.

"Hannah, they told me at the police station what happened to you last night. I warned you that you were risking trouble."

And you could easily be the one who attacked me, she said to herself. The only clue she had to go on was the smell of her attacker's cologne. She stepped closer to Perez to get within smelling distance.

"Are you following me?" she asked, still not close enough to get a decent whiff.

"Looking for you, yes. Following you, no."

She moved her nose closer to Perez's neck.

He looked at her like she was mad. "What the hell are you doing?" he said, stepping down a step.

"Nothing." Nothing was right. Perez wore no cologne that she could detect, although it didn't mean that he hadn't worn any the night before. Hannah racked her brain trying to remember if she had ever smelled cologne on him the other times they had been together, but both her brain and nose came up blank.

"For your information, the county forensic lab did the tests on that rock you brought in."

She snapped to attention. "It was covered with drugs, wasn't it?"

He shook his head. "No. Clean as a whistle."

"That can't be true."

"Why not?"

"Because I went to that church. The people were hallucinating. They had to be drugged."

"Well, they weren't. People can make themselves hallucinate strictly on their own power."

"What about the list of church contributors? Have they gone through those yet?" she asked.

"Not all of them, but it turns out that some were dummy corporations. On that count you may have been right. It looks like the Church of Revelations could be a front for laundering money. And it turns out Swanson had a criminal record.''

"For what?''

"Embezzling. He did some time fifteen years ago for stealing money from a trucking company. He was an accountant. After that he found religion but got thrown out of one church for stealing. Looks like he set up a deal with the Revelations church to launder drug money. That's what a lot of the big donations apparently were.''

"So there could easily be other people who would have wanted to kill him.''

"Possibly, but to help your sister the police have to make the connection between those people and the lunch guests at Lisa Lempke's. Those are the people who could have stolen the knife with your sister's prints on it.''

"I'll just have to make that connection myself.''

Perez took hold of her forearm. "Leave this to the police.''

Hannah jerked her arm away. "I can't leave it to anyone. This is my sister's welfare we're talking about.''

"The police are working on it.''

"They're not exploring every option. They've got other cases to work on. But this is my only focus. It's important I stay involved.''

Frustrated, Perez turned away a moment, then faced her again. "Hannah, think about the Weeping Stone,'' he said, his tone now calmer and slower, as if he were speaking to a child, which annoyed Hannah. "There's a message for you there if you'll pay attention to it.''

She pressed her hand against her chest. "A lesson for me?''

"Yes. Believe it or not, even at our age life has things to teach us,'' he said with irony. "You were dead sure that rock was covered with drugs and it wasn't. You see, it didn't have to be.''

"What are you talking about?'' Hannah asked, irritated that he would criticize her.

"That people can start believing things because they just plain want to believe them, and those beliefs, religious or otherwise, can make them do stupid things." He paused. "Like breaking into buildings and stealing things. Like believing that someone who wants to be their friend is leaving amputated fingers on their porch."

On the defensive, Hannah drew herself up. "You could easily have left that box on my doorstep."

"But I didn't. Hannah, you're so busy scrounging around trying to dig up facts that you're missing the big picture."

She missing the big picture? She opened her mouth to give a sharp retort but couldn't think of any.

"I appreciate your advice, John," she said more harshly than she intended. "I have to go now. I have things to do."

A bucket of ice cubes down his boxers would have been less chilly, and she regretted her remarks as she walked away from him. But she had too much pride to turn back and apologize, even though deep down she knew he was at least partially right. She *was* missing some important information. She had to be or else she would have had the murders solved by now. And if she didn't latch onto the answer soon, her sister could very well be tried for murder.

Hannah liked to consider herself a sympathetic, loving person, but when it came to garden pests, she could lop their little heads off without compunction. And today Attila the Hun couldn't have shown more gusto in annihilating any bug even contemplating ingesting a mouthful of her prize roses.

Wearing her own form of pest-eradicating military garb— faded overalls, tattered baseball hat, leather gloves, nose mask, and rubber gardening clogs—she spent the lunch hour initiating a frontal attack, squirting the pests with an environmentally friendly pest spray she mixed herself, taking out all of her frustrations on the insects. The Rose Club festival was that afternoon and she had to get her entry in the competition ready. She considered giving up the idea

of entering the contest, but then decided, as a show of re-
spect to Arnold Lempke's prowess as a rosarian, to enter
his Summer Surprise hybrid. She would enter it in his
name, and she felt that Lempke had been competitive
enough to have wanted her to enter her own rose as well.

With a groan due to the previous night's exploits, she
got down on her knees and inspected the bush from which
she would take her entry. There was a bud just opening that
would be perfect.

Perez was such a vexing man, she thought for the fifty-
sixth time in an hour as she gave an unwitting aphid the
business end of her spray bottle. She was definitely attracted to him, more so every time she met up with him.
And his lack of cologne certainly lessened the odds of him
being the previous night's attacker. Still, he could wear
cologne on some days and not on others. Men did that, she
supposed. And as far she was concerned, he was still a
murder suspect and could have easily left the disgusting
finger on her porch.

Taking no prisoners, she asphyxiated another aphid with
an especially volatile blast. Though Perez seemed like such
a thoughtful reasonable man. But then, what did she know
about people? In a thousand years she would never have
guessed that there could be a murderer among her circle of
acquaintances. And in a *gazillion* years she wouldn't have
thought that Kiki, who in college had joined a sorority so
she could mix with the "right people," would now be
clothes-swapping chummy with a jailed prostitute-spiritual-
healer. Anyone with a brain bigger than a walnut knew
damned well that Chantal had probably been "healing" a
body part that was suffering from nothing more serious than
lust, Hannah decided as a cucumber beetle bit the dust.

When she heard Naomi's back door open, she put down
her spray bottle, removed her mask, and went to the fence.
Relations between the women were still slightly strained
from Hannah's earlier remarks about Red Moon, and when

Naomi saw her, she said only a chilly hello. But within seconds she was at the fence, too curious about what was going on to let minor annoyances impede her. Hannah filled her in, her brief synopsis taking a good ten minutes. Naomi stood there, spellbound, becoming increasingly agitated as she listened.

"Such dark forces at work here," she said, shaking her head. "But, Hannah, you've got the brains and the stick-to-it attitude that will solve this case. You are going to keep working at it, aren't you?"

"Of course, I am." Hannah paused, considering her question before she asked it. "Naomi, when you were channeling for Mary, did you ever think that Arnold was not taking good enough care of her?"

"To be honest, sometimes I wondered. Toward the end she seemed so doped up that she couldn't even take part in the channeling. But I'm no nurse, Hannah. I didn't feel I was in a position to judge."

They said their good-byes and Hannah returned to her gardening. Her instincts told her she was close to the truth, yet the information wasn't quite coming together and it was very frustrating. As she stooped down she kicked over the marker that sat planted in the ground in front of one of the bushes. She was righting it when an idea began to take form. It was the marker that had started it. She picked the marker out of the ground and stared at as she recreated Lempke's rose garden in her head.

"My Lord," she muttered, tossing down her spray bottle and walking over to her potting shed, where she kept a tattered rose encyclopedia in one of the drawers. Thumbing through the soiled and water-stained curled pages, she finally found what she was looking for. After reading the page, she closed her eyes, not believing how stupid she had been. Something about that garden had bothered her, something that was terribly wrong. And now, at last, she knew what it was.

TWENTY-TWO

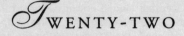

$\mathscr{I}$N TOO MUCH OF A hurry to walk, Hannah, dirt still clinging to her face, drove the Cadillac to Lempke's house as fast as prudence and the speed limit allowed. She stopped the car in front, got out hurriedly, then halted, forcing herself to walk slowly and casually to the front gate. She didn't want to attract attention. But as soon as she got inside, she jogged down the gravel path through the side yard to Lempke's rose garden.

The plants had suffered from lack of attention since his death. Withered blossoms stood untrimmed, turning brown under the sun, and dead petals lay scattered on the ground, as if the roses were grieving the loss of their caretaker. But new healthy blooms were abundant, the roses still thriving from the meticulous care Lempke had given them for so many years.

She approached the flowers gingerly, her steps slowing with reverence. For Hannah, a well-tended, beautifully planted garden was a spiritual place, more like a church than some of the imposing, concrete buildings claiming that title. With its carefully planned abundance of foliage and flowers, a garden was one of the rare occurrences in life that God and man created together.

For Arnold Lempke to have created this lovely patch of earth he had to have felt about his garden as Hannah did about hers. He must have loved and nurtured it, finding a deep satisfaction that eluded him in the rest of the chaotic world.

Stepping farther into the yard, she noticed the meticulous layout of the bushes, the canes painstakingly pruned, the carefully written-out metal markers in front of each bush, then stooped in front of Lempke's exquisite hybrid, its white and red petals delicately ruffled, richly fragrant. Looking down at the dirt and grass below it, she winced when she saw the blades of grass covered with an oily black substance that must have been Lempke's blood, baked under the sun.

The marker stuck in the dirt in front of the hybrid rose read SUMMER SURPRISE, but Hannah knew from her rose encyclopedia that a Summer Surprise was no unique hybrid. It was a standard floribunda with lavender blossoms, one that could be ordered out of most rose catalogs. It was a hardy rose, disease-resistant and a steady bloomer, but paled beside this lustrous streaked beauty Lempke had created. His rose had a fiery depth, a profusion of delicate glossy petals unfurling with such majesty that looking deep into them, you felt you had gotten a glimpse of God's paradise. What had been quietly nagging at Hannah, even though she hadn't realized it, was that Lempke's hybrid was bearing the wrong marker. And Lempke would never have mismarked his own rose. No rosarian makes that mistake.

It took only a few moments for Hannah to identify the real Summer Surprise, its lavender flowers easily discernible among the other bushes. Kneeling in front of it, she examined the marker with an ache of sadness. It read MARY'S SORROW. Lempke had named his precious hybrid rose after his wife. Sue Olsen's suspicions had been right. Lempke must have felt guilty over the way he had treated

Mary in her last months. That's why he named his rose after her. But why had the marker in front of the rose been changed?

Hannah pulled the Mary's Sorrow marker out of the dirt. A flexible two-by-three inch metal rectangle bore the name of the rose, the letters printed in heavy black ink. Along each side of the label were thin narrow spikes the thickness of an ice pick, though several inches longer. The spikes looked rusty even though the soft metal label appeared new. Hannah inhaled sharply as she realized the truth.

It wasn't rust on the spikes. It was dried blood.

"Of course I remember you," Sue Olsen said. "How can I help you?"

Hannah cleared her throat. "Did Lisa Lempke ever contact you regarding her mother being taken out of your facility?"

"Yes, she did."

A pang shot through her. This was the response she had hoped not to hear. "When?"

"A few weeks ago. I thought it was strange that she would want to talk to me so long after her mother's death. She said she had been thinking about things and had some questions. I told her exactly what I told you. She was quite upset about it."

But she could have been more than upset, Hannah said to herself. It was quite possible that she felt murderous.

$\mathcal{T}$WENTY-THREE

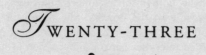

$\mathcal{O}$NCE A YEAR AND ONLY once a year the Hill Creek Rose Club invited the public to tread upon its hallowed grounds. These festivities were a source of immense excitement for the club's more socially inclined members, who relished showing off to the Marin County masses how enchanting their little club was, and how desirable and unattainable membership in it was to the likes of them. Perhaps as a sop to their consciences, all proceeds from the festival were donated to the local elementary schools.

Hannah was always pushing to open the club grounds to the public every day, but the idea was soundly squashed at each annual meeting, usually by Wanda, who felt the unwashed heathens incapable of respecting the nasturtiums.

On festival day the club members roped off the gardens, restricting people to the stone paths, with the games, music, and rose judging situated on the large lawn area. Behind all this stood the grand "cottage," stalwart and intimidating, a reminder to everybody of what *real* money could do.

The day had started out overcast, with a heavy layer of fog in from the coast, but by late morning the sun had burst through. By noon, the time Hannah arrived, the day sparkled, the smells of food mingling provocatively with the perfume of the flowers. In one hand she carried a perfectly shaped Mr. Lincoln and in the other an equally luscious Mary's Sorrow, both in rubber-topped bud vases. Her mind, however, wasn't on the flowers. She hastily dropped the blossoms off at the rose booth, politely brushing off Bertha when she tried to corner her for a discussion of mildew on one of her hybrid teas.

Hannah walked briskly through the food and beverage booths. An all-female marimba band had struck up a bouncy tune and a river of people admired the gardens, with others lining up at the wine, veggie burrito, and sushi concessions. Children squealed in the games area as they participated in politically correct, nongender-biased, nonviolent, self-esteem-building amusements.

As she passed the dunking booth she heard a splash and saw Naomi grimacing, a large dark water mark spreading up her canary-yellow caftan. Spotting her, Naomi waved with desperation, arms flailing, looking like a huge butterfly doing a spasmodic Macarena, but Hannah pretended not to see her.

"Where have you been?" Lauren asked when Hannah arrived at last at the beer booth.

"Sorry I'm late. Has it been busy?" she asked, a rhetorical question since there were no customers.

"Not at all. This beer's all domestic. But the organic juice booth across the way is a madhouse. Apparently there's an article in this month's *Holistic News* about antioxidants in guavas that—"

"Lauren." Hannah interrupted. "I need you to cover for me."

"What's wrong? You look worried."

"I can't discuss it now, but I must take care of something. It's important."

Lauren acquiesced easily and Hannah marched off in search of Lisa Lempke. Although she wasn't positive Lisa would be there, she figured the chances were good since her school was one of the festival's beneficiaries. The crowd was thickening and it was hard to find anyone, especially someone as petite as Lisa. As Hannah wove her way through the throng she saw Wanda and Walter at the pottery and foot-reflexology booth. Wanda gave her a polite wave while Walter smiled tightly.

Hannah was ready to give up on finding Lisa, at least for the time being, when she spotted her standing away from the crowd near a small garden of knee-high red salvia, deep in conversation with Crayton and two other women. They were all smiling, holding wineglasses.

At the sight of Arnold Lempke's daughter, trepidation swelled inside her. Hannah thought she knew what had happened to Lisa's father. And more than that, she also thought she knew why. But now, faced with the possibility of at last confirming the facts, she found her resolve faltering. Part of her wanted so much to be wrong. She took a deep breath, then approached Lisa.

"We have to talk," she said, drawing a disapproving look from Crayton. "Please. Alone."

Lisa tilted her head slightly, seemingly dismayed for a second, but then her smile returned. "Sure."

Crayton's eyes darted anxiously from Hannah to Lisa, then to the other women. If she and Lisa had been alone, she would in all likelihood have insisted on Hannah speaking to them both, but under the circumstances, she only nodded and, with a strained smile, asked Lisa not to stay away long.

The band switched to a ballad as Hannah steered Lisa away from the crowd.

"You're not drinking," Lisa said with a trace of slurring in her voice. Her eyes were dull, a touch of red lipstick smeared on her teeth. She was tipsy, Hannah realized.

"No. I never do." She watched her a moment then slowly pulled the garden marker out of her purse, holding it carefully by one edge with a white handkerchief.

As soon as Lisa saw it, her hazy grin collapsed. Although the sounds of the festival bubbled around them, the immediate environment around the two women seemed oddly still as Lisa's eyes fixed upon the marker. Seeing the recognition and fear on Lisa's face, and grasping why she was responding this way, Hannah felt sick. It was the moment she had dreaded. Her theory about Lempke's murder had to be correct.

"I checked my rose encyclopedia," Hannah said, her tone soft, the words slow. "This marker was stuck in front of the wrong bush. It belonged on your father's hybrid."

Lisa gave a small shrug, feigning disinterest. "What of it?"

"I think this marker tells the story of why you killed your father."

Lisa straightened with a jerk. "You're talking crazy. Maybe you should start drinking to clear up your head." She turned and took a step toward the relative safety of Crayton, but Hannah took her arm.

"I know what happened."

Lisa yanked her arm free. "You know nothing." Her voice was full of animosity. "How could you possibly know anything?"

"I know this much. You found your father in the garden," Hannah said with new intensity. "After you killed him, you changed the marker because you were afraid it would point to you as the killer."

Hearing these words, Lisa's face softened slightly. Hannah placed her hand on Lisa's as she continued. "The rose was named after your mother. Your mother is why you killed him. You thought he had killed her through neglect."

"That's not true." Lisa was shaking now, her eyes turning pink.

"You have to go to the police. You must see that. The way it probably happened, it might not actually be murder. The weapon you used shows that you didn't plan it. You were enraged and hurt. You had a right to be. That might make it manslaughter.''

Lisa's breaths came heavily now. She gulped down the rest of her wine. ''What weapon? What are you talking about?''

''The marker. You used the marker to kill him.''

''That?'' Her eyes grazed the marker before returning to Hannah. ''The police said my father had a single wound from some weird knife.''

Hannah held up the marker, bending the flexible metal label so the two spikes came together, forming the equivalent of a single blade. Lisa looked at it and this time her eyes stayed. In its normal shape the marker looked benign, but in the manner that Hannah held it, it was a deadly weapon.

''Your father's blood is still on the spikes. And my sister is in jail taking the blame for what you did.''

Lisa pressed her fist against her mouth, her face crumbling, the facade she had carefully crafted over the past week coming apart. Hannah thought perhaps she would run to Crayton or run anywhere, for what little good it would do her. But she didn't. The marimba band struck up a lively tune, children laughed, and a horn joyfully blared as Lisa stood there silent with despair, as vulnerable as a frightened child, quivering and beaten, huge tears forming in her lightless eyes.

''I'm not sorry he's dead,'' she said. ''After I found out what he had done to my mother, how could I be sorry?''

''Please tell me what happened.''

Lisa gave a deep, shuddering sigh. ''I'd suspected for a long time that he hadn't been taking proper care of Mom. I'm come by to see her and she'd be lying in urine, her nightgown filthy. I'd clean her up, and I'd ask him about it. He'd make some excuse. I'd believe it because I wanted to believe it. Then she really started going downhill and I asked him if we should put her back in the nursing home, where she'd get more help. He told me he had called Sue

Olsen and that she told him Mom was better off at home.''

"What prompted you to talk to Sue in the first place?''
Hannah asked.

"I couldn't think of anyone else to talk to about it. After
Mom died I just kept thinking about her and thinking about
those last months. I felt guilty, too, you see. I should have
done something. About ten days ago I called Sue. She told
me that Daddy had never called her. That she had gone to
see Mom and had asked him to get her help, but that he
refused.''

"So you went to see your father?''

Lisa nodded. "I went to the house to confront him with
what I knew.'' Her gaze moved away from Hannah. "And
there he was in the garden, tending to those roses like they
were babies, giving them more attention than he had given
my mother.'' She stopped her story there, her eyes locked
on something in the distance.

"Then what happened?'' Hannah prodded.

"I saw the name on the marker. My mom's name. I took
it out of the ground,'' Lisa said, her eyes again on the
marker. "I held on to it awhile, just because it had her
name on it. The cheap bastard shouldn't have been allowed
to use her name.'' She took another heavy breath. "He was
saying horrible things to me. And I hated him so much.
When he turned his back on me, I just shoved the marker
in his neck. I didn't think about it. I just did it.''

Lisa was crying now. Hannah knew she should have
been repelled by what she had just heard, but all she felt
was pity.

"What about Reverend Swanson?''

Lisa didn't seem to hear the question. "I loved my father.
In spite of what he did, I loved him. I want you to know
that. Whatever terrible thing he did, he should have been
punished by God, not me.''

"Most likely he will be,'' Hannah said. "What happened
to Swanson?''

Lisa hesitated, her hand moving to her head, where she grabbed a hunk of her hair. "You see, I felt terrible," she said, her voice so low Hannah had trouble hearing her. "I was sick with guilt. I had to talk to somebody."

"And you talked to Swanson?"

"I didn't expect forgiveness. I just wanted to talk, that's all. I couldn't hold it inside anymore. But he used what I told him to make me do things."

"To make you sleep with him?" Hannah asked, her mouth open with shock. She hadn't thought much of Swanson as a minister, but she hadn't suspected the man would blackmail some poor grieving girl into sex.

"It repulsed me. I don't like men like that. I don't think I like them in any way, really. But especially not that."

"So you went to his house to sleep with him?" Hannah asked. Lisa's face told her the answer.

It was odd, but at that precise moment Hannah suddenly remembered the softball game so many years before when Lisa had struck out so many times and she herself had comforted her. Up until then she hadn't thought much about the incident, but now it came back vividly. She remembered Lisa's face at thirteen and her expression of complete hopelessness. But she couldn't comfort her now the way she had then.

"Why try to make it look like my sister did it?"

"The police suspected her anyway. It seemed the easiest way to go." Lisa looked down at her shoes then up again. "I'm sorry, Hannah. You were good to me."

"I have to call the police. I have to give them this marker. You must come with me and tell them everything that happened."

Lisa nodded. Perhaps Hannah should have been afraid of her, but she wasn't. Lisa looked too small and helpless. Then out of the corner of her eye Hannah saw Crayton looking toward them anxiously. At that moment she feel compassion for Crayton. She and Crayton were alike, both caretakers, the strong taking care of the weak. Crayton took care of Lisa the way Hannah took care of Kiki. Sometimes, taking care of other people was a draining occupation, especially when those people bashed into walls at every turn.

TWENTY-FOUR

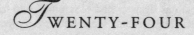

"*I*T DOESN'T TAKE MISS MANNERS to know that if someone frames your relative for murder, they're off your list for social calls," Kiki said as she and Hannah meandered down a gravel walkway at Urban Farm, Hannah's favorite nursery.

Hannah considered the new shipment of cosmos with a knowledgeable eye. "If Lauren wants to visit Lisa in jail, that's her business."

"Well, it's my opinion that Lauren should reconsider. It doesn't look right." Kiki said the words with a touch of haughtiness born from the fact that the *Marin Daily News* was planning a two-part, front-page feature article on her, the wrongfully incarcerated Hill Creek matron, complete with color photos. Kiki was going to provide juicy, and no doubt exaggerated, details on what it was like to be in the local jail, and she was relishing the attention.

With outrageous gall, Wanda had telephoned that morning to announce that she was planning a welcome-home lunch for the ex-prisoner, and all of Kiki's Rose Club friends, the ones who had previously dumped her like last week's tofu, would be in attendance. And to further assault all decency, Wanda had coyly suggested that Kiki might want a photo of the two of them in the newspaper article— Kiki as the falsely accused, Wanda as the friend who stood by her in her time of need.

What began as disaster had blossomed into triumph, and the fact that Kiki's friends were faithless hypocrites didn't seem to bother her in the least. Not only were they back, they were in the throes of, so to speak, penal envy. And when they saw how much weight she had lost in so short a time, they would probably all begin blatantly shoplifting just to earn a few days behind bars. After all, if colonic cleansing could have its day in the sun, why not jail?

Hannah picked up a pot of Mexican sage, examining its deep green foliage. The selection at this nursery was small, but the plants they carried had been nurtured like newborns, each an example of radiant green perfection. The ambience of the place was wonderfully serene, the plants displayed on weathered wooden tables under vine-covered trellises. At the end of a walkway water bubbled from a rustic stone fountain, the happy sound welcome to Hannah's ears. It had been one hell of a week.

"We should feel sorry for Lisa," she said, inhaling deeply, savoring the smell of jasmine that wafted from a nearby cedar fence.

Kiki's nose crinkled. "Oh, pooh," she said with a flop of her hand. "Let's feel sorry for her victims. She sent my poor Arnie to his Maker." Once certain her sister was watching, she theatrically lifted a hand to her forehead. "Eventually we would have been married, you know."

Hannah opened her mouth, a sarcastic retort prepared to explode like a cork from a champagne bottle, but she clamped her teeth shut. Her sister had only gotten out of jail the night before and was still celebrating her homecoming. In a victory for self-control she said, "And let's not forget Reverend Swanson. What a terrible way to die."

Kiki raised her shoulders toward her ears and made a

face. "Why on earth did Lisa cut his finger off?"

"To frighten me is what she said on the way to the police station," Hannah replied, her brow furrowed. "She said she thought I was very close to discovering her as the murderer, though at the time she wasn't at the top of my list."

"Lisa just doesn't seem like the finger-chopping type."

Hannah gave her a sidewise glance. "You can pick them out of a crowd, can you?"

"You know what I mean. So bloody and messy. Lisa seems kind of timid."

Hannah had been thinking the same thing, but facts were facts. Lisa had confessed and was now behind bars. Immediately after their conversation at the festival, Lisa had gone to the police with Hannah, leaving Crayton and her friends without explanation. She confessed to both murders, to leaving Swanson's finger on Hannah's porch, and to attacking Hannah inside the church. Now, with the murders solved, Hannah was of course relieved to have Kiki home, but she felt no pride in solving the murders, only a terrible sadness for Lisa.

Despite what the young woman had done, Hannah had trouble seeing that kind of brutality in her. She didn't approve of killers claiming they were victims in order to escape paying for their crimes, but Lisa really *had been* a victim. Lempke had horribly abused her mother, and Swanson degraded her in a manner no better then rape. Naturally Hannah was horrified by Lisa's actions, but at least on some level, she understood it.

Kiki was unencumbered by such ambiguities. All that concerned her was the fact that she had entered jail a caterpillar and emerged a butterfly. The butterfly paused, took off one of her red high-heeled shoes, and shook out a piece of gravel. While balanced on one foot, she began to wobble, and Hannah took hold of her arm to steady her.

"I told you not to wear those shoes in here."

With her shoe back on, Kiki got both her feet on the ground as solidly as her nature permitted. "I just feel so svelte, I wanted to dress up.'' She walked a few more steps, then stopped, her footwear not allowing simultaneous thinking and walking. ''You know, I remember when Lisa was on that softball team with Lauren. The poor little thing could barely toss the ball, remember?''

Having moved to the next table of plants, Hannah paused. Of course Kiki was right. Lisa had been a hopeless athlete. It would have taken some strength and coordination to kill a man with the spikes from a garden marker. But at the time Lisa's adrenaline had been pumping, which could perhaps explain things.

''You don't need a lot of coordination to cut a finger off if the knife is very sharp, I suppose,'' Hannah said.

Kiki raised her eyebrows. ''Well, that knife *was* sharp. When I used it that day at Lisa's, I almost cut my own finger off.''

Hannah picked up two plastic pots of lemon geraniums, handing a third to Kiki. ''Let's take these.''

''Then can we go to the Book Stop? I want everybody to see me,'' Kiki said. ''Give me your opinion. When I walk in should I pretend not to see people, you know, like I'm still drained from the jail thing, or should I smile and wave?''

''Smile and wave, I think. With the back of your hand facing your public like Queen Elizabeth,'' Hannah answered.

Kiki gave a slight sneer that Hannah thought she must have learned during her incarceration. They were halfway down the aisle when she stopped again, this time rather suddenly, bumping into Hannah. ''My God! Do you know what I just realized? Red Moon was right.''

''You almost made me drop the plants. Right about what?''

''Red Moon said 'two ones standing side by side.' Don't you see?'' Kiki drew the numbers in the air with her finger. ''Two ones look like two *L*s. Which stands for Lisa Lempke.''

Hannah chewed on this a moment, finally muttering, "You're right." Squinting her eyes, she concentrated, remembering the sessions with Red Moon. "He also told me to look to God's soil. And then the murder weapon turned out to be stuck in the ground."

"Ooh, and remember that eerie part when he said something about how the corpse rose? Arnie's hybrid rose was named after Mary and she was a corpse. Am I right?"

"Yes, you are," Hannah answered slowly.

Kiki shook a finger at her. "And so you have to admit that Red Moon is real."

The troublesome thought settled in Hannah's head, but she quickly shook it off the way she would an annoying insect. "I admit nothing. Let's pay for these."

Smug in the knowledge that her point had been made, a grinning Kiki followed her sister to the checkout stand inside the store, where pots, gardening tools, and accessories were sold.

She leaned on the counter, her chin resting on her fist. "You know, I wouldn't mind getting to know Red Moon better. He sounds so awfully virile, being an Indian and everything."

Hannah pursed her lips as she put the plants on the checkout counter. "You have a crush on Red Moon? Now I've heard everything. He's not even human. He's vapor."

"You're just embarrassed because it turns out he's real. And you shouldn't talk to me that way. Chantal says I'm very sensitive and spiritual. I think you're going to like her, Hannah."

Chantal, who was expected to be released from jail in a few days, had been invited to dinner the following week.

Hannah rummaged through her handbag for her wallet while Fred, who knew her from her frequent visits to the shop, rang up her bill. In his twenties, Fred was a fervent organic gardener who specialized in medicinal herbs, and he and Hannah had had many lively conversations about organic pest control.

He pecked at the computer keyboard, a machine that seemed out of place in this botanical environment, with its wind chimes and gardening paraphernalia. "That'll be eight twenty-two. You're not going for those new hyacinth bulbs?" he asked.

Hannah shook her head. "I think it's a little late in the year."

"These are a new variety. You should try them. Or ask your friend Naomi. She bought a bagful."

Busy counting out her money, at first Hannah barely noticed what he said. Naomi had accompanied her to the shop several times and Fred had been fascinated to learn she was a psychic, a fact Naomi always managed to drop into any conversation. You could be discussing cow manure and she would somehow connect the subject to Red Moon.

An idea hit Hannah. Her head popped up. "Hyacinth bulbs? Naomi? When?"

"About a week ago, I guess. She asked me a lot of questions about how to plant them. I told her to talk to you if she had any questions after she got home."

"Good Lord." Hannah tossed a ten-dollar bill on the counter. "Come on, Kiki. I must go home."

Kiki's face fell. "I thought we were going to the Book Stop."

"Please go without me. I'll pick you up later." Hannah grabbed the geraniums, which Fred had boxed, and pushed Kiki toward the door.

"What about your change?" Fred called after her.

"Buy yourself an espresso on me," Hannah replied.

"What's going on?" Kiki asked, irritated. "Suddenly you're all fired up."

"I have to find Naomi. I think I know how Red Moon got his so-called psychic information about Lempke's murder."

Naomi's house was an old shingled craftsman's style cottage similar to Hannah's, though smaller and not as scrupulously maintained. The shingles were dusty blue, the color of a robin's egg, with white trim, and the front door was painted a glossy bright red. A bunch of dried herbs always hung from the tarnished brass door knocker to keep the house free from disgruntled spirits.

Other than a few boxwoods and a hydrangea, Naomi's flower beds were fairly empty, and there were many bare areas, a fact that always bothered Hannah. But on one side of the house there grew an abbreviated row of shrubbery, green and hardy thanks to Hannah's fertilizing it last fall. She had to straddle this foliage to get close to the window, the one facing west, which she knew belonged to Naomi's "spirit room," the place where she channeled for her clients.

Hannah had noticed Naomi's battered SAAB with its faded "Free Tibet" bumper sticker in the driveway as well a new Mercedes she didn't recognize parked behind it. Probably a client. Having tried the doorbell and receiving no answer, she knew Naomi was in the middle of a session. But she couldn't wait.

"Of all days to wear a skirt," she muttered as she pressed her body close to the wall beneath the window, stiff leaves lodging themselves annoyingly in her Maidenform panties. If she heard Naomi inside, she planned to tap discreetly on the window to get her attention.

Not able to hear anything, Hannah stood on her tiptoes, her hand shading her eyes, and peeked over the window ledge. She couldn't see a thing. In a matter of seconds a piercing screech came from inside the house.

Hannah stumbled backward and fell bottom-first into the shrubbery. Then she heard a crash inside followed by more insane shrieking. The wood-frame window opened with a whack and Naomi's head stuck out. She looked down at the human sprawled in her shrubbery, first with rage, then with amazement.

"Hannah, what are you doing?" she said through gritted teeth, trying her best to keep her voice low. "You almost scared Mrs. Hargrove into a heart attack. She thought you were her dead mother.''

Hannah modestly pushed her skirt back down around her calves. "I want to talk to you."

"What are you thinking? I'm in the middle of a session. Red Moon was about to give Mrs. Hargrove some advice on her granddaughter's wedding. She's going to be very angry at the interruption."

Hannah hauled herself out of the bush and stepped closer to the window, her expression stern. "I *know* about the bulbs."

Naomi grimaced, mouthed a silent *oh shit*, then slammed the window shut so hard it made Hannah's teeth hurt. Within two minutes she flew into the backyard wearing a saffron caftan that would have made her look like a Burmese monk except for her huge hoop earrings and bright coral lipstick.

"Is Mrs. Hargrove all right?" Hannah asked.

"Middling," Naomi answered, out of breath. "I've got her doing a snake-shaman war chant."

"Is there such a thing?"

"Not really, so let's make this fast."

The two women stared at each other as each waited for the other to break the silence, for they both knew a large messy truth was about to be spilled and that it wasn't going to be pleasant. Hannah spoke first.

"I just saw Fred at Urban Farm. He told me you bought hyacinth bulbs and I know you hate gardening. You bought them to plant in Lempke's garden, didn't you?"

Naomi's usual placid countenance turned turbulent, reflecting the conflicting thoughts bouncing around her cranium. She had carried the mammoth secret inside so long, the pressure building inside her like a late baby, until now, grateful she no longer had a choice, she burst with the truth.

"I had to, Hannah. After what he said at the cocktail party about Red Moon being a fraud," she said, the words rushing forth. "He told everybody that Red Moon said there would be hyacinths growing in his garden. I had to make good on it, didn't I? I thought I planted them before Mary died, but you know I'm hardly a plant expert. So after what Arnold said, I went to the nursery to check, and darn it if I hadn't planted amaryllis bulbs.''

Hannah listened to this raptly. ''You were in Lempke's garden planting them when he was murdered?''

Naomi held up her hand, her thumb and index finger pressed together. ''Not exactly.''

''What exactly?''

''Well, if you must know,'' Naomi replied, pulling her shoulders back, trying to look dignified, ''I was on my hands and knees trying to get the damn things in the dirt. I was in such a hurry I'd just grabbed some salad tongs from the kitchen to dig with and they weren't working well.''

Hannah winced at the image. Naomi continued. ''So there I was, crawling around, tonging the dirt like crazy so I could get the bulbs planted and get back to Whitney Jansen before she came back to her body.''

''Excuse me?''

''Whitney's been coming to me for years to be hypnotized so she can have a past-life experience. She says she's getting in touch with her past life as an Apache princess, but truth is, she just naps. At least half an hour, always. So you see, I didn't have much time. As soon as I heard her start to snore, I ran the two blocks to Arnold's. I was on my hands and knees in the middle of his flower bed when I heard the door open. I panicked and hid in the bushes.''

''Good Lord, Naomi, what did you see?''

''I was too busy crawling away to see much of anything, but then I heard Lisa's voice.'' Naomi shuddered, the memory of that day returning. ''She and her father argued. Not yelling. Something more intense than that. Full of hate.''

''What about?''

''You have to understand, I couldn't hear everything. But I know they argued about her mother, about him taking her

out of the nursing home when he shouldn't have." Naomi
hesitated.

"What else?"

Naomi gave her spirit-room window a worried look.
"Well, there was a little more talking I couldn't understand.
Then he called her a lesbian." She turned her gaze back to
Hannah. "Which Lisa may or may not be. It's none of my
business and she's entitled to sleep with whomever she
wants."

"I imagine Lempke wasn't so open-minded," Hannah
said.

"Then, if that wasn't bad enough, he called her a dyke.
A 'dirty dyke' he said, and that she was sinning. Then he
said, 'You shouldn't be allowed to corrupt people.' "

A pang of disgust squeezed Hannah's insides as she
imagined Lempke's harshness. "I suppose he thought she
shouldn't be a teacher. What a thing to say to your own
daughter."

"Oh, Hannah, he used the words so hatefully, like they
were a curse. Such a repulsive little man."

"Then what happened?"

Naomi took a breath to fortify herself. "Then I heard a
kind of thud followed by a bigger thud." Again she shuddered.

"Why didn't you tell the police?"

Naomi, normally unflappable, now seemed vulnerable,
and she looked at Hannah imploringly. "I didn't realize
then what the sounds meant. Later I knew if I talked to the
police, I'd have to explain why I was in the garden. You
know how gossipy this town is. Everyone would know I
was there planting those bulbs. They'd think Red Moon
was a fake and my business would be ruined. How would
I support myself? How would I live?"

Hannah shook her head at her neighbor's sad foolishness.
Just then there was a rapping at the window. Both women
turned and saw Mrs. Hargrove, feathered war stick in hand,
giving Naomi a peeved look. Seeing her, Naomi marched

in place and moved her fist up and down in a pantomime encouraging Mrs. Hargrove to continue her chanting. After Mrs. Hargrove disappeared from the window, Naomi continued.

"Hannah, I knew I had to help the police. That's why I had Red Moon give you information."

"You call that information?" Hannah said. "Two ones side by side? And that ridiculous thing about the corpse rose."

Naomi's brow knit in puzzlement. "The corpse rose? I didn't say that. That one must have come from Red Moon," she said, obviously pleased. "He can be so helpful."

"Oh, Naomi, stop it. You aren't going to expect me to believe now that Red Moon is real."

"He *is* real," Naomi insisted huffily. "Sure I throw in a few things myself here and there, but I only do it to make people feel good about themselves. Like telling Mary that the hyacinths would be a sign of life. I thought it would cheer her up. But Red Moon comes out of me and chats up a storm and I never know what he's said. Like that corpse-rose thing."

Naomi spoke with such conviction that, much to Hannah's astonishment, she actually felt Naomi was telling the truth, but this revelation was soon interrupted by more rapping at the window, this time with more vehemence. Mrs. Hargrove was shaking the war stick at them, looking like she was ready to go on the warpath herself.

Naomi waved at her and shouted, "I'm coming!" Then she turned back to Hannah, rolling her eyes in frustration. "That Mrs. Hargrove. Her and her dead mother are a pain in the astral. Even Red Moon's sick of them." She sighed. "Gotta go." She started off but turned back. "You see, I didn't think it would hurt anything in the long run to let Red Moon give you the information. I always knew you were smarter than the police anyway and that you could solve Arnold's murder."

"That was very wrong of you, Naomi," Hannah said, pressing her hand to her forehead.

"But you *did* solve the murder."

Hannah looked down at the ground, worried.

"To be honest, now I'm not so sure."

TWENTY-FIVE

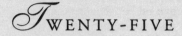

KIKI HAULED HERSELF OUT OF the Cadillac, slammed the door shut, and hands on hips, gave the Marin County jail a long, hard stare. If the jail had its own eyes, it would no doubt have responded likewise.

In a spasm of euphoria she had donned a tight purple skirt topped with a fringed western blouse, a long row of rhinestones dancing in figure eights across her breasts, her feet shod in pink cowboy boots—the whole effect a sort of Dale-Evans-turns-hooker fashion statement that raised Hannah's eyebrows when she first saw it. But with her new celebrity status, Kiki felt she owed it to her public to provide a little glamour in their humdrum lives, and Hannah was so glad to have her home that she kept her mouth shut about the outfit, including the unseemly display of rootin'-tootin' cowgirl cleavage.

Kiki thought that Hannah, being such a close relative, should also jazz up her normally conservative ensembles with some brighter colors and jewelry. Hannah declined the suggestion, choosing dark pants and a mustard cotton sweater.

Hannah entwined her arm with her sister's as the two began the long walk to the jail. The parking lot was so crowded they had to park the Cadillac in the farthest corner, and the jail, which was part of the larger civic center, seemed miles away. The sky was clear and Hannah enjoyed the sun's warmth on her shoulders.

"Are you sure you want to go to the jail? You could wait in the car if it makes you uncomfortable," she suggested.

"Oh no, I'll go, but the only reason is because I've decided it's my Christian duty," Kiki said, her neon-pink boots clomping against the pavement.

"The only reason you're doing this is because you want to visit Chantal while we're there," Hannah replied with a knowing smile.

Kiki gave a little shrug. "Well, that, too. I want her to see this outfit. She told me she loves a cowgirl look. She said that sometimes she wears cowgirl outfits when she does her spiritual healings. She calls them fantasy healings."

At this last statement, Hannah's forehead furrowed, and Kiki continued. "I still don't understand why you made the appointment to see Lisa. You and Lauren are visiting her as much as you visited me."

"That's not true, Kiki. Like I told you, I have to talk to her. I still have so many questions."

Kiki stopped walking just long enough to stomp her boot for emphasis. "Hannah, you're so hardheaded sometimes. You and your theories and your overanalyzing. Lisa Lempke confessed!"

And Hannah knew that Lisa's confession would be even more compelling now that she had convinced Naomi to go to the police. After Naomi's story came out, suspicion would lie even more heavily on poor Lisa. Yet there were still things that didn't sit right with Hannah, and she felt that if she didn't try to confirm the facts now, the truth might be lost forever.

"I'm sorry, Kiki, but since I helped put Lisa in jail, I'm responsible to make certain she really belongs there. And to do that I need to talk to her at least one more time."

Kiki muttered a vague disapproval, then spat out, "Darn it, these boots are too small. My feet are starting to kill me and we're not even a third of the way there."

"You've had those boots over twenty years. I know because I remember you bought them after you saw *Urban Cowboy*. You know that your feet get larger as you age," Hannah said.

"Oh, don't talk about aging like we're fossils."

"But we *are* getting older."

"Maybe you are, but I'm not. Not so it shows, anyway. It's my bone structure." Kiki silently mouthed an *ouch*. "Darn these boots. Maybe they shrunk. I don't know why we couldn't have taken a limo like I wanted. I'm famous now, and people expect these things."

"One article in the local newspaper doesn't make you famous, and we can't afford to drive around in limos."

Just then they passed a large van and saw Crayton unlocking the driver's-side door of her Volvo.

"Oh good! Crayton can give us a ride to the entrance," Kiki said, shouting out "Crayton!" before Hannah could stop her. They were only a few yards away, so when Kiki trotted up to Crayton, Hannah had little choice except to follow.

She wore jeans and a faded red sweatshirt, her long red hair pulled into a haphazard ponytail. With no makeup and dark circles under her eyes, she looked ghostly. She also didn't look especially pleased to see them.

Crayton's expression was grim and became grimmer as Kiki and Hannah got closer. The door of the gray Volvo swung open, and she stood beside it.

"What are you doing here?" she asked, her voice an odd monotone.

"We're visiting Lisa," Kiki answered brightly.

As soon as Crayton heard this, her face distorted with

resentment. "Can't you leave her alone? You've done enough harm." Her rancor was now so obvious even Kiki noticed it, and she gave a little gasp of irritation.

"Crayton, please—" Hannah began but Kiki interrupted.

"There's no need for rudeness, Crayton," she said, her new notoriety having boosted her confidence. "It's understandable that you might blame Hannah for Lisa being in jail, but you see, now Hannah doesn't even think Lisa really did it."

"What are you talking about?" Crayton asked.

"This really isn't the time," Hannah said, but Kiki could not be stopped.

"You see, Hannah thinks Lisa wasn't strong enough to kill someone with a single blow. We talked about it this morning. It was my idea really," Kiki said with pride. "I was the one who remembered Lisa on the softball team."

Crayton looked baffled and Hannah didn't blame her. Hannah stepped forward to pull Kiki away, but at that moment a breeze drifted in their direction, rustling the leaves of the tree behind Crayton's car and wafting the aroma of her cologne directly at Hannah's nose. As her arm stretched out to nudge Kiki backward, Hannah got a whiff of spice and musk, her nostrils flaring slightly. Then, like a bloodhound lifting its snout, she gave the air a few quick industrious sniffs. After that she froze, her eyes wide. She knew the smell. It was the cologne her attacker had worn that night in the church.

While Kiki rambled on about Lisa's lack of softball skills, Hannah's mind raced. Lempke had been killed by a single blow. The wound on his neck proved it, and what Naomi heard in the garden corroborated it. Naomi had heard two thuds—the thud when the garden marker hit Lempke and the larger thud when he hit the ground.

"I suppose Hannah has a point. It probably has to do with biceps or triceps or whatever," Kiki prattled on, mindless of the storm gathering around her. "But the truth is

that little Lisa was—if I can say this without hurting anyone's feelings—Lisa was a weakling.''

Hannah realized now with certainty that it was impossible for Lisa to have killed her father. She wasn't strong
enough physically or emotionally to have committed such
a brutal crime. But Crayton was.

''Of course, *I* was a cheerleader in high school. We did
jumps and cartwheels,'' Kiki said as Hannah grabbed her
arm in a vain attempt to get her away from Crayton, but
she was so relishing talking about herself an earthquake
wouldn't have distracted her. ''Made it easy for the boys
to look right up our skirts,'' Kiki added with a twitter.

For Hannah the truth became a spell settling slowly on
her. Crayton must have been with Lisa the day in the garden when she confronted her father. Naomi heard only
Lisa's voice, but it didn't mean Crayton wasn't there. She
and Lisa always seemed to be together. Naomi heard
Lempke say ''dirty dyke'' as well as ''you shouldn't be
allowed to corrupt people.'' But he didn't say those words
to his daughter. He said them to Crayton. He accused her
of corrupting Lisa.

Hannah closed her eyes as she pictured the scene in her
head. Crayton standing silently next to Lisa, her anger
building as Lisa confronted her father about his treatment
of her mother. Crayton watched the argument, enraged by
the cruel words Lempke hurled at his daughter as well as
herself. Lisa's story about her father's neglect of her mother
rang true, as did the story about Swanson blackmailing her
into sex. The stories *were* true. Except Lisa didn't murder
the men in a rage. She didn't have to. Crayton did it for
her.

Hannah's eyes snapped open, the sight of Crayton filling
them. ''You,'' she whispered.

Her thoughts must have showed on her face. Though
Kiki jabbered on, Crayton's gaze fell directly on Hannah.

''So don't you worry, hon,'' Kiki said, patting the hand
that had so recently sent two men to bloody deaths. ''Han-

nah's so smart. Always has been. She'll figure everything out . . ." She let the sentence dangle as something in Crayton's car caught her eye. "Is that a gun underneath the seat of your car?" She waggled her hand at the redhead while a growing sense of dread filled Hannah.

Hannah said, "Kiki, no," but her sister was in full throttle.

"That's so practical," she continued cheerfully. "The way crime's going these days. I want one myself. Just for protection, of course, but Hannah won't hear of it."

"We need to be leaving," Hannah said firmly, hoping to make a quick exit before Kiki got them killed, but Fortuna gave her skirts a little riffle, and within seconds Crayton had scooped up the small black revolver. Hannah froze. Crayton held the weapon in her palm, the barrel pointed away from all of them.

"I want you to stay here," she said.

Hannah felt as if all her blood had suddenly coagulated into ice. "Crayton, what are you doing with that thing?"

"I was planning to kill myself with it." She said the words calmly.

Hannah moved her hand to Kiki's waist, slowly pushing her backward. "Put it away, Crayton. There's been enough death. For Lisa's sake."

Everything about Crayton seemed to contract and harden. She looked at Hannah with loathing. "Don't mention her name. You're the reason she's in the terrible place she is."

Kiki raised a finger. "You know, honey, it's not all that bad."

"Shut up," Crayton spat. "Everything was fine until you pushed your nose into things." She directed these words at Hannah. "I tried to scare you off, but you're so stupid. So arrogant."

"I had to help my sister." A golfball-sized lump formed in Hannah's throat as she watched the redhead's fingers tighten around the gun's handle.

"It was her own fault," Crayton said, tossing a venomous glance at Kiki. "The disgusting way she chased after Lisa's father."

"Excuse me?" Kiki asked with annoyance. Hannah squeezed her arm to silence her.

"She's hardly the one to blame," Hannah said. "You killed two men. You tried to make it look like Kiki had committed a crime that you were responsible for. You took the knife she used that day at Lisa's house and used it to kill Swanson."

Kiki's mouth opened into a horrified *oh* as the reality of the situation finally hit her. She looked from Hannah to Crayton, then to the gun. "But if Crayton killed the reverend and Arnie, why did Lisa confess to it?"

Hannah had never been so frightened in her life, the trembling in Crayton's gun-toting hand bothering her most. She wanted to yell for Kiki to run, but she didn't dare. Perspiration had sprouted on Crayton's forehead, and with the fingers of her free hand she nervously twisted the fabric of her sweatshirt. She was coming apart, on the edge of losing control. Better, Hannah decided, to keep talking until she could think of something.

"She did it out of love, I suppose," she began, the words slow and measured. "And maybe out of guilt. Crayton was protecting her. She committed crimes that Lisa wanted to commit. But Lisa didn't have the nerve. Crayton did."

Kiki let out a fearful squeak. "Good Lord, Crayton. Stabbing the reverend's one thing, but chopping off his finger?"

Hannah gulped. Was her sister determined to get them both shot?

The edges of Crayton's mouth turned up. "It was a trophy. Lisa didn't like it much, so I gave it to you." She looked at Hannah. "But you didn't get the message."

"You must have resented the hold he had on her," Hannah said, trying to stall for time in hopes someone would walk by.

Crayton's mouth twisted. "He was a money-grubbing

fraud who tricked people with that stupid rock."

"But Lisa trusted him," Hannah said. "She told him what happened in the garden that day."

"Lisa looked up to him like he was Christ Himself. She went to that little prick for spiritual guidance, then he used what she told him to blackmail her into bed."

"And she was going to go through with it so he wouldn't tell the police you had done it?"

"She loves me. She wanted to protect me. But I protected her instead. Now get in the fucking car." Crayton was pointing the gun directly at them now.

"Oh my," Kiki said, putting up her hands like she was in a television cop show.

"Put your hands down, you cow," Crayton said. "You were a joke to Lisa's father. Did you realize that? He told jokes about you."

Kiki reared her shoulder back. "How dare you!" She looked at Hannah for help. The cow remark was a low blow, no doubt about it, but at that moment Hannah was too concerned about impending death to defend her sister's honor.

"Just get in the car. Front seat." Crayton looked at Hannah. "You drive."

Hannah's eyes darted around her, still hoping that someone would walk by, but they were hopelessly alone. "Where are you taking us?" she asked, trying to keep her voice steady, wanting to conceal her fear from Kiki.

"I left a note in my house giving enough details to prove I committed the murders so they'll let Lisa go. I was going to kill myself, only there's been a change in the plan. Now I'm killing you, too."

"Why hurt us?" Kiki asked tearfully.

"Because if you two had just stayed out of it, Lisa and I would have been fine. But you kept questioning her and she freaked out. She thought she had to confess to Swanson."

"Crayton, hand me the gun. You don't want to shoot anyone," Hannah said.

"Just get in the fucking car." Crayton spoke slowly, enunciating each word, then moved her gun hand into her handbag where it couldn't be seen. The bulge against the leather made it clear the gun was pointed at them.

Frightened, Kiki looked again at Hannah, but Hannah had no help to give. She walked past Crayton and slid into the driver's seat. Kiki walked around to the passenger's side while Crayton got in the back.

Hannah and Kiki closed their car doors, with Crayton closing hers last, the sound of it slamming shut resounding in Hannah's ears. A coffin couldn't have closed with more finality.

The keys dropped in the seat next to her.

"Start the car," Crayton commanded.

At first Hannah was so frightened that her hand couldn't move to pick up the keys, but hearing the order shouted a second time galvanized her into compliance. She fumbled with the keys, her fingers unable to manipulate the right one into the slot. This only heightened Crayton's anger. She kicked the back of Hannah's seat.

"Start the car, Hannah, please, before she shoots us," Kiki pleaded.

But Hannah didn't start the car. She knew eventually someone would walk by.

"Where are we going?" She could see Crayton in the rearview mirror, her face reddened, sweat beading on her upper lip.

"Start the car now! I can blow your goddamn heads off. It doesn't mean shit to me. Do you understand that?"

Kiki whispered "oh God" and started moving her lips, praying like crazy. With no other choice, Hannah started the car then buckled her seat belt. "Put on your seat belt, Kiki."

Kiki started to cry. "Oh, good idea, Hannah. Crayton's going to shoot off our heads, but we sure wouldn't want to get into an accident and get whiplash.'' The tears turned into sobs, but she fastened her seat belt.

Crayton directed Hannah to the closest exit out of the parking lot, dashing her hopes of finding a pedestrian and yelling for help. The problem was, if she did yell for help, Crayton might shoot them on the spot. Frequent glances into the rearview mirror told her that the redhead was looking increasingly frazzled.

On Crayton's direction, Hannah pulled the car into the avenue that ran adjacent to the civic center. Crayton then told her to get on the freeway. Hannah's stomach tightened. Once they were on the freeway, all hopes of getting help would be lost. But Kiki's use of the word *accident* a few seconds earlier sparked an idea. It caused her to remember an article she had read in the *Ladies' Home Journal* about what to do in various crime situations, including one in which an armed person forces himself into your car. Her current situation wasn't quite the same scenario as in the magazine article, but it was close enough.

Hannah turned the steering wheel, moving the car toward the freeway entrance. She gulped some air for courage, then slammed her foot on the gas pedal, causing the car to veer sharply to the right. The Volvo jumped a median and they were headed down the wrong side of the street, another car coming toward them.

Kiki screamed. Hannah turned the steering wheel right then left, making the car swerve. Crayton yelled at her, her instinctive fear of a head-on collision temporarily taking priority over murder and suicide.

A car heading toward them honked madly. It swerved left, running up a curb. Hannah swerved the car right, crashing into a cement pillar beneath the freeway. Crayton, who wasn't buckled in, flew into the rear side window, her head meeting glass with a thud.

Kiki just kept yelling her head off while Hannah unbuckled her seat belt and scrambled into the backseat, grabbing the gun off the floor.

"Get out of the car!" she shouted. Kiki unbuckled her seat belt, opened the door, and jumped out, while Hannah emerged from the rear door. The Volvo's right rear fender and door were smashed.

A few people came running to help. The man in the other car was marching angrily their way, pointing to his car, which had crashed into a parked truck, and shouting obscenities. When he saw the gun in Hannah's hand, he stopped in his tracks.

"Call the police," Hannah told him.

"Yeah, okay," he said fearfully. Hannah turned, looking for Kiki, not finding her at first. Then she saw her. Kiki had gotten out of the car and walked around to the other side. Crayton had opened the door and was sitting there dazed from the blow to her head, tears streaming down her cheeks. A trickle of blood zigzagged across her forehead.

Apparently recovered from the ordeal, Kiki swung her purse at Crayton and whacked her on the head twice before Hannah could stop her.

TWENTY-SIX

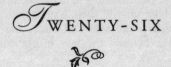

THE BALMY MEXICAN AIR BRUSHED Hannah's face as she sipped a virgin piña colada and watched the approaching shore of Acapulco.

Normally not one for travel, she had decided she deserved a rest after the murders and their nerve-racking aftermath, and on an impulse bought a ticket for the Acapulco cruise. It wasn't like her to do such a thing, but she was in some ways a different person than she had been only a week before. The past few days had given her new insight into life as well as herself. She had learned about the evil people could do, and the knowledge would always lie heavy on her heart. But she had also learned that whatever your age, life held fresh excitements and adventures if you only reached out for them.

And as far as women her age being expendable, by solving two murders Hannah felt certain she had proven that her skills and persistence could, at least on occasion, be quite indispensable.

Yes, it had been a fascinating week and a half. And now she could enjoy her trip to Mexico with a peaceful heart, for the Hill Creek body politic had not only returned to its former state of homeostasis, it was perhaps, like herself, better for the experience. First prize in the rose competition had gone posthumously to Arnold Lempke, and Hannah found herself quietly pleased that she had only taken second place. Lempke had not been an admirable man by any means, but someone who loved roses as much as he had, couldn't have been without some goodness, and she felt that, at least as far as his flowers were concerned, he deserved the tribute.

The festival was such a success that the Rose Club was excitedly planning a Fall Fair, this one without a dunking booth. On top of that, Detective Morgan, with Hannah's prodding, had asked Lauren for a date. This event was to take place during the two weeks the sisters were out of town, which Hannah felt was very wise of her niece.

Naomi's ancient water heater finally gave out, and right after the plumber told her how much it would cost to replace it, a light fell upon her and she had an amazing vision revealing that Red Moon could indeed communicate with little dead Bon Bon. Wanda was thrilled and was now seeing Red Moon twice a week.

Taking another sip of her drink, Hannah sighed with satisfaction and admired the view of the Mexican coastline. The pink-and-white hotels seemed to have sprung up like flowers from the lush green hillsides, and she could see red streaks of bougainvillea climbing up their edges. She had heard there were lovely tropical flowers in the town—birds of paradise, orchids, a dozen varieties of native lilies.

But this pleasant interlude was interrupted by a small belch followed by a groan that emanated from the deck chair next to her.

"If I eat another bite, I'm going to bust right out of this jumpsuit," Kiki exclaimed, her face obscured by rhinestone-encrusted sunglasses and the brim of a pink baseball hat with ACAPULCO stitched in gold across the front. "I don't understand why it's so tight. It fit just perfect that day in the shop."

Hannah cast her an incredulous glance. "Perfect? It practically took a blowtorch and safety goggles to get you out of it. What I don't understand is how you got into it this morning in the first place."

"I lay down on the floor while Chantal zipped it up. But it's like it's getting smaller as the day goes on."

"Maybe it's because at lunch you ate your weight in enchiladas. Not to mention the tequila."

"Oh, that tequila hardly has any calories at all. Besides, Chantal said the jumpsuit looks good tight." Kiki sighed with renewed contentment and took a bracing drink of her banana daiquiri. "I'm so glad she came on the cruise with me. She's almost as good as a man because she's so good at meeting them."

Hannah fought the urge to comment. As a favor, Detective Morgan had looked up Chantal's police record before Kiki invited her on the cruise and reported his findings to Hannah. Although she had been arrested for soliciting, the charges had been dropped and she seemed committed to getting out of the "spiritual healing" business altogether. And Hannah certainly couldn't discriminate against a person just because she did a little jail time, especially when her own sister had seen the wrong side of a cell herself.

"And John Perez deciding to come along at the last minute. What a surprise." Kiki looked at her sister over the top of her sunglasses. "Where is he?"

"In the gym trying to work off last night's dinner."

Kiki sighed. "I love a man who takes care of himself. Chantal thinks he's handsome. I do, too. But he only seems interested in you, Hannah. I think you're the only reason he came on this cruise. That's what I think."

The corners of Hannah's lips curled up. "Well, it turns out he's quite a garden enthusiast."

Kiki eyed her sister a moment but then relaxed in her chair. "Here we are, all of us having such a lovely time, after everything that happened. There's just one thing, Hannah . . .''

Kiki's sentence trailed off as a good-looking man wearing only a Speedo walked by them.

"You were saying, Kiki?"

"Oh, I was just thinking about poor Lisa. Do you think she'll be all right?"

"I don't know. Seeing your father murdered right in front of you is a horrible thing. But she'll pull through with time. Women can be very strong when they need to be."

The sucking sound of Kiki's straw announced the completion of her daiquiri. "Well, I'm going to find Chantal by the pool," she said, rolling onto one side, swinging her legs off the deck chair, and using the momentum to leverage herself into a standing position. "Are you and John coming to dinner in town tonight?"

"I think we're going to stay on the ship. It will be quiet with everyone gone, and the nights here are so lovely."

Kiki pressed her fist into her hip. "I just don't get it. I put all that effort into getting a man for this cruise and come up with zip, and here you are, not even trying, and you snag one."

"Well, Kiki, you had a man. It's just unfortunate that he, well, had to cancel."

"Just plain rotten luck." The frown on Kiki's face transformed into a smile. "But Chantal and I have outfits that are dynamite for tonight. We may get lucky."

Hannah wished them all the good fortune in the world.

Moonlight streamed in through the porthole, turning the bed into a puddle of silver.

"Let me see it again, Hannah," Perez whispered.

"Why?"

"Because it's beautiful."

Hannah laughed softly and unbuttoned her blouse. Perez pulled back the fabric and smiled. She twisted slightly and the moonlight fell across her skin. Hannah's chest was a smooth landscape, her breasts replaced by a wealth of images—roses, lilies, and ivy tattooed across her skin, the colors rich and the detail in each flower quite extraordinary.

"You're a garden, Hannah. A walking, breathing garden."

Hannah very much liked the idea of that.